SCARLET OAK

SCARLET OAK

A NOVEL

Angie Weiland-Crosby

ISBN: 978-1-7371551-0-2
ISBN: 978-1-7371551-1-9 (eBook)

First Edition: February 2021

Edited by Leah Weiss
Formatted by Melissa Williams Design
Cover Art by iStock.com / George Peters
Cover Design by Angie Weiland-Crosby

Published by Autumn Rising Press LLC

www.angieweilandcrosby.com

inquiries@angieweilandcrosby.com

For the Leftovers

Part One

The Forest Realm

Smis-Speak

I exist in an unseen world. Okay, perhaps I overstate my plight. Some see me. The magical tree sprites in the forest realm. The soul-boy who lives in the bluebell house. And, of course, the newly dead.

More to the point, my name is Smis, an acronym for my fullest label, *Southern Maryland in Shadow*. If you'd rather be spoon-fed in cliché, I am a Grim Reaper. You see, we are not one, but many, covering territories that span the world. My region is dotted with farms and forests and small towns and, at times, smaller minds. But the job remains the same— to usher those who have passed to their final destination. I choose to dub it either the *Light* or the *Dark*.

Painfully, and sometimes with pleasure, I move in and out of shadows, as I am a shadow myself. But on this night, only terror finds me—and the soul-boy. He sits alone in the kitchen of the bluebell house. No matter that a Thanksgiving meal with all the fixings rests before him, he doesn't eat.

Instead, he listens to his parents screaming upstairs. He cannot talk. If he could, I'm certain he would say something profound, such as, "Even the cranberry sauce is bleeding, so wounded, so sad."

All right, that truly is my thought. I use it to avoid imagining his truest suffering. After all, I am Smis, with a dark reputation to uphold. The soul-boy jars me from this rumination. He opens the front door, not so quiet. But quieter than the yelling. He runs with flapping hands and his most haunted hum. The world labels him in a cliché, too—autistic. Still, I call him the soul-boy. We've met before, you see, years ago.

The soul-boy rushes to a weathered shed near the house and enters only briefly. He then exits with a bag that he lugs over his shoulder as he sprints the snaky length of the driveway. Unable to resist, I swoop and stand strange before him, a broken man's crooked shadow. He sees me—this I know. He even tries to touch me until the tiniest twig-of-a-sprite flies from her pin oak tree and circles us. Round and round and round. For a moment, we are mesmerized, calmed. Love must feel a little like this, I believe.

But soon, the magic snaps apart, and the twig sprite sails back to her tree that leans into the bluebell house. At this moment, my nonexistent heart tells *me* to intervene. *You're the only one left to do so.* However, on this night, I am bound to say . . . *No.*

And so, the soul-boy wanders into the forest alone.

Chapter 1

During my fiftieth year as a tree sprite, I finally faced death. I did so while hunching beneath the moon that struck with foul light my only friend. There, Sycamore rested in her tree's hollow. Sunlit eyes forever shut. Wings folded into her chest. And moss trampling tufts of hair, her little body starved. No nuts, berries, or insects would she ever feast on again. Sycamore adored the red, ripe berries from a nearby holly tree. So I snatched a branch, plucked two, and placed one on each wing. Then I raced back to my scarlet birth oak as grief spun my heart like a cyclone.

"Come, Scarlet, sleep in my hollow."

When my forest father, Horace, spoke, his voice murmured in my sap-flow without outer sound, as was customary of a tree and its sprite. On this autumn night, his tone warmed even while the rest of me shivered.

"Come, child, the night is cold."

I didn't creep to his hollow. Instead, I remained firm on his branch. So he rocked me with such tenderness that I nearly let him know that I loved him. But the moment passed, and I could tell he'd fallen asleep to his own rocking.

Restless, I scaled to Horace's tallest branch and squatted with my tears. Here, I aimed to commune with Nature's extraordinary madness. I so wished for her to ease my heartache. But the full moon, typically a friend, only gawked, and the stars clanged and chattered, shunning my company even more so than usual. As my misery grew, that's when I heard the *crackle, crunch, crackle*. At first, it appeared distant, and so I considered it my imagination. But as the noises progressed, quickened, intensified, I sat up, even stiller. Peered below with hawk eyes. It couldn't be. It shouldn't be. But it was—a human visitation.

I'd never seen a human up close. So I studied the golden boy as he dropped a bag and paced around my tree with his hands flapping. Miniaturized on Horace, I dug into my bark-skin, picked it raw, and twirled the thin gray-black branches of my hair. My beady eyes softened as my fingers fidgeted like the carpenter ants that climbed down Horace's trunk. I supposed I was beautiful in some way, like this boy. My body never told me so. And my sap-scent, at times, shortened my breath, panicking me.

But then the boy hummed a language that felt near. In fact, his human-speak buzzed into my soul, and my grief warmed a bit at the gesture as I kept watch of him circling Horace. Little did I know at the time that this sound was atypical for a human. If I had known, then things would be much different. There were other details I missed as well, such as he wasn't a man, but he wasn't necessarily a boy, either. He lived somewhere in between, and that place troubled him.

With this in-between sorrow, the boy rested against Horace's trunk. Surprisingly, Horace slept on in his weary worn way, which only tempted me. For no matter that, unlike a human, I breathed magic, I sensed enchantment as the boy's tears rippled from his cheeks—dewdrops of mystery so blue that I wanted to catch and cradle them in my tiny hands, swim in their origin, taste his story.

Even the moon seemed to lower with a want to do the same. Whether the moon prompted what came next, however, I'm still unsure. But I sensed a beast, one that appeared peaceable, drink the boy's tears. Suddenly, the boy froze. No sound. No tears. No magic. But I'd soon learn this peaceable beast proved to be most dangerous, as a violence lodged in its quiet and calm, and it was patient, calculating, waiting for the proper moment to feed.

In the stillness, the boy looked up once, and I could have sworn he stared through me, unfazed. My heart wept, as I longed for this boy to know me. But for the time being, I tucked him into memory, settling on delicate as his defining feature. He housed a delicate soul. I wanted to hold it, rock it, find an unbreakable bough for it to rest upon, allow the moonlight to warm it until it blushed into the color of sunlight, and then see myself in it. I would smile, defying everything that haunted me on this night. I'd even hum to his soul and become a part of him.

Horace would scold me for such foolishness (as he often did), and for a moment, I thought he awoke, his branch shook so. But I soon discovered it wasn't Horace at all. It was the boy, grabbing my oak and climbing. He scooted his body along a sturdy limb beneath me and set to work, knotting a rope he withdrew from his bag. At the time, I didn't know it was a rope, a wicked human-thing. I only found it an odd item, and so focused on it.

In that instant of my turning from the boy, he leapt with the rope around his neck like a deer with such grace, and

Horace, always dependable, dangled him. At first, I thought it may have been a self-soothing human thing to do. But when the boy gagged and sputtered and winced and cried, I knew his pain, and he knew mine, because I sprinted down my tree and crawled onto a nearby branch. Hung from one hand. Peered into his eyes as they fell. Our souls locked into the peaceable beast, and his lips struggled for this sound before he died. I spoke it for him, my very first attempt at human-speak . . .

"No."

And he was gone.

Chapter 2

I lifted my body, scampered along a branch, climbed down Horace's trunk, and detached from my birth oak. Once I did so, I morphed into largeness, a version of myself that looked closer to a spring-born human. Fearful, wearing my moonshine skin, brown root eyes, raven-hued hair, I walked to the boy. Well-mannered sprites told me I was beautiful even without wings, but as I approached the boy, my lovely memory of him vanished. This haunting picture took its place. His body paled and his lips blued as he hung limp, long hair swaying with the wind. I cringed and ached in all my aching parts.

But then, something quite amazing happened. Yes, he was gone, insomuch as who he was before the hanging. But no, he wasn't gone-gone. Instead, the boy opened into pieces of wonder. First, his soul exited in a blue prism of light that pushed through him in a spherical shape and flew past me. It then rested in a warm glow on the branch where the boy hung and gazed to me for direction.

Guiltily, I remembered my wish to hold his soul. And so I refused to look at it for too long, and I didn't cradle it once.

Instead, I returned my thoughts to the body, wondering why Horace slept on.

"I'm not asleep," Horace said. "I've heard, and felt, and witnessed everything."

"Then why didn't you stop the boy?" I asked.

"Humans like free will . . . or so I've heard."

"You should have done something."

"Why didn't you?" Horace asked.

I cupped my trembling hands, tears filling and slipping through them.

"When I looked in his eyes, they spoke a different story. It wasn't a tale about dying at all."

"Humans have no place here. The forest's magic isn't theirs. His soul belongs to me, now. Nature's law."

Grief-stricken, I silenced and bowed my head. I doubted this was Nature's law, no matter how many times I listened to Horace's wisdom about soul-things and all matters human. You see, Horace informed me at an early age that what little magic a human did possess lived in his soul. The last living person or thing to touch a dying human owned his soul.

"No gratitude?" Horace asked. "You were admiring his soul?"

"It doesn't mean I wished him dead. I just wanted to soothe it. Take the pain away. And then, perhaps, some of mine would leave me, too."

The boy's soul levitated and floated into Horace's hollow, settling in the kindest spot.

"You can visit it as you wish. Perhaps now you'll forgive me for clipping your wings."

I only wished I could forgive Horace for severing my wings at birth, disabling me. But even now, I couldn't. Still, silence and shame overwhelmed me, especially as I turned from the soul aware that visitations remained in my power. Instead, I viewed the body. Another piece left it—spirit that matched his form—soldered with gauzy yellows and golds. No matter the beauty, the spirit moved broken. It landed morose and crept like a beetle to the nearby sugar maple tree, named Stein, crouching, straightaway rocking, rocking, rocking. My mind thrashed. Surely, this piece was meant to be well but wasn't. This piece that refused to die but already had.

Again, I knew from Horace's preaching that the human spirit was meant to move to the Light or Dark, and horrendous Smis, Death's shadowy undertaker, guided the spirit to where it belonged. But this spirit stayed, paralyzed in its rocking.

I raced to Stein and peered into his hollow to find his cuddly sprite, Sugar Maple, fast asleep. Old, wise Sugar Maple, always so compliant and dutiful. She could tune out the fiercest thunder and slumber on, but hear the tiniest rustle-hum and rise to service. Oddly, on this night, wrapped tight in her wrinkled bark, she slept on, unaware.

So I walked around Stein and stood a respectful distance from the boy's spirit. Already, he had transformed. The golden hues faded to starched grays and whites, eyes fully gray and sullen. His fingers locked into each other, and he rocked like a mockingbird's ceaseless chant. His sound, at once so hypnotic, now shrieked. If he was aware of my existence, he didn't show me. And so, I sat near him and waited to see what came next.

That's when tree sprites detached from their birth trees—morphed from miniature camouflage to largeness—and flew toward us. On most days, their flight inspired awe and jealousy, as I longed to flap wings alongside them. But today I only experienced thankfulness for their presence as they stood in a pack, gazing woefully to me and then to the boy's body and spirit. I stared at them, recognizing now more than ever the subtle traces that lingered regardless of their near-human masquerade: flecks of bark in toenails, sunlit twigs in hair, blushes of leaf tones on skin.

But then, tree-belting inflexible Prickly Elder pushed his way toward me, and my relief evaporated as he glowered at me in his thorny faced way. He was the eldest tree sprite, and I often wished he'd hunch a bit, act his age, limp in his spindly body. Instead, like always, he fanned his wings higher and stomped his wrinkled feet with the forest's strength.

Prickly Elder opened his mouth to rustle-hum but didn't. Tree sprites, one must know, communicate with a mix of rustle-hums and visuals. While our language threads us together into a cozy oneness as magical folk, it remains imperceptible to the human ear, especially since it sounds like leaves rustling with the wind. But to the tree sprite, every rustle-hum bears a dialect from one's tree, nuances only we can know within a common language every tree sprite can discern. On the occasion when a sprite feels overwhelmed with senses that bear too much, we speak primarily through mind-pictures.

In this instance, Prickly Elder axed a horrific visual into my mind: Horace's first cruelty. My wings—gone! In response, I axed my own outrage into him (a picture too cruel to share) and then stood with defiance. Prickly Elder poked my chest with his spiny finger and rustle-hummed.

"Scarlet Oak," he said.

A few other Scarlet Oaks quivered, as I was one of many. In my forest realm, trees named sprites in their likeness.

"You brought us this human tragedy by not only defying but challenging Nature and her cycle of extraordinary magic. You mourned Sycamore's passing instead of accepting our one honorable way to die . . . along with our birth tree."

I refrained in this moment from commenting on the unfairness of living and dying tied to one's tree. Instead, I stared at the boy's spirit as he continued to rock, naive to the goings-on around him.

"I didn't mean for *this* to happen," I finally said.

"Who do you think will come find the boy? Humans. You've conspired in a human's death. You've brought shame to Horace, and danger to us."

"I didn't call him to the forest," I said, refusing to make eye contact.

Prickly Elder soared and whipped above me, and as I dared to look up, he slapped my face with his crusty right wing. The scent of sap and sour bird eggs leached into my nose.

That's when I heard the horrible hissing sound of *Smissssss*. In a flash, tree sprites flew to their birth trees and morphed back into tiny camouflage, even Prickly Elder. I wanted to do the same, but I couldn't leave the boy's hopeless spirit. So I sat beside him, combating fear. I wondered over which shadow Smis would assume, as he could contort into any shadow and camp out to serve as a reminder of his presence. His favorite incarnation always tormented—a human.

On this night, however, Smis snaked the chilled ground with force, a shadow reflective of the crackly brown leaves spitting up. I stood. Screamed an earth-shattering squawk to warn the spirit to run. But he didn't. The boy's spirit drew more into his rocking and away from the life still left around him. My heart hollered, this time, begging Horace for help.

"There's nothing I can do," Horace said. "We must submit to law."

"The boy's lost," I said.

"He's no longer a boy . . . but a spirit."

"A broken spirit," I said, "that longs for peace."

"The peaceable beast did little to help the boy."

Vexed, I was furious Horace had eavesdropped on my thoughts, the entire night, it seemed. But there wasn't time to be so for long. Smis now stood upright a foot from us in the form of Horace's darkest most deliberate shadow, sizing me up with keen interest, wondering, no doubt, why a tree sprite would even dare to ask a lowly thing as a tree to interfere with his process. But Horace was *my* tree. So far from simple and so close to great, that I knew Horace could outwit Smis if he truly wanted. I was so certain of this, I rustle-hummed.

"May we have the boy's spirit?"

I could tell Smis understood me as he inched closer.

"I know we're not on the best of terms," I said. "But perhaps if you listened to me just this once, bent to my will, I'd learn to appreciate you more, even admire you."

Where I found the courage to converse so closely with Smis fell beyond me. But I didn't diverge from doing so, worried he would take it as weakness.

"You smell of pine, and I find pine delightful," I said.

In fact, Smis smelled like *no-thing,* and he certainly wouldn't smell like pine, even if he owned a scent. More like the most pungent marshy odor. And as I imagined, whiffing this unpleasant aroma, Smis rose from the ground as a blinding shadow that matched the boy's form, hovering near the spirit with ill will. Stunning even myself, I squirmed in between the two. Coldness swooped through me. I wobbled but did not fall. Still, the boy's spirit only rocked.

It was then that Smis schooled me, and this is how I came to interpret it, plain and simple. Smis meant to take the boy's spirit to the Dark. He killed himself. His body would return to the earth. The soul belonged to Horace. And this is *what was*, and *always had been*. Enough said.

Smis stiffened like the forest in summer's harshest hold and sizzled my skin, as I'd imagine a forest fire would salivate to do. But I labeled myself as an impossibility that wished to push the possible. And so, the chance to help the boy's spirit, it stayed with me. Burrowed into my soul as purpose. It was what *would be.*

Smis would have none of this. Knocked me down. Blew me (or flew me) to Horace's tree trunk. Rapped me with it. My head struck hard, and all things dizzied around me. Worse yet, Smis unleashed the horrific sound of a million crows flocking, cawing, pecking.

Then came Horace, my tree who loved me. He leaned his longest branch, scooped the boy's spirit, and raised it to the moon. Surprisingly, Smis hissed and returned as a splatshadow on the ground. For what reason Death's almighty undertaker relented to my oak, I didn't know.

"The spirit . . . move it to the Light," Horace said. "Make an exception."

"No," Smis said.

"My sprite says his eyes didn't intend death."

"How could the boy *not* have intended death? He hung his body from a tree. Your sprite is delusional."

Horace did not speak in return, although his temperament

with Smis took on a softer energy, and I misread it as Horace's strict affection for me, and perhaps the boy.

"You wish to give more to your sprite who takes?" Smis asked.

"Take pity."

I was even more confused by the intimacy with which Horace and Smis now communicated. But my thoughts moved elsewhere quickly as a long awkward silence occurred, one in which I imagined Smis coddling the peaceable beast. Finally, Smis raised upright, contorted himself into a tall lean human's shadow. When he turned his face to the side, his nose grew crooked and sharp as Horace's most irascible branch as his lips strangely quivered.

"I'll give one cycle of seasons to your sprite to provide proof that the spirit belongs to the Light, not the Dark," Smis finally murmured. "One cycle, and that's all."

I dared to step closer to Smis.

"Thank you," I said. "Thank you. Thank you."

"Not so fast," Smis said.

I swallowed my breath.

"You do realize what this means."

Of course I didn't. Logic bypassed me long ago. Only heart-wrenching emotion navigated my sap-flow.

"You'll have to move beyond the boy's spirit to gain that proof."

I stared at the boy's spirit, rocking alone in his agony. I imagined swimming deep through soil and severing Horace's roots with my teeth an easier feat than reaching him.

"And if you leave your birth tree for more than a cycle of seasons . . . you know Nature's law. You'll never be able to morph back onto Horace in miniature form. Not ever again.

No cozy sleeps in his hollow. No warm, safe, symbiotic love for the two of you. You'll forever exist on the outside of Horace . . . in your more human form."

"I won't need to leave Horace at all," I said with the scarcest confidence. "I can reach the boy right here in the forest."

Smis gazed to the boy's spirit. His lips trembled once more, and he stared at Horace's final scarlet leaf fall in slow motion.

"Be sure you're in miniature on Horace before his last leaf falls next autumn, proof in hand."

I nodded and then looked to Horace as he bowed to Smis while still holding firm the boy's spirit. Smis, however, did not return the gesture. Instead, he shrouded us in a chill so deep it mined my quietest pieces, freezing them to black ice. In this state, my breath trapped, and I couldn't see, hear, think, or feel, although I tasted Smis's red wild-berry poison on the cold of my tongue. Smis then carved my rustle-hums, licked its sound like honeysuckle, leaving only fear's fleshy skin. I shivered as he pocketed my sweet flavor, slipped into my shadow, vanished.

Chapter 3

Morning's spidery light hung alongside the boy's body like a faithful web. I kept close in my tiniest form, if not staring at the horror, at least keeping it company. I paced back-and-forth from Horace's branch to his hollow, checking on the boy's pieces as if, somehow, I could will them back to a living body. But the spirit only rocked, and the soul stilled in its glow of patchwork blues. Vertigo eventually stopped this hopeless quest, and I settled on a branch above the body. I tried to weep. No tears showed up.

Sprites peered from their respective trees, but only one ventured near the body. Soothing to my soul, I saw that it was Sugar Maple. She crawled from her hollow, burrowed up Stein's trunk, and scampered along the branch that leaned to us, nearly touching Horace's longest branch. Here, Sugar Maple bowed her weary head. Rustle-hummed her signature moonlit hymn, the one she typically reserved for a tree sprite's passing. Such a kind gesture. I attempted to hum with her, but my voice cracked, its enchantment seemingly gone.

Sugar Maple took pity. She opened her eyes wide as the forest's expanse, and she showed me that love was always in her to give. I moved to the end of Horace's longest branch and took her hand in mine. Together, we sat as the sun grew higher and prouder, and the day flew on like locusts. It was only when dusk greeted us with the sound of humans that Sugar Maple dropped my hand. She urged me to camouflage and then sprinted as best she could to her hollow.

I crept and positioned my body in a triangular nook of Horace's trunk and branch. Rather than pick my bark-skin, I placed my hand over my heart and tapped my bare feet to its swift beats, reminding myself to breathe.

The humans rushed our realm in two waves. The first consisted of three men garbed in blue jay colors and armed with man-made light. For the second, however, humans arrived in a flurried pack, like snow clouds: white garments and faces, coldness, and silence. The men paced in strange patterns around the body, only their footsteps crackled. They brought their human-things and set to work, detaching the rope and placing the body on a stretcher. Still, no human-speak. Only terrible motion.

But then the father limped into view, hand on his heart, mimicking me while bringing sound to the horror of our heartbeats. He threw himself onto his son, cradled their love and wept, and wept, and wept. His anguish spun, panted, pleaded, and pushed through his body, and for a breath, I believed it looked my way, meandered through the forest, and entered me without permission. My heart opened and howled and vibrated the same. In the nucleus of despair, Horace's love for me bared itself—suffocating, dutiful, and affectionate as it was.

I wanted to rustle-hum, roar, crawl into Horace's hollow and sleep—to not feel the darkness that flooded me. Then, the boy's name left the father's tongue.

"Finn, Finn," the father said. "Finn."

The sound chimed—a magic psalm in between rustle-hum and human-speak. And so, I fixated on the loveliness of the boy's name; I played it in a delicate loop in my mind, as if tracing and retracing the sun with my finger. *Finn. Finn. Finn.* It saved me. Even to this day, it does much the same.

Now I proved capable of watching distant, but still close. I noticed things I couldn't have easily recognized in pain's beast-hold; how the father was an outsider to the forest realm but not a foe. His body showed telltale signs of Nature's wear: the aged skin that cracked, the bristled gray-tan shrub on his lower face, the oily thicket of gray and sun-colored hair on his back, the harsh angles and muscled curves of his body, the calluses on his fingertips. Whether the father was a proud strong oak like Horace, I wasn't sure. But I suspected so.

"John," a man said, patting his back. "John, it's time."

The father's name was John. I didn't have time to admire his name because now two men pulled John from Finn's body to cover it with a white cloth. Again, John howled horribly. But I refused to let it overpower me. I cleansed the pain and kept a steady eye on the happenings below. If only John could see his boy's spirit against Sugar Maple's tree. Plainly, the spirit was there, still rocking, unaware. And so I tossed some acorns in that direction. The men looked for a second, but then, purposeful as weeds, they turned to carry on with their business.

John, however, wandered in the direction of Finn's spirit. He stood near Stein and hugged his body into his strong arms. For a moment, I thought he may have felt his son. But, no. Instead, he glared at the branch that took his son without peering into my tree's hollow.

I'll never forget John's long, tear-soaked stare. He meant my tree harm. Still, I knew that whatever came next, I must go with him. John needed me more than his son's spirit, more than Horace, more than Nature and her extraordinary madness. I belonged to him in some inexplicable way.

"No," Horace spoke into me. Stern. "Stay."

I wanted to tell Horace, "Yes, I'll stay. I'll be faithful to you, as you are to me. We will never separate, not like John and Finn." But there lived a larger voice in me—perhaps grief's voice—and it spoke past rustle-hums and human-speak. It told me to leave Horace . . . to go, go, go.

"Please," I said. "Please let me give to John, and you give to Finn."

I couldn't help it. I visualized my wings and the axing of them, and knew then that Horace would yield to me. Horace's branches, of course, weighted with the image, and his hollow grew cold and guilty.

"Stay, please," Horace said, somber.

"I'll come back," I said. "You're my tree."

I watched Horace stare at John—father to father—and could feel my tree's pleas to keep me safe. As John turned, I sensed that Horace complied with my wishes. In this moment, I loved him more than ever before. I patted his branch and crept down to the base of his trunk, studying the rescue workers as they carried the body until the opportune time to follow arose. Then I slipped and morphed from Horace. Walked like a human without wings and lifted his final scarlet leaf from the ground. Holding it gently, I turned back only once to kiss my forest father with warm-root eyes. With every step from him, I wondered how much Horace ached to let me go.

Horace-Speak

My hollow aches the most. My branches can find companionship with the wind. My leaves come and go without much distress. I know they'll return. Perhaps not in the same way as before. But a return is inevitable. Part of Nature's extraordinary madness. My hollow, though, it's meant only for Scarlet, and now she's gone.

How can a thing born from within grow limbs that then carry it so far away? And how is this natural or Nature? I stand and wonder because there's nothing left to do. And also, because the boy's spirit isn't the most engaging distraction. It rocks and mourns—nothing more, nothing less. And I'm stuck beside it, no escape. Loyal to my word, I'll look after it. At least offer my shade, as fate would have it. But to give more?

Oh, I wish I wasn't so much a giving tree as a taking tree. I'd take Scarlet back. Then I'd give the boy-spirit to Nature, thrust it backwards into her void or Smis's shadow (whomever will take it first), so that circumstances weren't as they were. I miss her. Scarlet.

True, she's only just left. But my hollow's a burning lonely cavern of memory. The feel of what she felt inside of it—gone. The air of her breath. The whisper of her rustle-hums, for good or bad. The essence of the only tree sprite—and, in human-speak, child—I've ever known.

Scarlet's all there is and was to begin with, I now know. Be well, Scarlet. Be brave. If words can't find you, speak from the soul.

Chapter 4

As soon as I walked from Horace, camouflaged tree sprites rustle-hummed my intent with leaf-blown sound to each other—their voices traveling far and wide through the forest realm. Worried, I didn't speak (barely heard my own breath). Instead, I followed the men at a safe distance and hid in dark shadows, not behind trees. Still, my community warned and scolded me as I passed.

"Turn back. Turn back. Turn back. You belong to Horace. You belong to Horace. You belong to Horace. Tree sprite. Tree sprite. Tree sprite."

Nature's extraordinary madness did not stop me. I trudged on, fielding the curves and crunches of the forest and keeping the human-speak close. Oftentimes, John paused, fell to his knees, and the men were forced to lift him up. Each time, I knelt on the cold ground and replayed the beauty of Finn's name, struggling to overcome the force of John's pain.

It went on in this pattern until the men neared and passed Prickly Elder's tree—a devil's walkingstick. Autumn's end had already unleashed its cruel way with the tree—snatching its large overshadowing leaves—and rendering it bare and small, ugliness on full display. Beneath the jaded moonlight, the skeletal tree glowered at me with sharp spines and deep dark berries and broken ridge bark. As I glared back, I understood why Prickly Elder appeared so unpleasant. Haunted, I crept and tiptoed, hoping to bypass him.

Prickly Elder, however, eyed me from the bark in miniature form, more hideous than his tree: spiny skin with endless pricks, crusty moth wings, and soul juiced with the night's wickedness. I tried to look away but couldn't. His quiet rustle-hum chilled my wing scar.

"Scarlet Oak, you leave Horace, and the forest realm . . . you grow into human, and away from tree sprite."

Prickly Elder placed a picture in my mind, but it seemed unimaginable. I blocked it—won't even speak of it here— and there I didn't speak, either.

"There's no coming back."

Boldly, I took a step closer to the devil's walkingstick. I gazed into the openness of Prickly's eyes, searching for a different truth. I didn't rustle-hum to him, but thought to myself, *I'll come back. You'll see.*

Prickly Elder closed his eyes and camouflaged so deeply in his tree I couldn't find him. Something about Prickly Elder growing so small and offering my passage a choice frightened me more so than if he'd plumped himself up and bullied me to stay. I stood there for a long time, until the men's voices and footsteps grew into echoed whispers. It was only when I couldn't hear them at all that I closed my mind and told my feet to run.

I ran, the wind on my back, leaves tangling my hair, the moon on my face, the forest at my feet. I gasped. Feared. Fell a few times. But I didn't think. Not once. Only ran, longing for my wings in a way I'd never done before.

I caught up to John and the men only because grief stunted their journey. John had keeled over near some pines. His breath, powered like a gale, and together with the pine scent, I dizzied. It was then that I heard a rescue worker say, "A panic attack." John's pain pelted in me as the men did their best to soothe him. I took it, and waited, and watched.

When the unpeaceable beast passed, John stood again and followed the men that held his son. Only leaves cracked beneath them, and whispers from breath were heard. This went on until the border between the forest realm and the human realm arose. I hid, and gazed, and wondered. Never had I traveled this far from Horace, and certainly never to the edge of the forest realm.

This was how I experienced it—as if trees folded and fell, and space parted ways to an uncharted view. Yes, Nature still had her hand in its surroundings, but human-things dotted her color and vastness. I wished to go on and on, documenting the differences, but John's sorrow diverted my attention as he leaned over the white clothed body and begged Finn to come back to him, to live. I couldn't bear the intensity and so instead, marveled over John's aged Chevrolet truck.

In a flash, I imagined it delicate as a bluebird's egg. Yes, the color matched, a pale blue, but the size didn't. I realized it was in the way the truck sat so alone—apart from the larger vehicles with harsh lights—that made it feel so, as if with the sparsest touch it might crack open and tear to pieces, no nest beneath it.

I continued staring at John's truck, away from the lights that pierced my eyes, until whirs and rumbles sounded. I glanced back to find the body tucked away and John standing with only one man. John's unpeaceable beast roared, and by far, this outpouring encompassed the worst of it. I covered my ears. Closed my eyes. When it passed as best it could, the man patted his shoulder and walked away with his head hung low. Everyone and everything left except John, grief, and his truck.

The moment grew urgent, prompting me to morph into what I must. Offer a tiny gesture. Open John to the possibility of another realm. One in which his son still lived in spirit. His soul dwelled in my tree.

I caressed Horace's scarlet leaf, and ever so slowly, I walked beyond my birth father and the forest realm's secrets toward another father, and the human realm's secrets . . . stepping closer, and closer, and closer . . .

Chapter 5

It wasn't as I hoped from John. No tears or human-speak or gust of relief. It was, instead, a peculiar shock (I presumed), as if a weeping willow tree sprouted feet and tiptoed from the forest, carrying a scarlet oak leaf as a pitiable offering, and then hummed in a way that no human could believe a weeping willow to sound. Nature quieted alongside my rustle-hum, making it more pronounced, and we stood gazing in each other's grief-eyes.

I stole the first step closer, and John straightaway stepped back. He dashed to his truck, reached for a weatherworn tan jacket, and handed it to me. It was only then that I felt my nakedness in a way I never had before. I took the garment, draped it backwards on my shoulders, and when I stopped there, he moved forward, nervously, placed my arms in their rightful spot, and fastened the buttons. As the small buds on my chest pressed against the cold itchy fabric, I daydreamed winter's moon to have grown limbs and hand-dressed me in a shadow. My head hung low, and shame followed. John lifted my face with a gentle finger and gazed so deep into my russet-root eyes that I worried he knew all of my secrets.

"Somethin' happen in the woods?" he asked in a whisper. "Tell me now. What happen, to have ya come creepin' out like that, no clothes? Should I call the police?"

I didn't understand human-speak yet, so I stored all of his words and sounds deep in my mind and soul for future decoding and feeling. But I understood the emotional complexity of his eyes and knew he meant me no harm. In fact, I imagined the whites of his eyes dandelion seeds, blowing secret wishes into mine. The browns of his eyes, however, quickly buried this want as he readjusted his body, even took a step back.

"This ain't no place to be wanderin'."

John looked past me for a moment, as if perhaps I was an illusion the forest sent to rattle him all the more. He then readjusted his eyes on me, confused. This lasted for a good stretch, and I fidgeted in my bare feet until he finally moved to me, placing his hand on my shoulder as if to confirm I was there.

"Come on, then," he said. "Cold out here. Lemme drive ya home. Parents'll worry."

He trembled when he said "parents," as if the word swallowed into his heart's concave to never be spoken again. I struggled to find language other than the last word his son spoke. But *No* echoed three times in Finn's tone, even as I tried to stop it.

"No?" he asked, sorrow rushing back to him.

My heart twiddled in my frame and then shook so much so that I stepped forward, leaned against his pale blue truck. To calm myself, I lowered my nose, smelled its metal skin, and then placed my ear on its frostiness. Listened to the quiet. My actions distracted from his grief—this I knew by the way the furrow in his brow twitched in a different configuration.

"You okay?"

I stared off into the distance, wondering what to do next.

"You gotta come from someplace. Ain't born from the woods."

John's grief returned in a violent rush, and suddenly he keeled over, unable to breathe. He didn't cry. My presence seemed to dry that part of him up. But his chest heaved and undulated like sore moving clouds. It hurt me, but I knelt at a safe distance all the same—respectful of his space. When his breathing calmed, I stood and extended my crimson leaf to him, a simple offering that followed me from Horace. He squeezed it in his palm, never looking to me. Finally, he spoke.

"You'll be comin' home with me. My wife'll see to it ya find where ya meant to be."

He stood and opened the door. I understood his gesture, and so entered the truck and rested on its worn cream seat, only a tad comfier than a moss-topped stump. John shut the door and slipped into the seat on the other side, turning the motor to life. I didn't look at him, and he didn't look at me. But I heard every variation of his breath.

As we moved, the truck's interior reminded me of Horace's hollow—still but warmed with air, whirring with energy. No matter, fear snatched my soul with raw tentacles, directing me to return to the forest. And so I rustle-hummed Finn's name in my mind to self-soothe. Soon, however, my thoughts returned to Horace. I couldn't help it. He was there—apart and a part of me. His voice beckoned with the tender tone that lulled me to sleep: *"Be well, Scarlet. Be well. Be well."*

Part Two

The Human Realm

Smis-Speak

I live in the soul of all things. I slip in and out through shadows. Right now, I'm cloaked in the moon's shadow, resting on John's blue truck bed, skygazing. I finger the stars. *Chink. Clink. Chink. Clink.* I hear Scarlet's thoughts and contemplate my own.

The tree sprite feels me when I'm unseen. She hears what others can't hear. She tastes me on her lips. *Chink. Clink. Chink. Clink.* The stars know me, too. They twinkle to Smis. Submit.

There was a time when I longed for something more than what I am. More than the cruel shadow the living run from and condemn. There even existed a time I hoped for Love.

Yes, Love!

Chapter 6

The truck didn't wander very far, but even so, sleep took me. I only awoke when the motor stopped breathing, and turned to John as cool moonlight struck him. I closed my eyes again and listened to his heartbeat, rustle-hummed in my mind Finn's name. But this time, my soul blew it past my lips. John shook much in the way Horace did when frightened. He looked to me, and although I couldn't see his eyes too well, I felt them, pining orbs that wanted to know and not know, to be with me and not be with me. Then, he whispered these words.

"By God, ain't you a strange bird."

Time would eventually decode the word *bird* for me, and I'd soar with the likeness. Soar! I loved birds, whether strange or not. But for now, I simply ceased my rustle-hums of Finn's name and struggled to stop tapping my toes on the gravelly floor. John turned from me and stared through the smudged window. The moon and stars mixed with artificial red, blue, and yellow light, illuminating for me the distant house.

We were parked at the top of a hill overlooking a windy

dirt driveway. In order to gain access, John slipped from the truck and opened a metal gate attached to barbed-wire fencing that traveled the perimeter of his property—locking in tight his brand of Nature's madness—farmland I'd come to know. The driveway, too, snaked the territory, protective, dividing it east and west until its mouth eventually touched the bluebell house.

An odd description, the bluebell house, I know. But that's how I experienced it at first glance—a drooping blue flower of a house, beautiful in its fragility. A closer inspection, true, revealed Nature's work to distress the house's exterior, make it less of a bluebell flower and more of a weatherworn tree with a few aged forlorn stories. But I didn't have the view, want, or knowledge to look at it that way, then. I'd much rather think of Finn's house as a fragrant bluebell.

Once I saw the house, of course, I studied it, nursing the strongest desire to know its unique soul as much as I wanted to understand those who lived there. Its dark windows, however, eyed me with secrets to hide, and the woods enclosing the farmland towered, intent to do so as well.

Flashing red lights distracted me as we moved slowly up the long loneliness of the driveway. I watched John squirm near the gate and listened as the car approached, and a man wound his car window down, perched to speak. I twiddled my fingers for John.

"So sorry, John," the man said. "God bless ya'll real good."

"God ain't blessed nothin' bout these past days," John said.

John tapped the car twice, and I dipped lower in the truck's seat as the man drove away. John returned to me, and we traveled through the gate and down the driveway at a slug's pace. I could sense his want to reroute the truck, race back to the forest, hover over his dead son's body, remain there, not here, not wandering to the bluebell house to unload what was and wouldn't be again. I placed my hand near his, careful not to touch him. I hoped the gesture might ease him in the unease. But he only took his hand and placed it with the other on the steering wheel, the whites of his knuckles shining.

We stopped a short distance from the bluebell house. John leaned across and maneuvered the seat backwards, and I understood he meant for me to not only remain but also stay hidden for now. I abided by his wish, although I lifted my head high enough to watch through the window. As he left and neared the porch, a lean, pale, poisoned mushroom of a woman threw herself outside and slammed the door behind her. She stood before him so still that I worried John would turn to stone with her. Then she slapped his face twice. The sound hurt my ears, but I didn't cover them.

"John Hawes," she said, "it's all your fault. All yours. That woman in there you claim to love . . . she's devastated. No, worse than devastated. She's dead. She'll never live again. You killed her, and so you've got some nerve even showing up back here. Go on . . . go someplace else where you're wanted."

John didn't speak one word. But his body trembled as much as mine did when Prickly Elder scolded me. He must have dammed his rage deep in the ruggedness of his landscape to not lash out. Thankfully, Finn's mother, Helen, exited in a tattered gray robe, hair extending like wildfire, and limbs just as fiery as she gripped the poisoned mushroom woman.

"Go on home, Sandra," Helen said, curtly.

"You need me," Sandra Cummings said. "When will it

dawn on you that you need me more than him? Now's about the time you'd know that . . . when that man's killed your only son."

"Go," Helen said. "Leave."

"God is your Lord savior, not this man . . . not the way you've made this man, and his land, and his way, yours. Look what it's brought you, Helen. It pains me to see . . . to see you this way."

Sandra tried to stroke Helen's hair from her face, but Helen pushed her away and instead grabbed John, pulled him into the bluebell house. Slammed the door shut. Sandra gazed at the stars. She star-spoke to them (something cruel, I'm sure, although I couldn't hear what she said), and then she hobbled to her car. Sped off.

I rose in my seat and fixated on the rickety front porch, hypnotized by the dim blue bulb of light that hung from its ceiling, swaying soulfully with the wind. Magnetized to the melancholy, I moved closer to the house. Rooted myself footsteps from it, enchanted with the porch's sparse items: empty planters on the windowsills, a round wooden table holding a teapot and teacups, and a few saggy chairs. Most interesting, a weathered silver ax perched upright in a shadowed corner. I wondered over the curiousness of human-things and wanted to examine them closer, but fear moved me back to the truck.

As the moon sunk, John returned to me, and this time Helen walked behind him. She pushed past him. Her tear-stained face peered through the truck window, and when I didn't appear clear enough for her, she rubbed at it fiercely with her green robe. Once more, she stared at me, and I stared back, and in that startling gape I labeled Helen Hawes a rolling rainstorm of a woman. Like the unpredictability of a rolling rainstorm, she frightened and entranced me with her choppy watered eyes. It was John who pulled her back, opened the truck door, motioning for me to exit. I obeyed and stood as far away as I could from the two.

"She jus' come walkin' from the woods, like I say."

"My boy just hung himself to death, and you bring me back a naked tramp," Helen said, and then beat John's chest with her fists.

John withstood every punch and refused to fight back. I wanted to kick Helen, and it pained me not to do so. But John's eyes told me to stay still, to allow his wife the room to do what she must. Her punches soon mixed with words—a tornado of human-speak. I did my best to store them. How could I not? She glared my way as she punched, speaking to me as much as to her husband.

"Did she see Finn? Was she with Finn? Did she do something to Finn? Something perverse? Was she with someone who did something perverse to Finn? Has she told you anything, anything, John? Tell me everything . . . everything you know. A girl just doesn't come walking from the woods, naked, knowing nothing. Police say it was suicide. Suicide, John. Suicide. But maybe, just maybe, this girl knows more. Knows it wasn't that at all."

"Helen . . . girl ain't talk, as much I can tell. I told ya that."

Helen ceased striking and fell to John's feet and rippled beyond a rolling rainstorm, longer, too. John stooped over and tried to lift her. But she pushed him away.

"Just leave me alone," she said as she sobbed, staring back-and-forth between us. "If you, or you, won't tell me the truth . . . both of you . . . go."

Helen reached into my aloneness and echoed in chambers I'd never heard. The sounds—oh, the sounds. Even to this day I have nothing to liken them to. I keeled over, unable to blunt her pain. Helen, for all her grief, noticed, a maternal instinct taking hold. Slowly, she crawled to me, knelt, and looked up into my eyes. I couldn't help but think of Finn, and how I'd done the same.

Helen gazed into me with a forest's strength, wildness. To counterattack, I tried to process her many human pieces, but there were too many, most awfully the grief part, and so I turned to worry. I worried that she could smell my sin— my want to hold her son's soul. I worried she could see my severed wings. I worried she could feel my connection to Smis. After all, she was a mother—the most powerful human blessing and beast. She could sense these things . . . and more . . . and she did. This I knew when she pushed raven strands from my face, studied me deeper. Her fingers traced my cheek. I honored her with stillness.

Then, this strangeness happened. The rolling rainstorm piece of Helen switched off. The lines in her face softened, and her brown-gray nest eyes spoke to me . . . *"Do not fear, child."* Helen rose, and she took my hand, so cold, so firm but still kind in some sort of warm-forgotten way I knew once birthed in Horace's hollow. She walked with me to the bluebell house. She didn't look back to John . . . not once. She opened the worn wooden door. Of course, I followed. And then, she closed it behind me.

Chapter 7

I half expected to divorce myself from Horace as I entered the human realm. But I didn't feel that at all. Instead, I read my oak more acutely by way of the dim lighting, wooden floors, paneled shimmery walls, golds, greens, and browns of the décor, including the dewy plants hung in macramé and the air warming around it all. No, it wasn't a death from Horace but an earthen reminder of my birth father. Horace existed here, somehow, even while there in the forest realm.

My next impression of the bluebell house centered on its life force. At one time, this place rooted in happiness; the residue circulated in a pleasing energy, even lifting as an enchanted dance of moonlit dust motes. I stood in the entryway and allowed myself to greet it.

"Stay," Helen said.

I remained in that one spot, charmed and sorrowed. Helen rushed up the timber staircase ahead, returning with a floral nightgown. She guided me to a goldish green bathroom and handed it to me, closing the door behind her. Here, the light shone harsh as the brazen sun, but I refused to close my eyes. Rather, I removed John's coat and draped the smooth garment on my body, permitting it to rub my wing scar in a lovely way.

Afterwards, I glanced into a rectangular mirror framed in distressed wood above the sink, tapping and rubbing it and wondering over the bluebell house's magic. The mirror's surface felt nothing like my own. No, there were not two of me. I was one. As this realization dawned, I imagined how I'd appear in miniature form on my oak, picking my bark-skin and feeling overall ugly. That's when Helen opened the door. Stared at me gaping at myself.

"Who are you?" she said, her voice strangely silken as a spring breeze.

I didn't understand to speak and thus couldn't respond in her language. But I did turn from the mirror to acknowledge her with my eyes.

"You weren't born and bred in the woods. So we're going to put some tea on and have a chat. You'll tell me everything I need to know. Men, they aren't good with talk, and they seldom ask the right questions, or know enough to understand there's more questions to ask."

Helen confounded me. Not just her words, but also her actions. What happened to the rolling rainstorm of a woman from outside? Where did she go? This woman who took her place, she economized her grief, tucking it tidily away. I followed her to the kitchen and wondered over her hiding places. Could it be there . . . in the orangey kettle? Or there, in the magic water she drizzled into it and allowed to bubble on the harvest-gold stove? Or there, in the tea bags or the sugar she scooped from mushroom-shaped containers? Where? Certainly, not hidden there in the flower-patterned wall.

I sat on a chair that squeaked and placed my hands on

the wooden tabletop. Then, I waited for Helen to sit, too. Eventually, she handed me a mug. I touched its round part, not its handle, and spilled hot liquid, parts splattering on the hem of the nightdress she gave me. Helen wiped me first, and then the floor. She poured tea once more, placed the mug before me and sat to my left, gawking all the while.

I waited for her to sip from her mug—watched like a hawk—and then mimicked her movement. The tea tasted like the peppermint plants I loved near my forest realm's brook. My heart smiled.

"So, tell me, child . . . who do you belong to?"

I took a sip and tapped my toes.

"You must have a voice somewhere in that body," Helen said. "Speak it. Speak it clearly now, before another moment passes."

While she stopped speaking, she didn't stop staring, and I intuited in that stare that she'd continue to do so all night long if I didn't release one sound. I adored the peppermint tea but not so much the way she examined me. So I did it. I rustle-hummed my tree's name. *Horace.* Tears dripped from Helen's eyes. Fierce tears. Neat tears. Tears hand-sewn by sorrow's craftsmanship.

"Can't speak, child," Helen finally said. "Only hum."

She placed her hand over mine and she bowed her head. Helen Hawes, the rainstorm-of-a-woman, returned. But this time, the rainstorm lulled—it didn't roll. My hand warmed even in its want to shiver. And we stayed like this until my peppermint tea cooled. Not speaking anymore, not looking anymore, not wondering anymore. Eventually, Helen stood, opened the brown refrigerator to autumn's air, and withdrew human food. She sliced, and placed, and put it before me.

"Leftover turkey," she said, "and pumpkin pie. Didn't get to eat it this Thanksgiving. Eat. You look hungry."

I tasted a little of each but couldn't eat (no matter that both were delightful). So Helen guided me to the stairway. With each wooden footfall, I thought of Horace and all the steps I'd taken until this point with him and for him, and all the steps I'd left to take. I also pondered how the climb seemed simple, unlike the ascent on Horace's bark to branches. The steps only creaked—didn't crackle with my weight—yet still spoke to my soul in a quiet, unspoken space. The moment we reached the top, I longed to retrace my journey over and over and over again.

Helen stopped at a blue bathroom upstairs, and she offered me a plush towel and pointed to rosemary shampoos and creamy soaps in the bathtub. I stared at her, puzzled, and she read my confusion. Without words, she turned a knob as warm water trickled like summer's rain. Then she took the nightdress from my body and helped me inside. She touched my wing scar, studied it, but said nothing.

Helen then baptized me in humanness as she lowered my head beneath the silver spigot and scrubbed the forest from my hair. Her fingernails scratched like Horace's bark, but in a soothing way, and a mixture of emotions flooded me as I closed my eyes and thought of Horace, tears running down my cheeks. When she rinsed my hair, I sat up, and she handed me the soap, held my hand with it, and scrubbed my arms. She then stood back, motioned for me with her eyes to continue. It was then that I cleansed myself of every forest scent that kept me close to every part of Horace.

"That'll do," Helen said.

She extended her hand, and I finished as she wrapped the towel around me and then used part of it to dry my arms.

She left me to continue and returned with a different night-dress, plain, not floral. She slipped its cottonness over me, and it touched my wing scar in a startled way. She then used the towel to fight the wetness of my hair, and she studied a few strands with such interest, I thought she might detect subtle traces of my origin and interrogate me once more. Instead, she placed those strands neatly on my back, and opened the door. I followed.

We walked down the hallway to a cedar door. Gently, she held and turned its knob before entry. I didn't look around and try to experience too much, mostly because the room shivered with nighttime, only a small lamp offering the sparsest grim light. Helen moved with intent amidst it. She patted a modest bed (such a heavenly human sleep-thing) and threw a heavy quilt on it. She fluffed two pillows, folded the quilt down with precision, and signaled for me to approach. I slipped beneath the quilt and cozied my wing scar on the sheets that stuck like spider webs. My head rested in unrest, appreciative still of the pillows that channeled lush clouds.

"There you go," Helen whispered. "Sleep, child."

She took a seat near the bed and continued to scrutinize me. I closed my eyes. I didn't open them until her heaviness lifted and saw itself through the door. Then, I stood. Tiptoed to the window. Placed my hand against its cold. I looked through its glass to a world I knew better but hardly at all, anymore. For a moment, my rustle-hums quivered and I trembled in my entrapment behind the glass.

That's when I saw John in the distance, through a window carved into a small weathered workshed. Moonlight hugged his back as he hunched over something unseen. I longed to walk outside. Peer through his looking glass. Comfort him in some tiny way. But I could hear Helen's anguish unleashing itself in her room. Finn was gone, and I had watched, not helped. Guilt paralyzed me to this spot, and Smis locked me there, chaining me in his no-scent (that I only wished smelled of pine). Smis told me, "*Stay.*"

Smis-Speak

I enter the bluebell house. Fly the wooden stairs. Trespass in Scarlet's shadow. I don't apologize. It is mine to take. I whisper to her . . . *"You took me on, you give to me."* Scarlet hears me; but she won't speak.

"Speak," I say. *"Speak."*

She won't.

I want to hurt her in the way I hurt.

But I don't.

"Stay," I say. *"Stay in my shadow."*

Scarlet does, but not for me.

Grief listens. Grief stays willingly.

My only friend.

Chapter 8

I woke, not in the tradition of the forest realm with sliced sun or tepid rain or breathy fog on my face. Instead, I rose to Helen's cold touch, and human smells, and Smis's snide shadow as he parked in the room's corner, smiling. I didn't return the nicety.

"Breakfast," Helen said. "Come."

When she stood at the doorway and didn't leave, I got up, adjusted my nightgown, and followed. I didn't commune with the steps or Horace like the night before, mostly because I wondered if John would be downstairs. Indeed, he slouched in one of the four yellow chairs, his hands folded on the wooden tabletop. Once I neared, he pointed to a chair beside him. I knew to sit there, and not on the chair Helen leaned on, realizing it was Finn's.

"Pancakes," Helen said, placing a stack before me with warm butter.

She showered them with syrup, and as she did so I could smell old sweet Sugar Maple beside me. Helen then lifted a fork, sliced the pancakes for me, and placed a bite on a prong. She gave it to me and folded my fingers around the handle, guiding the food to my mouth.

"Girl knows how to eat," John said. "Jus' 'cause she ain't talkin' . . . that don't mean she ain't know how to eat."

"Just because she *isn't* talking," Helen said.

John bowed his head. He didn't eat. Helen busied herself at the stove, never taking a bite. Shamefully, I devoured the pancakes with the fork, quick to pick up the use of this silver human-thing.

"I'll be takin' her to town when she finishes up," John said. "Find out what we can about her."

Helen slammed the spatula on the countertop and stared at John with venom fit for the nastiest snake.

"You'll be doing nothing of the sort. *I'll* take her," Helen said.

"Helen," John said, his voice quieter.

"Don't *Helen* me. This day . . . it'll be difficult enough to get through, and the only reason I'm standing to get through it is that girl right there. The girl that came from the woods that killed our son. So I'll see her through, find out myself. You've work to do. The farm can't take a day to grieve. Neither can you."

"We need to talk," John said.

"The only thing left to say is Finn's dead. Dead. Never coming back. Talk over."

Helen didn't cry. Rage replaced the tears, and I feared first for the spatula that she tightened in her grip. And then, of course, for John. I didn't fear for myself. Somehow, I knew Helen wouldn't hurt me—that I was the sliver of wilted light keeping her heart from death's complete eclipse. Then came the sound at the front door. *Rap-a-tap-a-rap.*

Rap-a-tap-a-rap. Rap-a-tap-a-rap. I liked it very much. Softer than a woodpecker's tap. Respectful.

Helen and John did not share my sentiment. They both looked to the other with panic in their eyes, neither one moving, as if stone-shadows themselves. I mimicked their stillness. *Rap-a-tap-a-rap. Rap-a-tap-a-rap. Rap-a-tap-a-rap.* The sound refused to go away.

"Hide the girl," Helen said in a whisper. "Hide her."

John didn't speak, although his eyes cradled so many words, even that one that his son said last . . . *No.*

"If you still love me at all, John Hawes," Helen said, her whisper more forceful, "then you'll hide her."

John relented to his wife's demand. He patted my shoulder, took my plate, and I followed him into a pantry. It was dark, but I could smell the many human-things surrounding me, one that smelled of pine. Cleaning things, I later learned. Detergents and soaps, bleaches and brooms, mops and sponges. Things used to erase not only dirt but also horror.

"Stay," John said. "Jus' for a bit."

I understood John more and more, and not through his voice, but rather, his sorrow shimmer—a woeful glow that soul-spoke. And so, when he closed the door, I imagined holding not the plate of pancakes, but Finn's blue soul, so that when John came back, he would know his son was alive in some way, still beautiful. A few tears splashed the floor, even with the knowledge that the best of hollows harbored Finn's soul.

47

Voices, however, plucked me from my thoughts, and I cracked the door open. I watched as a man in black garb entered and stood, a brown hat held rigid against his chest. Helen cried, and John leaned against the counter, his head hung low.

"I'd like to offer some . . ."

"No," Helen said. "No, Father Will. No words handpicked from God and heaven and the angels above. God turned his back on us, and the angels flew off with him. Finn's dead. Dead. Not with God. Dead. And he'll be six feet under the ground, soon . . . and before that, on a cold slab, picked apart, primped, and then placed in a coffin. I won't look at him that way. I won't come to church for a funeral. And I sure as hell don't want anyone to see Finn that way, either. No one knew our Finn, anyway. Not truly. We'll say our goodbyes in our own way. Our way. Just us."

Much to my amazement, Helen and John united with a look to each other.

"I understand," Father Will said, his eyes a different shade of grief.

"Do you?" Helen asked. "Do you truly? Do you understand something growing inside your own womb . . . inside the most sacred holy space of your womanhood? . . . And then that child's ripped from you, and hung on the cold branch of a tree, killed, while God sat propped up all powerful and mighty in heaven with his angels and watched. Watched. I gave my heart to God, my time, my soul, my blood. Even gave Him a second chance, one too many times. Very few Sundays in my lifetime I missed going to church. Very few. But God paid me back. He waited, and then watched my son suffer alone and die."

"God isn't interested in paybacks . . ."

"Don't you dare preach me a sermon about God and heaven," Helen said. "Leave. The door's that way."

John's head lifted, and he looked at Father Will, not at all apologetic for his wife.

"John, you'll be needing some sort of burial," Father Will said. "I'd like to extend an offer to oversee it. If here's where you want to bury Finn, I'll oversee it for you. Even help as best I can with the arrangements."

"Wanna help me, that it? Wanna help me now?" John asked in a whisper.

Father Will didn't move, and the room grew silent. It went on this way for what felt like forever, until Helen finally spoke.

"We don't need religion to bury our son," Helen said.

"But you do need some help. And I'd like to give it."

"Time to go," John said. "We'll think on it. Let ya know by tomorrow."

"By phone," Helen said. "We have one of those, you know, hanging right there on the wall. Sure you can manage to find our number in the phone book. Save yourself the long drive from town to check up on people who aren't equipped for company."

"Not God's way . . . not the Southern Maryland way, either," Father Will said. "We reach out, touch, give a hand to our own."

I noticed John's face redden and his heart's want to slash its rugged seams, roar. Father Will averted his gaze from John, noticing as well, and instead looked around the kitchen nervously. He didn't extend his hand to either John or Helen, reading their resistance. However, his gaze did find mine—for a flicker—and so, I shut the door. When

I heard his footsteps near the pantry, I held my breath. But he walked past. Didn't intrude.

"Again, I'm so sorry," Father Will said.

"Sorry ain't ever undone what's said and done," John said.

The front door opened and shut. Silence spun, anxious, in the kitchen as I waited until Helen came to me and took my hand, walking me from the pantry's shadow. I stood as still and respectful as I could with my plate. Helen took it from me and doused more maple syrup on the few bites I had left to eat as John sat. Then Helen and I did the same. I finished eating in complete silence, save for the hum of pancake melting in my mouth.

Eventually, I returned to the bedroom and rested on the bed. Smis was there. He camped out in the curtain's fluid shadow and eyed me, but with less of a smile. He picked me apart with his shadow-eyes, and I picked my scalp in response, fidgeted my feet, rustle-hummed horrible sounds to him in my head. He could hear me because he altogether stopped smiling.

"I mean to know Finn's story, and in it find your proof," I rustle-hummed, no matter how hard Smis seemed to press my vocal chords with his shadow-fingers. *"When I do, then I'll know how to help John, Helen, and most of all, Finn."*

Smis gaped at me in his broody, barely there sort of way. Of course he only wished me to speak at his direction.

"Stop fighting what is," he finally said. *"The story's over. Finn's gone."*

"His spirit isn't," I said.

"Broken and meant for me."

"Not if I can help it," I said.

"Can't outrun me, Scarlet, there in the forest realm, or here in the human realm. Can't win."

"Can't lose," I said.

Smis now smiled once more with sharp, fractured shadow-teeth reflective of my pain. I closed my eyes despite my sore throat and fell into a nightmare. Smis, of course, flew into the dark with me.

Chapter 9

Helen didn't wake me until the afternoon. She tapped my shoulders and then threw open the curtains as I stood. Then she wrapped me in human-things—an orange floral dress, scratchy knee-high socks, and brown earth shoes too big for my feet. She fingered the tangles in my hair while clucking her tongue in a curious way, and continued to do so as she wiped my face with her spit and fingertips. Next, she buttoned me into an olive suede coat with furry fox skin on its collar. The strange fox-death-coat repulsed me, but still I followed Helen when she signaled to leave the room.

At the last moment, I turned to find Smis still there. He pointed his crooked shadow-finger at my coat. Smiled. I hated him all the more. And as I thought about all the reasons why I truly detested Smis, Helen loaded me into John's blue truck and then took her place at the wheel, winding down the window. John stood, his hands on the door. His eyes pleaded with her. Helen didn't speak until she absolutely had to do so.

"You really gonna take her to town?" John asked.

"I said I would. I will," Helen said.

"But you hid her from Father Will."

"Wasn't ready," Helen said.

"Lemme come. No shape to drive."

"I'm fine. Need the drive."

John patted the open space where the window should have closed them off. He looked at me, so sad.

"Hopin' you get back to where ya meant to be," he said.

I wanted to rustle-hum so many things (mostly that I was scared), but other things, too. Where was Helen taking me? Would I see John again? What was this *town*? The sound *ow* hurt me, and the *t* and *n* sounds shut the pain in—no escape. But, of course, I didn't voice any of this at all—not in rustle-hum or attempted human-speak. I simply nodded to John and resolved to find my way back, no matter where Helen took me. Fear would not strip my will.

John stepped back. He didn't stop us when the truck rumbled and rolled, and *bump-de-bumped* on the dirt driveway. No, he stood as still as Horace in the summertime, while Smis loitered in the smallness and largeness of his shadow. I welcomed the break.

The truck ambled along many roads—some dirt, some paved, some winding, most flat, a few with modest hills. We moved through Nature's openness (more farmland) and Nature's guardedness (trees towering or weeping to the left and right of us). We passed human-things: houses, mailboxes, and a few cars. Some houses shaped themselves differently than the bluebell one, with smaller stories and less grief. Each time we passed a house, Helen sped up while pushing my head down with her right hand, hiding me. After a few times, I cloaked myself. We went on this way for a turtle's stretch.

The sun chose to set, and darkness caved into us. Nature

required sleep. But we didn't. We continued to drive, biding time, breathing with the absence of rustle-hums or human-speak, tears, or even a final destination. Then the moon returned, and Helen drove to where we'd meant to go.

"Leonardtown," she said. "When John asks, you nod. We went to Leonardtown."

Helen nodded her head to show me how.

"I don't lie," she said. "I'm like the summertime. Summertime can't lie. Heat forces all truths."

Helen then whispered to herself, "Like the summertime, I don't lie." I didn't understand what this meant. But one day, I would.

When we entered Leonardtown, Helen allowed me to sit up, the dark a useful shadow. We rode into the tiny town woven together with lights and noise and prim, antiquated build-ings. Some shops spoke in faint lights, others with bright lights, and I glimpsed humans gathering and mouthing stories (and shopping, Helen said). Colorful earthen clothes and gestures adorned these humans, different creatures yet the same. Some were even eating, speaking, and laugh-ing around cozy tables. I couldn't absorb or process it all—this influx of human-watching in their element—and when my head pounded and my ears rung with the stimulus and sound, I closed my eyes, covered my ears, imagined my wing scar protected from it all. Helen reached to me and patted my lap.

"We won't stay long," she said. "Only drive by the police station . . . so we don't lie."

She drew me into her lie with her honey voice. But when we rode past the police station, its energy churned my stomach—the same energy I felt watching beetles burrow in the dirt. Or worse yet, Prickly Elder eating them with lemongrass. Thankfully, Helen didn't linger here. She drove by, made a sharp turn, and I hoped we'd now return to the bluebell house. Instead, she cried, her tears rolling with that rainstorm of hers.

"Need to stop at High's," she finally said. "Get milk for Finn."

Obviously, grief spoke to her through the weeping that Finn's death was a fantasy and he'd be home safe upon her return. I experienced the reality for her: Finn hanging, and *no*-ing, and dying. I struggled to ax the terrible visual, but when we parked in front of a shop with the brightest of lights and too many neon colors, it stuck. I held my stomach, aching. Helen didn't notice.

"Stay," she said, wiping her tears while looking into the rearview mirror. "Stay right here."

She patted my leg hard this time, a signal not to move. I understood. And just like that, Helen darted into the false night with her whooshing cream coat and swept into the shop. I watched her inside as she wandered much like her son, confused, heartbroken. My stomach hurt in a way I'd never experienced. The human food wanted to leave me, and I knew to exit the car to allow it. I rushed behind a blue dumpster and emptied my body over and over again, wiping my mouth each time.

In time, two circular lights stared me down as I peered around the dumpster. When the car died, to my awful surprise, Sandra Cummings exited. I focused not on her energy (which still was very much the pale poisoned mushroom variety), but her eyes, which spoke to me from a distance. They echoed *I am hollow*, and not in a Horace's-warm-hollow way. No, in a Smis-hollow way. I then noticed a few other things. Her skin shivered white as snow, and little hair graced her head. She covered its sparsity with a red woolen hat and pushed a scarf around her neck, walking so slow, so laborious. Frankly, the moon could have walked better.

The more she struggled to move, the more I wrestled to restrain the rage rambling through my heart. When it pulsated, heightened, I raced from behind the dumpster and kicked that pale poisoned mushroom of a woman, even in her fragile state. I struck her right shin with my too-big earth shoes, and then ran away and hid again behind the dumpster. Trembling, I stewed in my horridness as my lips frothed like the milk Helen longed to purchase.

A man rushed first to Sandra, as he eyed the dumpster at the same time. I worried he'd find me, and so I wandered behind the store and through some grasses and trees until a dark road arose that led to houses. I heard the man's footsteps in the distance and raced on, even as I missed my naked body from the forest realm more than ever. The fox-death-coat only trapped heat. When I found a tiny house with dim lighting and a kind holly tree, I hid prudently behind a spruce.

The man ran past me, intent. But Helen, she stopped, felt me without even a rustle-hum. She called for the man. Told him she thought she saw me farther along on a road we wouldn't take. He sprinted in that direction while Helen rushed to me, grabbed my arm, and then discreetly we moved through the wispy dark.

She hid me behind more bushes.

"Stay," she said.

This time I did, waiting until she drove along, and the man wasn't visible. I hopped into the car, and she backed up and took a different street to reroute us to the bluebell house. Along the way, I worried she'd harm me, she shook so hard and wept even harder. But she didn't. When the shaking and the crying ended, she laughed. Yes, laughed! A large cracking tree of a laugh.

I thought her spirit finally broke—much like her son's—since the sound harnessed a rocking quality. But when it ceased, I knew she had spirit left to give. She held my hand and squeezed it. Helen knew I meant harm to Sandra, the woman who meant harm to her husband.

"We lie to John," she whispered. "Okay?"

She brushed some of the tangled hair from my face. I nodded, and she smiled.

"It's the fall, you see, not summertime. We lie."

I bowed my head, aware her fantasy died. But lies and secrets, they were still very much alive. It was something, even if it wasn't the son she wanted most.

Horace-Speak

The boy's spirit is broken, and so am I.
It rocks, and rocks, and rocks.
I weep, and weep, and weep.
We are a split-secret that aches in Smis's
    shadow.
The moon tries to help. Shines her many faces
    to us. Beams a craterous smile.
We are a secret. *"No light,"* I say. *"No light."*
"Look to your hollow. Blue light," the moon
    says. *"Secrets rarely shine so* beautifully."
But Finn's soul glows in me like a stranger.
I can't bear to look.
It's not Scarlet.

Chapter 10

Helen and I stopped at the top of the windy driveway to the bluebell house. The cobalt bulb hung and glimmered from the porch—an ode to Finn. A secret. As Helen breathed deeply, I opened the door and unlatched the metal gate like John did the night before. When I returned, Helen murmured in a loop, "... Alone I stand, heartache brushing the soul of my land." I kept quiet, and the truck surely refused to budge. Helen only gazed at the house, repeating grief's mantra. Finally, she broke free.

"Not home anymore," she said.

Home, I loved that word. *Home, home, home.* It strummed lovely—the hymn I'd imagine a hummingbird to hum in the nectar of peace.

"Finn was home," Helen said. "Finn was."

Helen began the descent to the place that would never be home again, even when her husband worked to make it so. We found him in the kitchen; roast beef and green beans on three plates, tiny bowls of applesauce, water-filled glasses, and the last of autumn's wildflowers in a vase at the table's center. The hope of home, even if hope had a better chance heating in hoarfrost than in this space.

"Knew she'd be comin' back. Felt it," John said.

Helen gazed at Finn's chair. She lowered her head, stiff for a beat, but then lifted her cheekbones and rounded and reddened its apples, fully present in her lie.

"We went to the police station. She stayed in the car. I poked the best I could . . . but there were no reports of a missing girl anywhere. None."

"Try again another day," John said. "Sit."

We took our coats off and sat. John's callused fingertips tapped the tabletop as he looked ahead, certainly not into us. No, John's spirit haunted someplace else. I chided myself for allowing Smis to stay so long. To counterattack, I imagined John stooping near Finn's spirit in the forest realm, smiling and mussing his gray-milk hair. But then Smis came around the corner in horrible human-shadow, hovering above the stove and staring at me, all while he dipped his shadow-finger in gravy. Stirred it.

"Gravy's boiling," Helen said.

She rose, lowered the heat, and returned to her seat. She didn't eat. Neither did John. *No son. No son. No son.* It rustle-hummed in my head, and so I tasted the meat to cease the sound. At the same time, Smis sat in Finn's chair, reaching across my plate to touch my food. I jerked the meal closer to me, hoarding my food and eating with savageness. Helen and John remained too distant to find it strange.

"Can't eat," Helen whispered.

"Go rest," John said. "We'll see to cleanin' up."

"Rest," Helen said, tears forming.

John knew not to speak more words, just as he knew not to help his wife from the chair, or hold her hand, or guide her up the stairs. Helen did all of it alone. I continued eating so as not to weep. John neither ate nor cried.

When I finished, John pointed to where I should stand near the sink, and he showed me how to wash dishes. He didn't dip my hands in the sudsy water to teach me. Instead, I stood at a respectful distance and solemnly observed the task.

During this time, Smis stole from the kitchen and slipped through the shadowed crack of the front door. He clinked the blue bulb on the porch and most likely snaked with the fiercest wind along the driveway, spitting up boring brown leaves. Smis, the wanderer. Off to do his brutal death-things. When he was gone, I surely breathed easier.

Once John completed the washing, he walked me upstairs. I averted his gaze and didn't speak even a whisper of a hum. He remained in the hallway after he opened the door for me and only nodded. He'd seemed to have run out of words for the day, so I offered the faintest smile.

Heavy-hearted, he walked off, and I closed the door, slipping beneath the quilt. At once, I thought of Horace, and then I bloomed into terrible hollow-sickness and longed for company, even if it was Smis. A strange musing, but not nearly strange enough, because Smis knew my secrets and still he kept me company.

To combat my thoughts, I stood and peered through the window. A light popped on in the workshed, and I could soon see that sorrow curved John's body in an awkward angle. Saddened, I imagined plucking grief from him in the way I excavated ticks from my bark-and-cream skin in the summertime. But quickly I recognized the flaw in my imagining. Those sapsuckers always crawled back, no matter how vigilant I was. You see, grief is just this sort of taker.

Chapter 11

The yellow phone on the kitchen wall rang relentlessly in the following days. Helen finally answered. She wept and yelled and then finally agreed.

"Okay, Father Will. You can oversee the burial. But no one else is to come."

Of course, the logistics loomed—the digging of the grave near the sunflower field, the arrival of the coffin, and the resting of it beside the earth's deep lonely hole—all of which John tended to, along with a few other strange men. Helen stood on the porch. A spectator. She didn't offer the men words or even a cup of her kind peppermint tea.

Father Will arrived on the cold, steely day of Finn's burial with only a Bible in hand. He *rap-a-tap-a-rapped* on the door in his meek and sorry way. John opened it and stepped outside while Helen rushed me upstairs. She placed me like a fresh plant in her bedroom, fingering my hair and watering my lap. Then she gazed at me with her blood-moon eyes.

"No hums," she said. "No noise. You're to stay here."

The windows in her bedroom refused me a view of the sunflower field. But as she pleaded with me, I recreated it in my mind during the summertime when Finn's spirit and soul were still companions to his body. In my vision, bright petals brushed Finn's sunlit hair, and cheerful brown seed-heads warmed his cheek's freckles. Finn couldn't contain such beauty in stillness, so he flew—arms outstretched as wings—palms brushing the flowers, eyes squinting to the sky, smiling.

I offered my daydream to Helen in my own palms. Of course, she found it odd. She took my hands in hers, put them on my lap, and whispered once more, "Stay." I nodded. She left. To deter myself from wandering and aching, I arced the Finn-sunflower imagining like a rainbow above me. But soon my fingers opened, and its loveliness slipped like sand through the cracks, and what remained weighted like a weatherworn stump: Finn's fingers scaling my great oak, tying a rope, hanging. "Finn'll be buried," John told me one night. I came to understand that this meant his motionless body arranged in a casket set to fall. My skin quivered at the thought of beetles finding him.

"*So much fear,*" Smis whispered.

From behind a mirror over a redwood vanity, Smis slinked and sat on the stool that accompanied it. He presented as a small shadow that only grew larger when I refused to face him (the corner of my eye told me so). Vexed, I closed my lids to darkness. But it only reaped this mind-picture: Smis marinating my fear's tree-bark-flavor, roasting my voice over a forest fire, then twiddling ashes between his shadow-fingers.

"*I'm not always a thing to fear.*"

"*Aren't you?*" I rustle-hummed. "*Then why, exactly, are you here . . . if not for fear's sake?*"

"*You're alone. You wanted my company.*"

"I never want your company," I said.

"Not what you mused the other night," Smis said.

I thought Smis was gone at that time. But was he? Did he miniaturize and creep into the bedroom? Morph into the tiniest of shadows? Eavesdrop? Or was Smis a mere part of my secrets and lies?

"Do you want to see the funeral's end?" Smis said.

"I'm to stay," I said.

"When have you ever stayed? Not when Horace asked. Not now, probably."

I turned my back to Smis, hoping he'd leave.

"Your choice," he said. *"But I'd watch. It's as much your ending as it is Finn's body."*

I didn't want to know what Smis meant, but the moment my curiosity overrode my resistance, he vanished. I cracked the room's door. Then shut it. But my fingers couldn't stop fidgeting with defiance, and ultimately, I tiptoed into the hallway and toward the room with the finest view. Once I arrived, I paused to deliberate, wanting to do the best thing for Helen, John, and Finn. Guilt wriggled around, harping on my misdeed. Certainly this was Finn's room—the only area Helen refused me access.

I pushed the door open and moved to the window that spoke to me. Once there, I touched the silky curtain, adjusting it slightly for a glance. A pin oak tree glared back. The towering tree was so close, in fact, that one of its branches touched the glass. Quickly, I shut the curtain.

No matter that I feared, I needed to see the sunflower

field and its fateful visitors. I didn't know why, exactly. And I suspected that, if I did, then I might race back to Helen's room and bury myself beneath her quilt to weep. So I pushed the *whys* from me, and *hows*, and *whats*, and what *ifs*, and all sorts of inquisitive language I hadn't yet formed but still communed with in some visceral part of my body—a part that didn't need articulating, that only knew.

Emptied from it all, I parted the curtain. Late autumn sheared the pin oak to its bare bones and offered wise spaces to see beyond the tree. I squatted to peer past the crooked branches for the best view.

In the background, sunflowers bowed their parched heads against a gray, laced sky. In the foreground, Helen draped her entire body over the coffin. She rested stiller than death while John stood a short distance from the coffin, detached from her. Father Will fumbled with his Bible, and Smis lowered his shadow-head. Questions returned in that knowing, wordless soul-gap. Why wasn't Smis gloating? Why did he bow with the sunflowers? Once more, this didn't align with my version of Smis as cold and cruel. I didn't want to know it, so I closed the curtain. Oddly, I smelled pine on my breath.

A few moments later, I composed myself enough to part the curtain once more. Smis was gone, but everything else froze in place. I longed to guide John to Helen, to direct his callused hand into her frigid fingertips, to imagine sunlight, and Finn's spirit, and the bluebell soul of the home they once loved. But this wish could only dwell in my strange musing, and as I lamented the fact, something curious distracted me. There was the tiniest movement in the oak's silver bark, and then nothing. Something. Nothing. It spooked me, but no more than Smis.

I didn't investigate further, and I certainly didn't search the room. Instead, I crept to the hallway and closed Finn's door with my gentlest touch. Then I tiptoed back to Helen's room and waited. In time, Helen returned—the same in body, but different. She indicated for me to leave with her silence. Respectfully, I obeyed.

I returned to my room and searched through the eastern window. In the distance, I found John walking with an ax in hand to a cold wet field, where he placed the weapon blade up and then sat beside it. Rain unleashed on John, first hard, and then soft, and then hard again. He remained stone-still, head bowed, never touching his ax.

I volleyed between observing Helen and John throughout the rest of that day. I studied Helen as she slept next to a half glass of water and some tiny white pellets glimmering on the nightstand, and then resumed eyeing John, the ax, and the rain. This pattern continued until dusk, when the rain ceased, and John stood to return the ax to the porch before venturing to his workshed. As the light glowed dimmer on his back, my curiosity heightened.

I descended the staircase, sure of one thing. I was a tree sprite—able to morph-as-I-must on my tree—camouflage from predators. Of course, I could manage discreetly peering into the workshed's window. I would discover what secrets kept John from Helen. Determined, I opened the front door, and that's when I saw him.

No, not Smis! Teenage life! He descended the twisty driveway like a dream figment—a moon-boy who carved himself free from its fullness and now walked Nature's soil, ripe and shimmery. Indeed, he sparkled with shiny skin, and long wavy brown hair, and chest tucked into a deep yellow T-shirt, and muscled legs sheathed in brown corduroy, and soul spinning with footsteps, his hands carrying a plate wrapped in aluminum foil. He was Warren Cummings, and he was meant for me.

I wanted to hold his hand and run away with him. Eat whatever warmed beneath the foil. Taste the smile I hope he offered. Leave grief behind. And as my body named these wants, it craved in an unusual way. A foreign way, not at all in the realm of tree sprite.

I was paralyzed beneath the hanging blue light. He approached me, shuffled his weight back-and-forth to each foot. I considered taking the warm plate, resting it on the table with the old teapot and the odd ax. But I didn't. Instead, I stared into him, and unexpectedly he did the same. My hair fell awkwardly in my face, covering my right eye. I didn't move it, and neither did he, but I did break the gaze to notice my bare feet.

What did he see? Whom did he see? In the wilderness of Warren, I couldn't tell. I couldn't even read his expression—too human. Still, I struggled to do so, and that's when the workshed's door banged, and John's hurried footsteps met me. He arrived out of breath as he stopped at the foot of the porch and glared.

"Warren," he said, eyeing me the entire time. "Whatcha doin' here?"

Warren turned from me and extended the foiled plate.

"My mom," he said, "she made you and your wife some supper. She's been cryin' all day. I know she doesn't always handpick the right words to say, but I know she cares, feels your pain."

John climbed the steps, took the plate with one hand, and used the other to pull me beside him.

"I'm sorry," Warren said. "For your loss. Finn inspired me, sir. Inspired me with his knowing of things unknown."

"Thanks for bringin' this, Warren. Goodnight."

Warren wanted to ask questions; this I could discern, even as he went down the steps and proceeded to walk slowly away. We turned to enter the bluebell house, and that's when Warren called to us.

"The thing is . . ." he said, "and I don't mean to cause you any more pain. But the other night, my mom was attacked. Well, wouldn't say attacked. She was kicked by a dark-haired girl she'd never seen before in the High's parking lot. And the girl ran off, and my mom said Helen ran after her with another man. And it shook her good. She's sick, you know. Cancer gives her bad and very bad days, rarely good. Can't imagine why a girl would kick a sick woman like that and run off."

"Awful," John said, and nothing more.

Warren studied me again, and I could feel the moonlight striping my face in strangeness. John didn't say anything more. Instead, he guided me inside, along with the plate of food. He shut the door and then moved the gold curtain ajar from the window, watching Warren until he reached the top of the driveway, hopped the metal fence, and drove off. Then John turned to me and stared, deep. So many questions without words.

"To bed," he said, pointing. "Been a long day."

I wanted to hold John but resisted. Instead, I walked the stairs and wondered about Warren with each step. When I reached the top, I stood in Smis's shadow. Stayed, even as I wanted to move. John slid the curtain from the door and studied the driveway once more before entering the kitchen to hurl the plate in the trash.

Smis whispered to me.

"John has secrets, too."

Smis grazed my hand, shooed me along to my room. I sat on my bed. Inspected Smis, the moon's silky underbelly shadow, as he stood at the window. For once, I didn't mind looking at him—almost beautiful in this light. I mused on him until sleep seized me, and whether it was a dream or not, I heard Smis brush my cheek. It sounded like the ring of rain, and tasted like cool peppermint. I tried to feel it, but Smis blew away, a no-thing that truly didn't want to be known.

Or maybe he did.

Smis-Speak

The wind breathes lonely, longing to be seen. Sometimes, even Smis has days like these. This is one of them, as I rest on the porch, a shadow of the ax that sits upright on the old wooden table. I search for myself in its weathered, tinny blade, but find nothing. I turn to the teapot—so benign. Ask it to comfort me. Pour me warm tea. It can't.

This is our secret. The ax and the teapot, each owns a soul. This is my burden. Even soul-things fear me.

Finn's body doesn't. I fly to it, rest in it, whisper, *"I know you well. Sleep. Forever sleep."* I mourn Finn's body in a way most humans fail to understand. I grieve its loss of breath, and movement, and wholeness. *"You are not alone,"* I tell it. *"You have me."*

The soul and the spirit reject me. They tell me, *"I have more life to live."* But the body holds me in its concave heart and allows my presence. It sleeps, and so do I. We may not dream, but we still and listen to what the earth tells us. The below has stories, too, and secrets. Some of them bring peace. This truth, humans never would imagine.

I bow my head to peace.

Chapter 12

Rain always soothed me in the forest realm. But on this morning, it slammed against the window—a cruel symphony of rage—warning me that I didn't belong in the bluebell house. Droplets haunted, even made my wing scar ache. No matter, I walked to the window, touched its smooth coldness, and stared through the glimmering glass to a life once lived. I was more a stranger to Nature now than her child. Still, I longed for Nature to work with me, to offer sun-powered will to my fingertips to heal John and Helen and Finn's broken spirits.

Perhaps if this happened, I could speak to Warren. Oh, this musing shivered my heart. I didn't cross the forest's threshold for Warren Cummings, but for the golden boy who swayed my soul. *Finn. Finn. Finn.* I rustle-hummed his name in my mind, and then allowed it to replay in human-speak.

When Helen opened the door, she stepped inside my heartache and her son's name-strumming. She motioned for me to come. We descended the stairs together and sat for breakfast without John. I devoured scrambled eggs, crisp bacon, and orange juice. Helen didn't eat, only stared faraway in her gloom, and once I was done, she didn't direct me to stand and watch her clean the dishes. But I did, all the same. When she finished the task, she wiped her hands so dry I thought they might crack. She then took my hand in hers.

We ventured along the first floor's dim-lit hallway to a room tucked in the womb of the bluebell house, a snug space cramped with books on old wooden shelves. Two red oak chairs with intricate leaf etchings rested against barren harvest gold walls on either side of a lone window. A brown beaded macramé hanger dangled from the ceiling near the window, accommodating a spider plant that searched for Nature's gray light pouring in and repelled the warm light cast from an amber glass fixture on the ceiling.

The book room presented as both wordy and simple, but that's not what stabbed my heart. No, it was the forest's crushing existence—too much of it—bludgeoned, dismantled, rearranged, and synthesized. Soul-sick, I didn't sit even when Helen did. Of course, she couldn't possibly understand my pain as she scrutinized me. So she stooped to her knees and proceeded to look for a selection that may suit me.

Helen was unaware that all books belonged to my birth realm. Yes, the stories laced humankind's voice in a spectrum from love to hate, but it cradled the forest's soul first. I knew this even before I came to learn this. My gut told me, and for this I wept, unseen. *Humans took from the forest. But did they give?* Musings like this flickered until Helen found the book meant for me, I supposed. She placed it on my lap and then gazed into me as if she knew a piece of me that I didn't. Of course, she expected something in return.

"Can you speak? Read?" she asked. "You hum. But you haven't said one word since coming to us."

In her prying eyes a larger inquiry existed—one that equaled the expanse of life and death—and in it hung her son, sure as a question mark. Indeed, I could read this pining for a son she would never hold again but in memory. Her pain eclipsed my musings and compacted my misery into a speck, so I rustle-hummed all of this.

"I saw Finn, and I was with Finn when he died, and I loved his soul so much, and Horace kept Finn's soul in his hollow, and I took on Smis for his spirit, and it will be yours, his spirit, one day, it will be yours . . . if not to keep . . . to at least know he's moved into the Light."

I hummed it so beautifully that it must have moved her soul—the shadowed part dying to live again. And that's when her anger flashed. She didn't slap with it. Or curse me. Or throw books or rip the plant that nearly touched our heads. Instead, she tidied her rage, tucked it in a neat row, like her books, and tightened her hair with bobby pins. She pointed to the picture book, a bid to direct my attention to it.

"TREE. This is a TREE. This book's title is *A Tree is Nice.*"

I've had many years to reflect on this moment. Why Helen chose this specific book, and said "TREE" so forcefully, as if she knew my secrets. But in truth she must have coddled a kinship and a loathing of trees, the last living connection to her son before he died. Naturally, she was drawn to trees in the same breath as she bonded to me, the strange girl the forest gave after taking her child. At the time, however, I didn't think any of these thoughts. Only looked to the picture, and then said as best I could . . .

"T . . . r . . . e . . . e."

Of course, I spoke with an odd tone. Her quizzical

stare told me so. No matter, she pointed once more and repeated . . .

"Tree."

I parroted the word many times, sounding unnatural with each try, closer, no doubt, to tree sprite attempting to speak human. She studied me while her lips mouthed the word, her eyes widening, feet tapping the floor. Finally, she took the book from me. Replaced it on the shelf.

"You can speak," she said. "This, we've determined. Still, you need to be taught to speak. I'll teach you."

For the remainder of that morning, she busied me here and there and everywhere throughout the house, naming things and coaxing sound from my tongue, lips, and teeth. It exhausted not only my energy but also something divine. To now see human-things as this, and that, and label it as such-and-such took the soul from it, the experience of being in all purity. Immediately I craved a oneness, a lack of knowledge, a communion with the heavenly energy that flowed into all things and interconnected rather than compartmentalized. This was a musing, but one Horace would admire. It meant he taught me something sacred in the forest realm—a know-ingness without a name.

"All things in the forest are one," Horace whispered like a lullaby in my sap-flow. *"The tree connects to the soil that connects to the next tree, and the next, and to the grasses, and sun, and sky, and clouds, and rain . . ."*

I'd never understood what Horace meant. But in this moment, I not only comprehended but also mourned the loss. For I began to realize, after all the cataloguing and sounding, and speaking, that I was becoming more human, and in doing so was stripping some of Nature's extraordi-nary madness. Where initially I felt one with the bluebell house, now it chopped into pieces, and Helen wielded the weapon. I accepted the pain, aware that I was giving her purpose: a gift insomuch as it was a loss, because I detected a flint of magic in her eyes for the first time. And that flint told me she was clever, too. Perhaps not Horace-wise, but Helen-wise. She could teach me, even as grief remained hard by her side, and some of her intelligence might benefit me if ever I saw Warren Cummings again.

"Your name. I wish I knew your name. Helen, Helen, Helen," she said pounding her heart. "I am Helen."

I understood her but couldn't yet interpret my name into human-speak. So, I echoed *"Scarlet Oak"* to her in rustle-hum. As I did, she brushed my hands delicate as a rose, a few tears soothing me.

"Beautiful sound," she said. "Like the spring rain."

I smiled because I knew even if she wanted to do the same, she couldn't.

Horace-Speak

I make a sound—even the tiniest crackle—and
   it is her.
I sway, and it is she.
I bleed my sap, and it is here, and she.

Her voice flows from my roots,
travels through my trunk to my branches,
rustle-hums with my leaves.

Scarlet Oak is her name.
I told her so.

Chapter 13

Humans marked winter's start in the year 1977 on December 21. Helen found me in the kitchen, and sure enough, her face matched winter's pallor, and her eyes bellyached its cold. Poor Helen (early autumnal, I'd suspected). But grief killed her color. Tugged at her age. Frosted her. Indeed, she looked terrible, even though she'd bathed, and dressed, and sipped a cup of green tea. Some days, I thought she presented sicker than Sandra Cummings. Grief didn't mind and, in fact, liked her that way.

I looked through the kitchen window to stop staring at Helen. Nature coated the farmland in spotty firstborn snow. In my forest realm, I knew winter by icicle lashes, shimmer frost on cheeks, moody magic flakes and shrill air in between them. And red ripe holly berries on tongue. And chilly friction beneath bare feet. And merry snow-spill from treetops. And blue jays' whispery *whirs* and *jeers*, and bright cardinals snug in Horace's hollow. But now, I experienced the eldest season through windows and Helen, the ice-ghost, and her naming of things as she refused me to venture outside with John.

Inside, Helen dissected days on a calendar into numbered squares beneath *December*, seven names accompanying each week (*Wednesday* I loved the best, no matter that Helen told me "Wednesday's child is full of woe"). But I can't say that I loved the human-way of greeting winter and time's passage more so than the forest-way. And I can't say that the calendar inspired me, either. Each day Helen pointed to it in review, I only thought of Finn, and how it was one more day that Helen hadn't seen or heard or felt him. And no flipping back of the calendar and fingering November 24, 1977 (Finn's death-day), would ever return him in body, soul, and spirit to her. A calendar—a horrible, hopeless human-thing.

It depressed me to encounter time in this way, and to watch it, and see plainly that it passed—forever gone. Yes, in the forest realm, I marked it by how Horace aged. But I didn't focus too much on it. Now, with time structured and visible, I studied it through Helen and John and their powerlessness to ever see their son wade through its fluid stream again. Because truthfully, Finn existed someplace, beyond the calendar's printed page. In a form Smis knew but I only glimpsed.

"I have to leave today," Helen said. "For a little while."

She held a brown leather purse in her hand as she motioned to the door and then pointed to John's truck through the window.

"I'll come back . . . soon," she said. "Stay inside. Too cold to be outside."

I nodded to her.

"Can you say 'yes'?"

"Yes," I said, matching her tone.

She held my chin and lifted my face to her.

"You can speak with *your* voice," she said. "When you're ready."

She spoke these phrases often. I didn't comprehend them, yet, as I didn't grasp so much of Helen. But I always nodded. However, the thing I didn't understand the most was her putting a halt on discovering the basics of me. Who I was, where I came from, why I seemed so strange-birdlike? If ever John made mention of "sortin' it all out," she'd stop him with a fiery look. It was both a blessing and a curse. Of course, I feared summertime's truths.

"Practice," Helen said, handing me the book *Trees are Nice*. "Look at the pictures."

Helen then whisked through the door and jumped into the truck. Already outside, John raced after her, and as Helen wound down the window, they argued until she cut it short, winding the window up and speeding off. John shook his head. Wiped his brow. He then headed to the bluebell house and, once inside, slammed the door.

John startled when he saw me and adjusted his temperament to greet me. He did this often. The wearing of a kinder face as he pushed his heartache behind his back. Yes, John and kindheartedness may have been well suited perhaps in his days with Finn, or as the sun swam on his face when he plowed, or through his first kiss with Helen. But kindness and death—the two hardly fit or flattered each other. And grief and kindliness, what a rarity!

"Helen ain't be comin' back for while."

I stared at John, confused. He didn't mind. John knew I was learning language but hardly understood it yet. Still, he spoke without forcing me to respond or parrot his words or label the house's soul-things. He simply talked to me, and I believed rather enjoyed my silence.

"Snow wantin' to melt . . . to sleep. Not much to look at," he said, glancing through the window.

Boldly, I walked to the front door and opened it. I smiled and turned. He appeared frightened, not of me but Helen. His wife feared too much, and I'd imagine winter as her greatest fear: the hoary frigid beast carrying me off in a single snowflake, melting me as if I never was, or would be.

"Cold," John said.

I grabbed the olive fox-death-coat from a hook and wrapped it around me. The corners of John's mouth twinkled.

"Suppose jus' for a bit," he said.

Invigorated by the chill, I strolled past the porch, turned left, and headed straight for the workshed, hoping John would invite me inside. Instead, he rerouted me past the workshed to the backyard. While farmland stretched east and west of the house, the backyard existed as a modest space a short distance from the woods. A few feet from the forest's entrance, a humble blue spruce shivered alone, the only tree to speak of. Immediately, I communed with its beauty and isolation.

John turned to notice my interest. He approached the tree, reverent, touching blue-spun needles, feeling scaly gray bark. His gaze grew faraway, close to Finn, I presumed. It took time for him to return to me, and when he did, he bowed his head, seeming to chide himself for showing me the tree, exposing his emotion. He started to wander, confident that I would follow. I didn't.

Rather, I tapped the stiff needles and inhaled the faint citrus scent, all the while combing the tree for telltale signs of a sprite. If the spruce birthed one, it didn't allow me that knowledge and instead chose to prick my fingertip. John rushed back to me and implored with his eyes for us to return to the house. But I wouldn't. John connected with the tree for a reason, and until he spoke it or showed it, I refused to budge. John honored my willfulness. He may even have admired it.

He then sat in silence near the spruce on the snow-laced ground as I rested at a respectful distance. A few tears slid down his rose-rugged cheeks. I wanted to cup and know them as much as Finn's tears. But I didn't move closer, and I dared not swipe them on my fingertips. Rather, I waited patiently as Horace in the wintertime, anticipating spring's thaw.

"My boy ain't speak," John finally said, his voice cracking. "Not a lick . . . not one word. Hummed. His way, ya see. Never heard him hum so big as when he'd pace 'round this tree."

John mimicked his son's hum, and it sounded like Finn's psalm as he circled Horace.

"Hum could put ya to sleep, it could," John said. "Or make you mad, sad, damn sight worried . . ."

John laughed through more tears.

"But them happy hums . . . they the best. Happy hums 'round this tree."

John shook himself from the reverie.

"Almost Christmas, girl. Folks right as rain shoulda been lookin' for ya. Why ain't they lookin' for ya?"

John spoke this with such intensity and confusion that I couldn't meet his gaze. I lowered my head. Traced the scant snow around me.

"And why ya hum? Why ya hum sorta like my boy? Dunno no family 'round these parts that have a child like our Finn. You walk out the woods like ya belong there. Ain't put no sense to any of it. We crazy grievin', Helen and me? But Warren . . . boy saw ya. Know he did. But still didn't say it at all. Not really."

John stopped speaking. I didn't look up.

"You the girl that kick his ma?"

John chuckled—a deep belly-thunder chuckle.

"Throwin' no blame your way for doin' it. But lyin' with Helen. Lyin'. Helen ain't try to find your folks. Know it."

I understood the word *lie* by this time, and resolved to keep doing it. I betrayed Helen by walking outside and didn't regret it, but I wouldn't betray my autumn lie with Helen, either. You see, I was loyal to Helen in her way, and I would be loyal to John in his way. I'd keep the secret from Helen about my journey with John to the blue spruce like it never happened—a soft snowfall sort of lie.

"Helen off to see her ma, today. Used to go on to church every Sunday with her ma. Kept Finn with me, and we come out to this tree. 'Round Christmastime, we put all kinds of stuff on it. Decorate it all up. Bows and bird seed, and candy canes. Then, we have ourselves our own kinda prayer. I'd like to think on it as love. A love hum, and a smile. Hopin' he knew it. Love. Hopin' he knew it."

John lowered his head. Like snowflakes, Finn's hums fell silent. But my heart still heard his voice. I'm sure John's did, too, as we sat there for a long while, allowing winter to morph as it must and gently dust us.

In time, I thought of how John's language differed from Helen's. His all tangled in soil and roots and earthen things. Then I listened to Helen's words in my mind—a precise bush of thorny red roses. What was their shared language? Finn, perhaps? I imagined Finn's hum stringing his parent's skyscape together like the sun entwining two lovely clouds.

Human-speak, it could be beautiful as much as it could be sorrowful.

That's when I turned and looked to the bluebell house to find Helen's silhouette chilling the window. Smis stood behind her, whispering into her ear, I was sure. Frozen, I didn't motion to John because to do so felt more of a betrayal rather than less.

At the precise moment Smis vanished, Helen slammed open the backdoor. John shook, snow crumbling from his face like a fallen prayer. I wanted to catch some of its pieces. Keep them tucked in the fox-death-coat's pockets to give back when the sun shone. But I couldn't. Not when Helen bolted to us—no coat on her back—and grabbed my hand, tight.

"Just what do you think you're doing? Keeping her out in the cold. Showing her relics of our son? Relics, not our son. Relics, John. No sitting by that spruce tree will bring Finn back. No wishing. Or hoping. Or doing whatever you do. God knows, it's not praying."

"Girl jus' wanna come outside," John said. "No amount of keepin' her locked up in that house gonna be good for her. Girl needs to breathe."

"She doesn't even have on proper shoes," Helen said, eyeing my slippers. "You didn't even look to make her wear boots."

John stared at my wet slippers—as if seeing them for the first time—and his shoulders drooped.

"Don't tell me you know how to care for her more than

me. Don't you dare try to tell me that. I'm a mother. No . . . was a mother," she said in whisper. "*Was*," she added, now raising her head, eyes of fire. "Never be again."

"You doin' a good job with her," John said.

Helen gazed at her husband for an uncomfortable spell before she spoke again.

"Seems to me you have work to do to keep this farm afloat. Can't be sitting at the heels of a spruce, thinking that'll bring Finn back. It won't. And don't even dare dress it all up with ribbons and candy canes or anything . . . *anything*, John. I won't have it. I won't have one single decoration in this house or on this property to remind us of the first Christmas without our son. Without our son. Imagine that. Christmas without a son."

"Hear ya, Helen," John said. "Hear ya."

He walked off, not in the direction of the bluebell house but to the dead sunflower field.

"He's not there, either," Helen yelled. "Won't find Finn at the grave. And my mom, she's not doing well . . . thanks for asking. Near death, John. She's near death, too!"

"Near crazy, not death," John called back as he kept wandering.

I imagined John melting her words and listening only to the hearty snow. So many stories in those snowflakes, one of them must have been Finn's. Just one. I wished that for him, and for Helen. I wished that Finn's spirit touched a sparkly snowflake in the forest realm and then blew it all the way to his father. And then John would touch it and smile and blow it to his wife. And she'd touch it and smile and blow it to me. I'd cradle that snowflake and place it beneath the blue light on the front porch. Then, I'd say, "*Never melt it away, please. Only warm it.*"

This musing kept me from heartbreak as I walked with Helen, her icy hand gliding me along. We entered the house, and she removed my slippers and placed them near the door. Then she motioned for me to stay, raced upstairs, and returned with two towels and fluffy socks, draping one towel around my shoulder and using the other to dry my feet. She unrolled the socks up my legs with more tenderness than I deserved.

We bustled straightaway to the kitchen. Helen pulled a chair for me to sit and then prepared hot chocolate on the stove, stirring it so gracefully that shame burned my insides. When she finished, she sprinkled marshmallows on top. Finally, she placed it down on the table and eyed me to take a sip. I did. It made some of what just happened better, and some of it worse.

"John doesn't have his senses about him," Helen said. "You don't go outside in slippers."

I nodded. I knew and loved the word *slippers*. A divine human-thing.

"You listen to me, next time," Helen said.

She touched her ears, and then mine, and she tapped her chest. I understood what she meant. A hierarchy dominated her mind, and she stood at the helm, like Prickly Elder. Guilty over likening Helen to old irascible Prickly, I wiped my mind clear.

"John, for all his gruff, he's a sentimental man. But no sentiment's going to change what happened, what was, what is, what will be. And sitting by that old spruce, it's foolish. He's foolish."

She shook her head, talking more to herself than me. She then stared off, lost in despair.

Smis walked in, respectful enough not to take a seat or

reach for my hot chocolate. I nodded at Smis, a strange thing to do. He bowed his shadow-head back, and together we gazed through the kitchen window. Outside, winter whooshed heavy and heartsick. For a beat, Smis seemed the same.

Smis-Speak

Winter knows me well. Reaches into my shadow-self and longs to feel bones, chill them, rattle them awake. *"I have none,"* I say. *"I can't be anything than what I am . . . a shadow."* Winter isn't satisfied. Blows kind, old snow to decorate me. Make me prettier, visible. The snow doesn't stick.

"Stay with me," Winter says. *"Do not leave."* But I can't stay. Just as I can't go. I can't be anything than what I am . . . a shadow. Scarlet knows. She sees what I am, and she knows my limitations. Scarlet and I (for as different as we are) we are still the same.

Scarlet isn't at all the sprite I thought she was. Not at all.

Horace-Speak

Come closer, boy-spirit.
Beneath my snow-light.
It might do us both good.
Come closer.
Yes, it's okay.
A little closer.
There you are.
Rock near me.
Or rest, if need be.
That's okay, too.
Stand.
Look.
See me.

Chapter 14

Helen kept me close during the days that followed, and I didn't learn anything more about Christmas. True to her word, she ensured the blue spruce remained in its natural state without ribbons, candy canes or birdseed. All the while, John tended to the farmland. No matter how I longed to observe his work, Helen never allowed me the opportunity. But on December 25, that all changed. In fact, the hopeless yellow phone sounded as the catalyst.

It rang early on Christmas morning as I sat in the kitchen. Helen refused to answer. Persistent, it chimed in a hapless rhythm, over and over and over, much like my thought patterns. Finally, John came inside and answered the call, much to Helen's displeasure.

"Go to the nursin' home," John said. "Your ma's in a bad way, today. Askin' for ya."

Helen remained seated at the kitchen table. Conflicted, it seemed.

"Need me to drive?" John asked.

"No," Helen said curtly. "No. Stay with her. Inside."

"Take the Impala," John said. "Not a lot of gas in the truck."

Helen grabbed my hand, kissed it, then rose to swipe her coat from the hook and slammed the door behind her. She jumped into the long, lean, tan car parked at the side of the house. Then she sped up the driveway, gray clouds racing with her.

"Be okay," he said.

He sighed and sat at the table, tapping it with his callused fingertips. I reached out to touch his knuckles—the tiniest gesture to calm him. He stopped fidgeting. Looked at me with a blue moon's melancholy.

"Christmas, today," he said. "Finn's favorite holiday. House and farm used to be so dressed up . . . fancy as a peacock."

I lost John to his memories but only for a few heartbeats, after which he returned, altered. Indeed, his cheeks appeared less sallow while his face brightened, warmed even like spring's first breath. He stood and pushed the chair to the table.

"Helen say no dressin' the farm all up . . . but Finn . . . that boy, he'd have wanted me to do it. Gotta do it for Finn. For my boy on Christmas."

He walked to the coat hook and grabbed my coat and winter boots.

"Go on, then," he said. "Put them on."

Respectful of Helen, I hesitated.

"Be back before she is," he said. "Love that woman . . . but she ain't always know what's right, what's wrong. Heart says what I wanna do's right. Gotta listen."

I obeyed because I'd grown fond of John, and because I wanted to know his relationship with Finn. And I obeyed because I was tired of being cooped up like a caterpillar in a cocoon, and, most of all, longed to know Christmas. Nature, also, beckoned me outside, and I suppose I minded her, too. So I slipped on the coat and boots while John flew the stairs and returned with a blue sheet draped over his shoulder, and together we left the bluebell house.

John didn't stop at the blue spruce. Sadly, he walked past without even looking that way. We entered the forest realm behind the house and dipped here and there, amongst branches, and rounded many trees and moved until a manmade pathway met us, then followed it deep and true. The forest air crisped with the promise of snow, and I reminisced with the woodsy pine scent that tickled my throat with nostalgia. The trees, however, stood aloof, and their sprites hid. So I focused on John's whistles and attempted to mimic his sound.

"Deep in the forest I stroll, to hear the wisdom of my soul," he finally said, singsong like. "You know, my daddy done said that, every time he'd walk into these woods, even though his soul surely seemed none the wiser."

John grew even chattier than usual with forest memories, and I could see that it divorced him from grief, if only for a little bit. I welcomed the enchantment and time's stillness as love moved us. All the while, I listened attentively, even if I didn't record every word. This part, though, I knew to keep and savor.

"My daddy used to take me on this here Christmas forest walk, and his daddy done it with him before . . . collectin' the greens. By God . . . magic, if ever there was. And Finn, he loved to do this every Christmas with me. Hum, and flap, and smile, he would. We doin' this for Finn. Helen'll have to understand."

John stopped and placed the sheet on the ground. He pointed below to the glossy evergreen.

"Get us some of that crow's-foot," he said.

He pulled and handed some to me.

"Go on, then," he said, motioning for me to place it on the sheet.

I did so, delicately, as if handling Finn's soul.

"Finn . . . he'd a scrunched them all up in his hands, smilin'."

John smiled and scrunched some crow's-foot. He was with Finn right now, not me, as he did so. Then he dropped it on the sheet and placed the sack over his shoulder.

"Keep goin', we will," he said.

We stepped further into John's charming memory walk, and it so entranced me that I ceased searching for camouflaged tree sprites. Instead, I grounded myself fully in the present.

"Right here," he said. "Jun'per. No . . . Ju . . . ni . . . per."

Oddly, he self-corrected his speech.

"Helen done give up tryin' to get me to speak proper, like her. But on Christmas, I try jus' a bit harder for her . . . make her smile at it."

I loved how John said *Helen* in a softer tone as he whiffed the juniper with his eyes closed before handing it to me, motioning for me to do the same. I inhaled it, a lovely pine scent, and missed Horace.

"Smell of juniper . . . like gin, my daddy say. Like gin. And he always smile so big after that . . . and even gotta little hop in his get-along . . . a little hope, too."

John's expression changed when he spoke of his daddy, and I had difficulty reading its complexity. I also wondered over gin, sniffing again to smell John's version of juniper before tucking it into the sheet.

In time, we stopped near a holly tree, where John clipped some branches laden with ripe red berries (all the while saying, "Finn's favorite . . . Finn's favorite . . ."). In this instant, my soul paid homage to my dear deceased friend, Sycamore, who loved to eat those same berries. Tears fell, and I couldn't dam them.

"What's wrong?" John asked.

I shook. Placed the holly against my chest, and bowed my head in reverence. John stared at me all the while, and for the first time I sensed him draw away from his magic space and into me. Yes. He searched me, wondering who I was, not who Finn was, or Helen, or his daddy. Who *I* was! Tenderly, he dried my tears with his bark-sharp fingertips, and he cradled me into his chest, holding me, patting my hair, echoing, "Here, here . . . here, here . . . ain't no use in cryin' . . . 'specially on Christmas." I longed for Horace, for my forest home, for so much more.

But now, John's body—so close to mine—swept me into a strange new territory. Human limbs—softer, warmer— heartbeat *tick-tock-ing* like the grandfather clock from the bluebell house. Breath flowing, growing, and hands soothing my back, as if trying to expel the sadness, pull it past me, and replace pain with peace. It was lovely, even lovelier in some ways than hugging Horace. But my heart squirmed, whispered, *"I love Horace more."* This truth drizzled through my sap-flow.

"Gonna be okay," John said, pulling away. "We find out who ya belong to, and we see to it ya get there."

I shook my head. Vehement. *"No. No. No."*

"Don't wanna go back?" John said.

94

I couldn't control my rustle-hums, and this is what I said.

"No, I can't go back. I'm here to save Finn's spirit, and to save you, and to save Helen, and Smis is here, too, and I can't be sure he wants me to succeed or fail. I can't be sure what Smis wants, now, because he doesn't scare me nearly as much. And I'm sorry for ruining your magic memory. Grief was far, and love was near. And Helen, I ruined her too . . . by stepping out from the bluebell house . . . coming here with you."

Of course, John couldn't interpret my strange language, but he accepted the many shades of my hums. This I could tell from his warm touch to my shoulders.

"You can stay," he said. "Stay with us. No cryin'. Now, let's get ya to where we're meant to go. We take these here greens, and we do something to make ya feel all better."

I smiled through my pain as we retraced the path, this time with John's silence. When we returned to the backyard, I thought we'd journey straight to the bluebell house. But we didn't. Instead, John walked me to the weathered workshed and eyed for me to come inside. I hoped to know John's secrets.

My entry, however, failed to cast light on his mystery in a way I could unwrap. Instead, old farm equipment cluttered the perimeter, aged cans slouched on shelves, and large cabinets hid things, mostly in weary silver drawers. John dropped the sheet of greens on a sizeable table in the shed's center. He opened a drawer for a tangle of grapevine and placed it down. Then he set to work, showing me how to fashion a grapevine wreath with nature's decorative greens and pops of holly red. John-speak directed each step, and at times he guided my fingertips to help.

When all was said and done, we stepped back. Of course,

I fixated on the wreath's fine details. But John, he studied me. Even saw me. Not that I was a tree sprite, Scarlet Oak. But rather, that I was alive, with a wish to comfort and love him. He then held the wreath with the tenderness I imagined he showed his son.

"Ain't Christmas without givin'," he said.

John opened the door and we walked to the truck with the grapevine wreath. Surely, I looked worried. But he coaxed me with reassuring eyes to enter, and so I did. We rode along the spiraling driveway and turned left down that lonely country road, traveling a mile or two, then right, onto a dusty driveway that led to a cozy windswept house. John parked a safe distance from it and turned to me.

"Stay," he said, patting my leg. "Helen'll have me for dinner if I done show ya to a single soul. But look. See. The givin' . . . it's the best part of Christmas."

I knew the word *stay* well. I also understood to hide myself from view, not making a sound or drawing attention. So, I dipped in the seat but ensured a good view as John carried the wreath to the front door. I cracked the window, hoping to hear.

John stood unsteady on the porch as he knocked. In time, an aged brown-skinned woman with a moonbeam smile opened her sunlit home and offered a soft embrace. She reminded me of Sugar Maple, and I longed to fling myself from the truck, run to hug her wisdom and warm sugary soul, and feel Sugar Maple's kindred spirit on human land. But I respected John and so sat witness as he placed the handmade wreath on her door and spruced it up, arranging a few pieces to make it more pleasing. All the while, the old woman smiled, smiled, smiled. Finally, John hugged her goodbye. Walked away. The woman called to him, the tremor of her voice so like Sugar Maple I nearly wept with forest-sickness.

"See to it you tell Helen I'm sorry . . . sorry for her loss. Miss Finn, John. Miss that boy."

John stopped and retraced his steps. He allowed the woman to hold him and he cried. I couldn't help thinking that he should be embracing Helen in much this way, grieving in unison. Still, I watched the love between them, so beautiful. In time, John withdrew and patted the woman's shoulder in the gentlest manner. She tried to smile as he cupped her face with his palms to soul-speak goodbye. Then he walked away, and I scooted down into the seat. I neither rustle-hummed nor moved, once he returned. No, we drove in quietness until nearing the farm.

"Name's Lucy," John said. "Lovely woman as ever was. Done take a wreath to her family every Christmas with my daddy. Finn, too. Best neighbors could hope for."

John was a good man. Helen was a good woman. Finn was a good child. But something caused Finn to climb a tree and hang. *What?* My mind swirled with theories. And I couldn't put it to rest pretty, like that wreath hanging kindheartedly on Lucy's door.

"Wish I knew your name," John said, clear as Helen would have said it, but with his voice. "Wish I did."

I wondered if he'd practiced this since my arrival. How to ask it proper like Helen, eliciting my truth. So vulnerable he appeared, I couldn't sit in stone-silence. So I rustle-hummed *Scarlet Oak*, hoping he'd cherish my name in the same way he relished his forest walks and wreath-making and magic Christmas memory. That's when Smis slipped into the backseat, tapping my shoulder.

John released a single tear to his cheek. I questioned whether it was grief's doing, or if my name spoke to Finn's happy hum—the pacing around the blue spruce hum that John treasured. The truck grew colder, and my voice blew fog-breath. But John didn't speak. Instead, he fidgeted his fingertips on the steering wheel.

"Shit," he said, jumping from the truck to open the driveway's metal gate.

Once he reentered the vehicle, John slammed the steering wheel with his palms to the words: "Shit, shit, shit."

Scared, I spotted the Impala near the bluebell house. John wouldn't turn to conspire with me. Instead, the truck moved sluggish as an inchworm along the driveway, and when it stopped, we both froze in our seats. That's when a shriek killed the silence. John raced to the backyard. I ran behind him.

There, the blue spruce bled sideways on the ground, and Helen rested on her back near it, gazing lifelessly at the still gray clouds. The ax in her hand shone guilty—sap on its blade, horror in its handle. I mourned the dead blue spruce but lamented my betrayal of Helen more. Swiftly, John dipped to brush hair from her face, rubbing her cheeks with the warmth he'd used with Lucy moments ago.

"Helen," John said. "Helen."

Helen's eyes mimicked a largeness more vacuous than

grief. She stared at the clouds, tears trapped somewhere in them. Dead.

"Get ya inside," John said. "Get ya inside. Cold out here."

My pain shifted to John's absence of tears. Where did they go? Perhaps they inverted? Froze into the sharpest icicles? Jabbed his heart? Pierced his soul? It took John finally turning to me to shake the wild thoughts from me. His eyes matched Helen's.

"Help," he whispered.

I moved to his side. He lifted Helen, and I held her limp hand. We walked as quickly as we could to the bluebell house, and once we entered, John rested her on the golden couch in the living room. We knelt before her, and we watched as her eyes shut. On Christmas morning, we waited for Helen's return.

Smis-Speak

I pace in the living room.
Grief follows me.
I stop.
Turn to Grief.
Go away.
Go away.
It's Christmas.
Grief, GO AWAY!
Grief-speaks.
"No place to go."

Chapter 15

Helen didn't open her eyes on Christmas until late that afternoon, when the sun gleamed through silvered clouds in luminous strings of light. We were there when she did. As she sat up, John gave her chamomile tea and shortbread. Helen accepted the small offerings, sipping and nibbling. Then she squeezed my hand.

"Sorry," John said. "Took her to Lucy's with a wreath."

Helen's eyes colored in a way that indicated she was imagining us on our forest walk, collecting greens, fashioning a wreath, driving to Lucy's, all while she suffered with her mother and without us. Still, she didn't anger. Instead, she softened and reached for John's hand, holding it tight.

"Sorry," she said. "Finn's tree."

"No need to apologize," John said. "Shouldn't have took her. Shoulda been here when ya got back. You needed us, and I took her away."

Helen silenced for a stretch, and in that quietness, dark forest-noise surely rattled her body. But in time, she spoke.

"You did the right thing. You gave her Christmas. She deserves a Christmas."

Helen bowed her head, tears streaming.

"And what did I do?" she asked. "I chopped down Finn's tree. Just couldn't see straight when I got home. My mom was the same as she ever was . . . not at all kind, even on Christmas, even *this* Christmas, without Finn. And she wasn't that bad . . . nurses just didn't want to deal with her themselves. Then I came back here, and I thought she left us."

Helen stared at me as if I was a gossamer cloud that might evaporate right before her.

"You were gone," Helen said, refusing to look from me, to keep me close. "Finn's gone. Too much. Took the ax and went out to the tree, and before I knew what I was doing, axed it . . . couldn't stop myself . . . even when I told myself to stop. Couldn't stop, John. The pain was too much."

But then Helen's load lightened a notch, whether by guilt or genuine contrition, I did not know. I only saw her brush John's hand, looking at him like weary worn winter smiles at spring before it passes.

"Give her a proper Christmas . . . in some way," she said. "Bring Finn's tree inside. Decorate it. Too tired to do it, John. But I'll sit here . . . watch."

"You want me to do that?" John asked.

"I killed the blue spruce," she said, shaking her head. "Can't take it back. But it deserves a proper burial. A beautiful one. Dressed up in ribbons and candy canes and fancy wooden ornaments. Don't bring all the Christmas stuff down. Just the ornaments. And the golden angel decoration Finn loved so much. I think she'd like it."

"Sure?" John asked.

Helen nodded. John rose slowly, and he headed upstairs to the attic and returned with a few cardboard boxes and an olive metal tree stand. He placed the stand near the largest window. Then he took a match and struck a cozy blaze in the fireplace and stoked those blues and oranges with care.

"Wanna help?" he asked me.

I followed John outside, and we both stood a respectful distance from the blue spruce, saying our own silent good-byes before we neared. I then searched for the spruce's sprite and continued to do so as John put on a pair of gloves and reached for the severed trunk, grabbed around it, and dragged it across the yard. And still I searched while opening the door for him. The spruce, however, shadowed its sprite. Refused to offer a mere glimpse.

John pulled the tree up the porch's steps and crammed it through the door, needles falling. Protective, I wanted to cradle them and weep. But I couldn't give myself away, and so instead helped John lug the blue spruce to the stand and position it, and I even held it upright for him as he screwed bolts against the trunk.

John opened the boxes of stringed colored lights, draping them on the blue spruce. He then showed me how to hang an ornament. We began with tiny wooden painted birds of all sorts, and dangled them on the branches much in the way that Finn hung from Horace. This act of decorating the tree broke me. Pain seared like lightning in jagged flickers. Each time, Finn sparked—a moving picture in my mind. How he swayed with skin blue, forest eyes reaching, red blood trickling, heart *tick-tock, tick-tocking*. Then stillness. The image came and went to the blinking of the Christmas lights.

All the while, Helen observed and blinked, too, but never lifted her body from the couch. It was only when John withdrew a brass angel chime from a box that she came alive. John set it on a tall marble table and placed four slim white candles in the holders attached beneath the chime. He lit them, and I gravitated that way as the brass angels flew in a circle, spurred by the fire—all pain lost in the fluid motion. Tree sprites, I imagined, flying round the seasons—round and round and round. Or perhaps orbiting their trees.

"Somehow, I knew she'd love it," Helen said. "Just like Finn."

I stared, hypnotized, even when Helen stood and approached, resting her cold hands on my shoulders to gaze with me. She tucked strands of hair behind my right ear.

"Finn's fairies," she whispered, and then looked to John as if guarding winter's magical secrets. "I call them Finn's Christmas fairies. Always will. Angels left us. But the fairy didn't. She's still here."

The power of Helen's words eluded me in that moment. But one day, they'd sweep me into her fantasy, on the day she named who I was, a *fairy*. But for now, Helen moved to the tree, and I could have sworn she searched every inch for its sprite, masking her curiosity by touching an ornament and gazing here and then another one and gazing there.

"Tree looks right pretty," John said as proper as he could to Helen.

Helen turned from the tree and acknowledged John's words with eyes that spoke to a time that had passed but once loved deep and silent.

"It's right pretty," Helen said, sounding so much like John.

She then glanced at the stairway.

"Go on up," John said. "Rest."

"Not hungry," Helen said. "Can you feed her? Just want to go to bed."

"Rest," John said.

Helen caressed my shoulder when she passed and

ascended the steps with her secret. When she was gone, John moved a good deal, placing tissue in boxes and putting them at the foot of the stairway. He looked exhausted. Still, he entered the kitchen and fried me chicken, and stewed green beans in bacon, and browned fresh biscuits, and placed the shortbread on a fancy holly plate. He gave me iced tea to drink, sweetened with so much sugar my tongue compelled itself to hum. John looked in my eyes when I did and finally, he spoke.

"Thinkin' we should call ya somethin' Helen and I can both say," he said. "Hum's mighty pretty, but I ain't know how to hum that pretty back. Not at all. And Helen does have ya talkin', if not so much to me, to her. But it's her words, I reckon, her voice."

I stood. Resolved that this was the right time, and so retreated to the book room, and selected a few encyclopedias I'd flipped through and studied, the way I examined ants as they traveled in patterns along Horace's trunk. I returned to the kitchen and set the weighted books on the table. Then I leafed through them, John staring as if it was the oddest thing he'd ever seen me do. Finally, I pointed to a willow oak tree and also to a weeping willow. I knew the willow oak bore resemblance to my tree but wasn't purely Horace. And I'd never seen a weeping willow, but considered it beyond beautiful. So, I tapped the word "willow" beneath each picture, and drummed my heart, naming not who I was but who I was destined to become.

"Willow . . ." John said, "name's Willow."

I nodded.

Afterwards, I opened another encyclopedia, and located a picture of a brook. I pointed to it with a smile. In my forest realm, I loved to visit the sparkling brook that flowed over rocks of many sizes and rippled unapologetically, aware that one must sometimes go, not stay. Go. Move. Explore.

"Brook," John said.

I adored how that word sounded in human-speak as much as the way *Willow* did. I nodded again.

"Willow Brook," I said in a tone like a strange bird, repeating it many times.

John's face warmed and worried all at once.

"Don't know no Brooks 'round here. Must have come from far away."

I didn't nod. Instead, I closed the books and stacked them neatly.

"Wulp . . . Willow Brook, you belong with us, now, and we should be cleanin' up and headin' to bed. Long day. Long day."

I returned the encyclopedias to the shelf in the book room, saying *"Willow Brook"* in a loop. Afterwards, I ventured to the kitchen and helped John clean. In time, we walked to the Christmas tree and stared together for a wistful beat before John turned off the lights. Then we climbed the stairs, John opening my door for me.

"Get ya some rest, Willow," he said.

He closed the door, and I gravitated to a window. I flashed to Finn's death, and then rewound that night in fine detail. There, I sat at circle time along with my fellow sprites as Prickly Elder delivered news of my only friend, Sycamore, and her passing. I still haunted while replaying his rustle-hums: *Nature dictates that we live by our birth tree, for it, and then die with it. There's no need to mourn for Sycamore, Scarlet Oak. She lived and died beside her tree as an honorable sprite does.* Of course, I rebelled against this notion, always longing to live fuller, longer. And in that moment, I ran from circle time, defying Prickly Elder's call to return.

But now, I wondered over the spruce's sprite, wishing to offer a token of benevolence—a final farewell, as I did with Sycamore and the ripe red berries. The thought refused to pass, so I waited for all house sounds to quell, and then tiptoed down the staircase.

Once in the living room, I turned on the tree's lights and searched its branches for the sprite. It took a while, but finally, I spotted her resting in death's stillness. The sprite was tiny, silvery and lean. But just as I reached to touch her, a soft knocking startled me. I jumped and turned. Warren Cummings peeked in, blue light shading him richer, deeper.

At once, I abandoned the sprite and rushed to the door, opening it with quietness and stepping on the porch. Straightaway, Warren gave me a package wrapped in golden paper and a silver bow. Regal it was, nowhere as bland as the cardboard boxes I'd seen earlier that day.

"It's a gift for Ms. Hawes," he said, "from my mom."

I took it in awe and then fidgeted my toes in my slippers.

"I know it was you that kicked my mom. But don't worry. I didn't tell her it was you, or that you were even here . . . with Mr. and Mrs. Hawes. You must be a relative?"

I nodded, averting his eyes.

"Not sure why you did it, but maybe with what happened to Finn and all, you just couldn't help gettin' angry with someone. But my mom's sick. So she wasn't the right person to kick. Pick someone who deserves it, next time. I can find one or two people I wouldn't mind you kickin' around."

Warren chuckled when he said this last sentence.

"So, what's your name?" he said.

I knew how to respond to this question. Relieved, I whispered.

"Willow."

"Willow?"

I nodded my head.

"That's a pretty name for a pretty girl."

Pretty. It was a favorable human word (I knew, since John named my hums *pretty*). I also knew Warren favored me in the way he gazed at me—here, there, everywhere.

"Mr. and Mrs. Hawes asleep?" he said.

I nodded once more.

"You sure don't talk much."

That's when I heard John's footsteps and then the door slam open. He glared at Warren and pulled me inside.

"Whatcha doin' here?" John asked.

"I brought Mrs. Hawes a gift from my mom," Warren said. "That's all. Didn't know she'd answer the door."

"Not to be rude on Christmas . . . but we ain't lookin' for charity."

"It's just a gift," Warren said.

"Well, next time, you be callin' us before ya visit. I'm right sure Helen'll appreciate it. But it's too late . . . no time to be creepin' up with a gift and givin' it to Willow. Willow's my cousin's girl . . . not from these parts . . . not all together with it. But she's helpin' us here. Helpin' Helen. We aim to keep her close."

"I didn't mean harm," Warren said. "Just saw her starin' at the Christmas tree through the window, and she looked so sad and lonely. Knocked on the window so not to scare her. Couldn't leave without followin' through with my mom's wishes."

"Call, next time, ya hear? All I ask."

"Yes, sir," Warren said.

"You a good boy, Warren . . . takin' care of your ma the way ya do. Told Helen your daddy not done right by ya. Leavin' you both when the goin' got tough. But you can't be comin' 'round here without callin' first. Talkin' to Willow in the dark. Only fourteen . . . fifteen years old. You're seventeen, son. Seventeen. Tell your ma we're fine, here. Jus' fine. No need to worry or send you to check in on us."

"I wasn't tryin' to do anything with her, sir. Like . . . just talkin', was all. And I'm not tryin' to check in on you. I'm sorry, sir."

"Sure Helen'll thank ya when she's feelin' better. But we're fine, here. Tell your ma so."

Warren turned without a goodbye and walked up the long driveway as John shut the door. I tried not to cry, aware that I'd hurt him.

"Willow," he said. "No talkin' to him alone, ya hear?"

John took the gift from me but didn't place it beneath the tree. Instead, he left it on the soiled welcome mat. He then moved to the blue spruce, lost in Christmas lights and all things Finn, I was sure. I traveled upstairs, leaving him to memory.

From the hallway, the faintest sound—so beautiful—traveled to me. *Music*, I'd later learn by name. But for now, I placed my ear against Helen's bedroom door and listened to its buttercup-in-the-wind melody, and golden sunset-sky words, and Helen's aching tears. I'll never forget how the three harmonized, as Helen longed to be with Finn, a part of that *Silent Night* that would *sleep in heavenly peace . . . sleep in heavenly peace.*

Horace-Speak

It is silent on this night.
Nature, Smis, the boy-spirit . . . no one makes a
sound.
The boy-spirit rests against my trunk, his soul
deepening in blue.
Then, one twinkling star greets Finn's
spirit-face.
The star dims, then brightens: brighter,
brighter . . . even brighter.
The boy-spirit hums. Stuns and soothes me
with his soul-voice.
He rocks, but not in distress. No, he rocks in
purity with the hum.
My branches sway gently, too, as Finn's soul
calms in my hollow.
Even if we don't sleep, we know peace in this
moment.
Heavenly peace.

Smis-Speak

I stand always at a distance in the forest realm. I fear standing too close. Yes, Smis can fear, too. But then the star, the hum, the rocking—all of it calls me—and I draw into Finn's secret world. A world within (how beautiful). A deep, soulful world from within.

When the rocking stops and the humming ceases, Finn rises. He looks into Horace's hollow. Touches his soul. I imagine it to hold a fine jasmine scent. Jasmine would smell lovely, wouldn't it?

Finn motions for me to come. I approach, and he points to his blue shimmery soul. Courteous, I stretch into his spirit-shadow for a closer peek.

The soul-boy almost smiles, and I nearly give my best shadow-smile in return.

Chapter 16

No matter that we shared some soul-moments on Christmas, they passed as coldness flaked around the bluebell house—warm memories trapped in an iced hollow. Indeed, Finn's Christmas fairies silenced in the attic. Ornaments hid in boxes. And the blue spruce and sprite disappeared in John's truck, driven to and deserted in parts unknown. My self-created name, *Willow Brook*, however, refused quieting or concealing or abandoning. *Willow Brook* remained.

This did little to soothe or cheer Helen; in fact, I think the revelation of my name frightened her. She mostly kept to herself. It was for the best, as a part of me resented Helen for the fallen spruce and sprite, no matter the strange beauty of a Christmas tree. At times, I wished to lash out. Hum a horrible scream—the sounds I used to make in the forest realm whenever I was alone (or as alone as I could ever be) and thought of Smis or Prickly Elder. But whenever these feelings stirred, I noticed John look to me with a wary eye, communicate in his own fragile way that his wife now existed beyond his fragility. I knew to follow his lead and remain calm.

John stayed close to me and my tortured musings during the last days of December. Helen allowed me to venture outside with a heavy coat and winter boots with him, even as the ground lay hard and barren. Silent as snowfall, John tended to things frozen, I'd say. The frozen fields. His frozen life and Finn's frozen death. Finally, on December 31, he spoke.

"Almost the New Year," he said. "Nineteen seventy-seven's hangin' by a thread. And 1978's comin' for us."

As this New Year crept up on us, my comprehension of human language and emotion rose in me like the sun, illuminating what had rested in the shadowed unknown. I understood in a way I hadn't before. John's words connected to the calendar, and human-time's chunking and labeling and naming. My wing scar ached when I thought of it, and even more so when I considered Smis's version (one cycle of seasons to prove Finn belonged to the Light).

"We used to stay up," John said, "Helen, Finn, and me . . . waitin' for midnight to bless us. 'Round that time, we'd head on out to the porch, drink ourselves some fine warm tea in them fancy teacups, make us a toast, and then we'd place my daddy's ax on the floor, each hop on over it, make us a New Year's wish. Out with the ol', in with the new. When midnight come, we dance and we laugh, and we get that there New Year off to the right start."

John shuffled his feet as if a soul-piece still lived in the past. I smiled at John. A fresh year was a lovely thought, and this memory even lovelier. And so I tried to imagine Finn's spirit dancing alongside his father's instead of rocking in the forest realm. But the vision slipped from me as John sat on the frozen field, and I did the same beside him.

"When Finn's littler, we take him 'round the house . . . to

the ol' oak tree outside his window. Finn loved to swing, ya see. One of his favorite things to do. And we had a wooden swing up on a branch. Built it myself. We'd put Finn on, and Helen and I . . . together we'd push him high, high, higher . . . like he's flyin'. Like a bird. Finn, he'd smile, and laugh somethin' crazy . . . even if he'd be so darn tired. You see, we want our boy to be doin' the thing he love the most when the New Year come."

John then shook his head, scrubbing all emotion.

"Whatcha think 'bout stayin' up with me tonight?" he asked.

Of course, he didn't expect a reply. We existed in an unspoken realm, like a bee circling a flower, each taking the other's want and giving freely just the same. But as the New Year approached, I aimed to deepen our relationship.

"Yes," I said.

John looked at me and chuckled.

"Well, what do ya know? Willow's speakin' to me, now. You don't have to speak. But sure like to hear ya."

John patted my shoulder with warmth, and that's when we heard Helen's frosty voice.

"John, bring her inside!"

We walked slowly back to the bluebell house. When we entered, Helen moved quickly and panicky in the kitchen, reorganizing, and cleansing and wringing her hands. John stepped in her path in an attempt to calm her, but she pushed him away. I had learned when *not* to approach her— to remain still and respectful of her mood.

"What are you saying to her out there?" Helen asked. "Hope you're not putting any nonsense in her head about the New Year. Because I want to make this plain and clear, right now. We aren't staying up, celebrating it in any way. Not without Finn. There's nothing to hope for or wish for, because the only hope or wish we have is impossible. Finn's not coming back. We let 1977 pass. Bury it. We don't honor it or what comes after . . . no music, no dancing, no tea or ax jumping or swinging. Nothing, John. I let you give her Christmas, but I'm taking New Year's. That's my wish."

John knew not to challenge Helen. Only sighed.

"You ever gonna open that gift from Sandra?" he asked. "Or should I toss it? Lookin' at it each day . . . makes me feel right sick."

"A gift? Really, John? That's the last thing you should be worrying over. How about the farm? Don't see you really tending to things that need to be tended to. Talking to Willow instead . . . And I'm quite certain the conversations aren't about how to keep this farm afloat. Take more of my dead daddy's money and throw it all over the place, why don't you?"

John's brow furrowed, and he looked at Helen with ire.

"That's how ya gonna play this?" he asked.

"Don't do that," Helen said. "Don't make me out to be the bad guy in front of Willow. I'm a mother, grieving for her boy. Barely breathing minute to minute. Look to the sky every day, and I can't ever see it in the same way. Always be gray, whether the sun chooses to shine or not. It'll always be the sky that never covers my son, lights him up, lets him float with its clouds, smile at them. You expect me to celebrate a New Year, a new sky? Never."

"Grievin' too, Helen. See the same sky. Same sky."

"You can't. You're not a mother," Helen said.

John lowered his head and rapped his knuckles on the counter three times, as if wielding an ax to his voice. He then walked through the front door. Slammed it.

I didn't look at Helen. Instead, I stared at the thin, faint threads of bark interlaced in my fingernails.

"Don't feel sorry for him," Helen said. "He doesn't deserve your pity."

I searched for the proper human-speak to comfort Helen but couldn't unearth it. And I daydreamed remaining by John's side until midnight and doing all those things he named. Both, of course, were impossibilities, so I fetched the only possibility around—Sandra's gift. I handed it to Helen. Eyed her to open it. She shut her eyes, her heart digging a grave for her soul, perhaps. When she came back to me, her eyes glazed like ice.

"Warren had no business showing up at our doorstep that late on Christmas. No business at all. I told Sandra, 'You need to take care of yourself. We're fine, here. Don't need your handouts, gifts, words.' Woman's stubborn as a mule, and ignorant as one, too. Only sees Finn's death as her opportunity to weasel her way back to me."

I tapped the gift to redirect Helen.

"Fine," she said, looking at me.

She unwrapped the beautiful paper with precision and opened the box, leafing through tissue to find a silver picture frame. Dusting the glass with her fingertips, she stared at the image reflecting back in a sepia tone, thinking and feeling something, that's for sure. Eventually, she placed the frame facedown on the counter. I lifted it: two young girls cloaked in checkered dresses, holding hands and smiling.

"Typical Sandra," Helen finally said. "Trying to resurrect

a past that she believes was ideal. Wrap it all up in a pretty silver frame. But if I didn't know then, I know now who she truly is. Knew it the moment Finn wasn't her version of a flawless child to match her picture-perfect son. We knew Finn was different when he was born. She only knew he was wrong—all wrong. I saw it written all over her face when she held him, the first time. Small minds have no business holding small bodies. Small bodies with large spirit and even larger soul. Finn was all of that, Willow. Beautiful baby. Beautiful boy."

I soaked Helen's words into my soul, especially the "beautiful baby, beautiful boy" part. Words truer than anything I'd heard Helen or John speak today in grief's swamp.

"Should have known, the way she treated John when we married, the friendship was over," Helen said as she sat down, unsteady.

She placed her face in her hands.

"Should have known," she echoed. "Called him an 'illiterate ass of a no-good farmer from a family just the same. Too good for him, Helen. Too much going for you. That man'll be your downfall.' That's what she said. The night before our wedding, I couldn't cleanse Sandra's words from my mind. They just ran through in a loop. And I hate that I can still hear them, and that on some days I even think them myself."

Helen shook her head.

"Willow, some people stick because you feel stuck. All you've ever known. I know better now, though. I have you, Willow. I have you."

Helen picked up the photograph and tossed it into the trash can. She returned, staring so far into me I could have sworn she saw a piece of Finn. She touched my cheeks with her palms and kissed my forehead.

"Sweet girl," she said. "Sweet, sweet girl."

Helen then took me to the book room, and we read books and practiced speaking until dinnertime neared. John didn't come inside. He stayed in Nature's tameness and wildness, and he stayed in his workshed, and he stayed trapped in his own field of pain. When nightfall came, still no John, even as Helen walked me upstairs for bed. I buried myself beneath the covers and listened for him to climb the stairs.

I fell into a black, cavernous sleep. Loud noises accompanied it. *Clip clops* on the staircase. A *bang* of a door. The *thump-thump, thump-thump* of footsteps on winter's floor. In time, I knew it not to be a dream. I woke and pulled open the window and watched as Helen propelled herself inside the workshed. She then flew outside, holding a wooden swing with two long ropes attached. Immediately, I ran—the ropes haunting me—tripping on the stairs. I lifted myself quickly and raced around the side of the bluebell house, toward thunderous voices.

"Helen, you done lost ya mind," John said. "You ain't climbin' that tree, puttin' that swing on it. You'll kill yourself."

"Then you do it," Helen screamed. "Put Finn's swing up now. There's no time to argue."

"You really expectin' me to climb up that tree at this time of night?"

"Yes!" Helen said. "Before midnight. It has to be before midnight."

Helen looked at her watch nervously.

"Only twenty-two minutes left 'til midnight, John. Hurry! Finn wants to swing."

"Helen," John said, his voice softer.

He came short of telling his wife the truth—Finn wasn't here. Would never be here again.

"If you don't do it, John Hawes, then I'll climb that tree myself and do it. Come hell or high water, I will."

John looked at me in the hopes that I could save his wife in some way. I didn't know how to do anything but fear in that moment, especially as Helen had wrapped her body around the pin oak's trunk and tried climbing it with the swing in hand.

"Stop, Helen," John said. "I'll do it. Jus' need to get the ladder."

Helen dropped, then shoved the swing into John's shaky hands.

"Be quick about it," Helen said. "Quick."

Helen trembled and shook like a leaf aching to fall until John returned with a ladder. He looked up—a haunting stare that made my soul shiver—and then he climbed that tree and attached the swing to a sturdy branch with the ropes. John stood on that ladder a beat too long, staring down, lost somewhere—not here. It took Helen walking to the swing, swaying her hand in an awkward position, smiling, talking into nothingness, to jar John back to us.

"There you are, Finn," she whispered. "I found the swing. You'll fly, tonight. Don't worry. You'll fly at midnight."

John descended, and Helen moved to the swing, placing her imagined son on it. Her face glimmered and shadowed with starlight as she pushed the swing in the gentleness and fear of a mother's hand. Each time the swing left her fingertips, she inhaled, and each time it returned, she exhaled. I looked at John, his eyes wet with grief, and I took his hand and held it tight.

"Helen," John finally said, "Willow be wantin' to ride, too."

John pulled me to Helen, who gazed at me in the most curious way, as if I were some sort of warm, aching memory.

"Of course," she said. "Of course. Give her a turn."

Helen removed her imagined son from the swing and eyed me to sit.

"Push her, John," she said. "Push her up, up, up . . . in the sky, sky, sky . . . so high, high, high . . . higher than the stars."

Helen's voice clinked in a faraway tone—too far for me to reach. So I sat on the swing and parted ways with John and Helen and their divided grief so I could fly. The thrill of doing so tingled my wing scar. And the stars—typically so cruel—sparkled over me with whimsy, telling me it was okay. *Abandon grief's footfall! Fly! Fly! Fly!*

As John pushed me, the wind brushed my face in wishing splashes, and I didn't even think to search the tree for its sprite. Instead, I closed my eyes and thought of Warren Cummings. Imagined flying with him, even as John counted down to the New Year.

"It's here," he said, quietly. "New Year's here."

That's when I opened my eyes and spotted the tree sprite. Camouflaged on the trunk, she pointed at me, not to come but to stay. I rattled. Fell from the swing. This jolted Helen to her senses, and she raced to me. Respectful, John waited for her to move and then swooped my body in his arms, walking with Helen at his side back to the blue-lit porch, past the fancy teacups, the ax, and the dancing that never danced, and into the bluebell house.

Together, they rushed me to bed, fussed over me as Helen ordered John to bring her some ice. He returned with ice chunks wrapped in one of his T-shirts, and he placed it on the soreness of my arm. John and Helen pulled up two chairs from against the wall and sat bedside.

"Perhaps music to help her sleep," Helen said, rubbing my head.

John returned with a magical human-thing—a record player. He plugged its cord into the wall and placed it on my nightstand. I sat up and watched as he set a record on it, the spinning, spinning, spinning. Then came the sound, so magnificent, something from the great beyond—a realm I'd never known. It slipped all pain faraway. Soothed my spirit, my soul.

"'Ave Maria,'" Helen said. "Finn's favorite song."

As the melody swelled, softened, danced for us, Helen and John guarded me with full-moon eyes until I fell asleep.

I dreamed of flying alongside the Finn I wish I knew, our wings stronger than the sound, more beautiful. But then Warren Cummings caught me with a rope. Pulled me down with the night, and Smis watched—didn't intervene. No, he watched, just like I did when Finn hung. Died.

Smis-Speak

Before midnight, I don't overthink it. Instead, I fly to the forest realm. Shoo fear to the wind. I take Finn's spirit-hand and soar with him to Helen's bedroom. We witness her crying. Finn looks to me, Smis, Death's great shadow-contortionist. I have no rope. I let go.

Finn's grayness gives way to glimmer-gold. He stoops down, touches his mother's watery cheek. She turns. Sees him. Smiles.

I give Finn that moment, and Helen takes it. Love.

I return Finn's spirit to the forest realm. Give him to Horace's warm keep.

Helen pushes a swing. Finn is here—in the forest—and there. Death has secrets if only humans wish to listen and believe. On New Year's Eve, Helen listens. She knows.

Chapter 17

The next morning, Helen slept long and hard as winter—a single pill in the human realm able to "rest her on up," according to John. We ate little and spoke even less at breakfast, until the hopeless yellow phone *ring-ring-ringed*, and John answered it swiftly and used more words than I'd ever heard before, mostly excuses as to why Helen couldn't go to the nursing home and "fix a mama that ain't no right to be fixed." John said the phrase "Ain't no fixin' her" so many times that it played singsong-like in my head. Finally, he slammed the phone down and looked at me.

"Need to go to the nursin' home . . . see to Helen's ma. Woman done past crazy and kept on runnin'. Helen needs her some rest. Take care of her, Willow."

I walked to the entryway and put on my coat and boots.

"Oh, no," John said. "Helen'll have my tail for dinner."

The truth was I couldn't stay. After swinging the night prior, my sap-flow fizzed to fly once more, only someplace far from the bluebell house.

"I'll be good," I said.

Of course, I knew John wouldn't refuse me. Not when

I'd given him my voice, so new. I even imagined him rustle-humming all kinds of reasons to take me in his head, and this thought lightened me.

"Gotta be quick bout it," he said. "And you ain't meetin' Helen's ma. Stay outside the door."

"Yes," I said.

John scribbled some words on a piece of white paper and placed the note on the table. We hurried to the truck, and it bumped and grinded and rattled as he drove, quick and tense. I didn't speak anymore. Only watched the landscape and listened to the sounds and savored wild berries on my tongue, and thought of Warren Cummings and all the places I might see him. When we arrived in Leonardtown, John didn't order me to hide. Instead, he looked from the road to me, back-and-forth, as if fearing I was fickle as fog, surely set to vanish.

"I'll be good," I said again.

This time, John nodded, staring straight ahead. When we entered the lonely lot, he parked a good distance from the building.

"You can come . . . jus' not to see Helen's ma," he said once more. "Not the best place in town. Death . . . you feel it here . . . waitin', visitin'."

The truck's aura grew thick and heavy, even with my cold breath, and I intuited that John carried a complicated history with death that preceded Finn. I looked to the back seat, fully expecting to find Smis eyeing me. But he wasn't there at all.

"Lemme get this said and done," John said.

We left the truck and entered a vast structure paved with bleach and gloom. The first thing I noticed were the aged humans, slouching in wheel chairs and on benches. Skin sagging, Nature was pulling their souls closer to the earth. Then I considered the airflow, how it chilled alongside the gray and white tiles, walls, ceilings, and furnishings, triggering memories of an ice storm's grip on my forest realm. Yes, that sort of frozen hopelessness. And John, he moved slowly through it all, even though I knew he wanted to be quick about it. Indeed, he took time to nod to each old human he passed, mumbling a kindly "How ya do?" Most didn't respond (not even with eye contact), but a few did.

During my journey through grief's realm, I thought of Horace and Finn and, of course, Smis. I wondered what Horace might look like as an elder, and how Finn might have aged. I wondered if Smis was truly old and feared showing me and so remained cloaked beneath the darkest shadows of humans and soul-things alike. I checked behind me a few times. Again, Smis wasn't there.

I peeked through open doors while passing rooms and spotted more old humans, positioned in more postures of woe. Some had visitors but many were alone. I wanted to sit in silence with those lonesome ones. Imagine what lives they led, how many footsteps it took to arrive here, and whether or not those footsteps proved favorable or miserable. I envisioned John in one room and Helen in another, and when I did, a tear escaped me. That's when John turned and saw. He stopped to gaze at me and wipe it.

"Sad, Willow, I know," he said.

He held my hand, and we moved faster. Outside his mother-in-law's room, John directed me to sit on a bench.

"Won't be long, now," John said. "Stay."

I sat on that bench, but I didn't stay for long. Instead, I stood and scooted along the wall, leaning against it and listening near the cracked-open door. A few moments later, a rose-scented woman wearing bright pink lipstick stepped from the room. I looked innocent enough, and so she smiled at me, relieved to see someone young, I'm sure. She didn't speak, "stay" or "go." Rather, she smiled into my life force and then hurried along.

"Linda . . . why you gonna give that nice lady such a hard time?" I heard John say. "Helen's sick . . . no way she could come and see ya today."

I peered into the room with discretion. As John's back faced me, Helen's mother perched like a vulture in her chair at the room's corner. Linda was not at all a match for her age— still so much fight. Her fierce energy rivaled Prickly Elder's. She leaned to the right, placing her wrinkled elbow firm on the chair, holding her head up with a spotty, clawed hand.

"Somehow you stacked yourself with enough courage to come around here. How many years has it been? Too many, and too little. Didn't ask to see *you* today. Can't die in peace with you walking these halls."

"Feel much the same," John said. "And you ain't dyin', woman . . . except in places you refuse to do anything 'bout . . . like your soul. Calm down. Act proper. Ain't no business actin' like ya do."

"Well, that's a right ridiculous thing to say to me. Act proper. There's nothing, nor has there ever been, anything proper about you."

"Nothin' wrong with ya," John said. "Playin' Helen and these nice folks here. Playin' them. Selfish as you ever was. God lovin' . . . God fearin' . . . God forsake ya, you ain't nothin' but evil. And I'm here to say . . . give Helen some peace before ya go."

I looked once more, to find Linda's face crack like Horace's bark as she unleashed a weedy smile.

"John Hawes, you may think I'm evil, but you were born and bred from it and carried it on, just the same. You calling me evil . . . there's no sense in it. But then again, you don't have an ounce of sense about you."

"Ain't got time for this," John said. "Did my duty . . . came and checked in on your sorry soul. You're unwell . . . but not in the way these folk think."

"Ain't got time for me," Linda said, mimicking John's voice. "Ain't got time for me . . . a *God-loving* woman. But you sure as hell got time when it comes to doing the devil's work . . . trapping my daughter, marrying her, giving her a son born from evil, and taking the child she so deserved. My daughter didn't deserve Finn. Absolutely didn't deserve to bear the brunt of your family's misdeeds."

John shook, and I easily thought he could have struck her.

"My husband, God bless his deceased soul, both of us . . . we did our best for Helen's sake. Gave you money to make sure she was properly provided for. But what did you do? Locked my daughter up from the civilized world, and when Finn came . . . marred and sullied by your name, your genes . . . you kept him from getting the help he needed . . . to turn into a proper boy . . . go to school, even if it was a handicapped school. It's shameful, John Hawes. Shameful what you did . . . and I haven't even started on . . ."

"Don't wanna start with me," John said, "'cause I'll finish ya."

"Doctors telling Helen her son's severely autistic because she was a refrigerator mom . . . a cold, inadequate mother that thawed out just long enough to conceive Finn. But what they didn't know is it was *you* . . . you were the evil, not her. You were! You sentenced her to hell, and then Finn came along with it."

"Hateful as you ever was. Didn't need no doctors tellin' us things. Finn was who he was . . . and we loved him for it. Didn't need no one killin' Finn's spirit . . . killin' us. We loved our boy . . . who he was. You only wanted to turn him into who he ain't."

"No turning someone into proper when they're born from evil," Linda said. "For the best . . . Finn's gone. Keep telling Helen that. It's for the best."

John's face mirrored the sorest sunset sky, a blood-red hateful orange and battered blue. Rage. Horror. Grief.

My wing scar burned with hatred, too. I merged into John's emotion, aching to hurt Linda even more so than Sandra Cummings. But I fought it for John, as much as he fought it within himself. I returned to the bench and sat there. Waited. When John exited, I rushed to him and took his hand in mine. Together, we moved swiftly through the nursing home (no more *How ya do*s). We jumped into the truck. Flew home.

Helen was still asleep when we returned to the bluebell house. I knew we'd keep our outing a secret when John wadded the note, threw it in the trash can, and then mumbled small talk. Helen often said to John, "I've no interest in small talk, right now. I'd rather we didn't talk at all." I wished to engage John in large talk, the kind that would ax him open and release his knotted forest of pain.

I could be John's ax. The thought remained with me for the rest of the day.

Horace-Speak

Prickly Elder has come. He sees Finn's spirit first, then his soul in my hollow, then me. *"Foolish oak tree,"* he rustle-hums. He circles us, stamping. Screams into my hollow. *"Scarlet Oak may die before you, now. She's growing more human. She'll die in human-time, not tree-time."*

Then come the *should haves.* You should have been harder on her. You should have dismissed her musings. You should have forced her to see and be and live as a tree sprite. The *should haves* are always the worst. They come from me, not Prickly Elder.

Some days, I push these thoughts from me and pull the boy-spirit closer. We speak in soul-language, now. I tell him . . . *"Do not listen to Prickly Elder. You are a someone to be saved."* When I say this, Finn's spirit ceases rocking, and he focuses with curiosity on all things—large and small. His spirit shines consistent with the sun.

When this happens, I feel light, not dark. Finn's spirit

touches my bark that pines for Scarlet, reassures me that spirit lives here and there, that Scarlet's spirit is here and there, just the same.

Scarlet even breathes in the spaces between Prickly's footfall, trailing him, telling him all will be well. *"It's okay, Prickly Elder. I will return. It's okay. I will return more beautiful."*

Chapter 18

G rief came calling forceful and restless late into that night, tapping John, tapping me. From my bed, I heard John wandering the bluebell house with heavy *clip-clop, clip-clops*. I imagined placing soft moss beneath his feet. Of course, I was aware that John required aloneness at times, as much as he needed air to breathe, and I should respect it, resist comforting him. But the more he walked, the more I worried, especially when he didn't retreat to his workshed as usual.

Eventually I heard him climb the staircase and open Finn's door down the hall. Again, I knew not to intrude. But there wasn't one imagining I could conjure to stop from doing so. I moved down the dark hall with quietness, not wanting to startle John, but also wishing my presence known. The door stood ajar, and I pushed it slightly. Then I spotted John, speckled with the moonlight's cream as he cradled a baby's romper. It was pale blue—the sky's whisper—and John whispered a memory of Finn. All the while, he held the garment with gentleness. When his murmuring ceased, he squeezed it and lowered his head.

I opened the door wider and stepped inside, a courteous distance. John looked up. He shifted uncomfortably, but I closed the door, stepping into his moonlight and placing my hand on his shoulder. The room's energy assaulted me—a mixture of hope and hurt. John must have sensed my discomfort, because he moved from me and opened the curtain for more light to breathe. He then handed me the romper.

"Finn's," he whispered. "Favorite thing he wore when he's jus' a baby."

"I'm sorry," I said.

I flashed to Finn's eyes stretching into mine in the forest realm. Guilt knifed my soul. To counterattack, I gazed around the room. There weren't many furnishings—a kind bed, an oak dresser, a modest bookshelf. Still, there were two notable things that drew me closer. First, a beautiful mural adorned the largest wall, featuring a blue sky with pregnant clouds and birds flying. Second, diverse painted wooden bird figurines dotted the dresser and bookshelf. I lifted one, a cardinal, and could feel its soul—a connection to the boy who once lived here. John looked at me with glassy eyes.

"Finn loved him some birds," he said. "Some days, you could find him flappin' his arms so hard outside after seein' a bird fly by, you'd have thought he'd fly on off with it. Helen, she'd shake her head when I'd say it . . . let me know she knew Finn better than me, and the flappin' . . . it's what made him different from us. But when he'd flap his arms, I knew . . . my boy wanna fly."

Tears packed my eyes. But I drank them. Dammed them. Refused their fall.

"Fly, Finn," I said, touching the wall. "Fly!"

John watched me, curious.

"You bein' a strange bird and all. I knew you'd like it."

Even in his heartache, John wished to give to me, yielding his pain so I could see Finn's room. Perhaps he wanted me to know that I belonged here in some inexplicable way, even if he hadn't the proper words to share this wish with me.

"Finn . . . he lived beyond us, ya see. And wherever that was, I'd like to think it was beautiful . . . like that sky there Helen painted for him. Folks ain't gotta mind to see that kind of beauty. You told, ya see, what beauty looks like, and if it falls under somethin' else, looks like somethin' else . . . it ain't worth nothin'. But Finn was. He was jus' that kind of far-off beauty, past us folks tryin' to do things the same, seein' things the same. Miss him, Willow. Miss my boy."

I held his hand, worrying that if I spoke, the largeness of his words might chop back into small talk.

"Folks too wrapped up in the big things, gettin' somewhere at some time, havin' some things big, and little things . . . damn sight too small. That's how they see my boy . . . a small boy with nothin' to give. Even in church, Willow, even in God's home . . . even then. That's why I kept him with us . . . on the farm."

I remembered Linda and John mentioned God many times, but I hadn't the understanding of God to know how to respond. Thankfully, John lifted the cardinal figurine from the dresser in his palm, studying it. He then shook his head and replaced the figurine on the dresser. In a matter of seconds, he wiped his emotions clean.

"We best be gettin' to bed," he said.

But I didn't move to do so. Instead, I wandered to the window and planted myself there. John must have understood that I wanted alone time in Finn's room.

"Jus' close the door behind you."

I nodded, and he left. The snow ceased its own brand of wintry weeping, and when it did, I focused on the pin oak tree that slanted near Finn's window. I gazed not only with eyes but also with senses, soul, and spirit until, like a mirage, the sprite appeared, camouflaged in snow and silver on a branch. She stared at me with small eyes the largeness of a secret. The moment I inquired further, gazed deeper, however, she scuttled across the branch and down her tree's trunk, into his hollow.

I imagined her a softer rope between the Finn I saw hanging, dying, and the Finn that once lived in this room. On the right day, I'd gently tug her (not tie her) to tell me her secret. On the right day, we would rustle-hum together.

Chapter 19

As winter trudged its weary way, John's farm lay fallow, coated with icy snow that could no more sprout a tomato, corncob, or turnip than old Horace could supply leaves on his branches. Still, John kept busy, and I followed him most mornings on his business. There were planting schedules and seeds to order and tune-ups for the tractors. He told me that in happier times, Helen would quote a favorite poet, William Blake: "In seed time learn, in harvest teach, in winter enjoy." John revealed that during the coldest season they did enjoy some things: snowfall, Christmas, warm fires, and, mostly, Finn. "Time with Finn and Helen fireside. By God, them the good ol' days. Jus' the three of us." The way his tone warmed like the fire he so missed, I imagined the three of them dwelling in the magical insides of a firefly.

There were other mornings when John rose first. He didn't wake me but instead journeyed outside to the spot where Finn's pine once lived. I knew this because I followed him in secret once and watched from a distance. John knelt on the earth. Bowed his head, and spoke to God. Yes, God! His shoulders grew heavy and stiff as the deep roots of an old oak set to come undone. And when he finally wept, his cries rolled like a thunder that couldn't be silenced. Whatever happened to propel Finn to hang and die, John felt more responsible than Helen. This I'd figured out long ago.

But on a Wednesday, February 8, 1978, I didn't search outside for John, because inside Helen banged and clanged, moving more than ever before. I found her tidying the kitchen in a bleach frenzy, armed with the nursing home's scent. She didn't look up to acknowledge me. Instead, she mopped the floor with strict muscle and strength of will. I didn't move to her, could already feel that she wanted her space and my arrival disturbed it.

So I returned upstairs and looked for John through the windows. His truck was gone. I tried not to worry, passing the time reciting words like *shock* (Helen had said the other day, "I'm in *shock* winter hasn't dropped more snow.") or *steal* (deer liked to *steal* her bulbs in the front yard) or *sieve* (she sifted flour through a *sieve* to make fresh bread).

However, when evening arrived and John still hadn't returned, I knew my duty was to check on Helen. I crept downstairs and spotted her in the book room. I watched her for a stretch, musing all the while. I'd discovered more about this treasured room by spending time speaking freely with John outdoors. He'd told me just the other day, "Helen used to work at the Leonardtown library . . . before Finn . . . place with loads of books. She quit the job to take care of Finn. So I made damn sure to build that room for her . . . so not to miss them books too much. Helen loves her some books . . . and 'specially poetry. But she loved bein' Finn's momma more."

I glanced through the doorway and watched Helen sit, despondent, on one of the red oak chairs. She held firm a book, I knew it well, *Here Comes Tagalong*. Helen had revealed to me one day that Finn loved this book about a young boy who wanted to tagalong with his older brother. She also revealed that Finn's secret wish, she knew, was for a sibling. Helen's eyes grew misty when she spoke of Finn and the book and the unspoken wish. And now, as she sat with this same book, she tightened her grip, all mist already expunged from her by the look of her red face.

She didn't know I was there—couldn't have—because she spoke words that didn't belong to that book. Oddly, the words sounded like rainbow rain. Later, I'd learn Helen was speaking pieces of the poem "Out of the Cradle Endlessly Rocking," by Walt Whitman. It seemed that a few branches of poetry mattered most to her—those that moved, swayed, and glimmered, even in her sorrow.

> Out of the cradle endlessly rocking
> Out of the mocking-bird's throat, the
>   musical shuttle,
> Out of the Ninth-month midnight,
> Over the sterile sands and the fields beyond,
>   where the child leaving his bed
> wander'd alone, bareheaded, barefoot,
> Down from the shower'd halo,
> Up from the mystic play of shadows twining
>   and twisting as if they were alive,
> Out from the patches of briers and
>   blackberries,
> From the memories of the bird that chanted
>   to me,

From your memories, sad brother, from the
    fitful risings and fallings I heard,
From under that yellow half-moon late-
    risen, and swollen as if with tears,
From those beginning notes of sickness and
    love, there in the transparent mist,
From the thousand responses of my heart
    never to cease . . .

. . . O past! O happy life! O songs of joy!
In the air, in the woods, over fields,
Loved! loved! loved! loved! loved!
But my mate no more, no more with me!
We two together no more . . .

. . . And again death, death, death,
Hissing melodious, neither like the bird nor
    like my arous'd child's heart,
But edging near, as privately for me rustling
    at my feet,
Creeping thence steadily up to my ears and
    laving me softly all over,
Death, death, death, death, death . . .

Helen ceased speaking with the words *Death, death, death,* but my heart-flutter told me these words weren't the proper ending. And sure enough, that's when Smis arrived and stood behind me. Helen must have felt him, too, because violence ripped from her heart to her hands, as she hurled the book and it shattered the window's glass. Smis seemed to draw me back into his shadow, while Helen grabbed more books from shelves and threw them through the broken window. She didn't stop until nearly every book either flew outside or littered the floor. I pulled from Smis. Didn't even turn to acknowledge his presence. Helen's anger was my anger—that Death gave such grief and took such happiness.

"Death. I hate Death, too," I said (thinking of Smis), moving to her.

I knew the word *hate* intimately, now. Helen told me Finn hated peas and hated carrots and hated squash. When I didn't like her mincemeat pie, she told me, "You hate this." I did, more than anything I'd ever eaten before.

"I HATE Death," I said again, emphatically.

It was only then that Helen's eyes found mine, and our hatred of Death melded us to this moment, intertwined us in Finn's passing. She held my hand in hers.

"Yes," she said. "I believe you."

I turned to glare at Smis, but he was gone.

"Forgive me," she said. "You're just a child. No child should see this. No child."

She stood and proceeded to pick up the books, although she came short of ordering them neat and tidy. Rather, she placed them slipshod on the shelves—a tangled nest. I helped her do so.

"It's Finn's birthday," she finally said. "On a Saturday morning, February 8, 1964, Finn was born to me. He came from me," she continued as she touched her hollowed belly, "through me, my blood, my spirit, my soul."

I nodded, respectful. I understood and didn't, all the same.

"We'll make a cake," she said. "You and I together. Finn would've loved you. You're like the sun and sky and birds— all things Finn loved. You're so much like Finn, too, that he would've wanted you to have cake."

Helen never asked me where I came from or who I belonged to, anymore. It was understood that I belonged here, in the bluebell house, and I had come to know I was this—the girl who kept her heart from full collapse. And so I followed her to the kitchen.

Helen set the oven and gathered ingredients to prepare a pineapple upside-down cake. When the time came, she guided me to place the pineapple properly in the pan and even allowed me to lick the batter in the bowl. She opened the warm oven, and heat poured out as I placed the *confection* (I loved this word!) inside. We then sat at the kitchen table.

We waited for the cake without many words but enough to learn that Finn savored pineapple upside-down cake slowly. He was also scared of the dark, and so they kept the lights on when he blew out his candles. And Finn would hum as they sang "Happy Birthday."

"He hummed like you, Willow," Helen said. "Sometimes, when you think I'm not listening, I hear you whisper-hum in your strange, beautiful way, and it brings me closer to Finn's spirit. You see, I must believe Finn's spirit is with me. If I don't, I might hang from a tree, myself."

There it was . . . plain, stark. Never before had John or Helen spoke of how Finn died, at least not in front of me. But now, Helen named it. I absorbed her pain and held her hand until the timer voiced its anxious little *ding-ding, ding-ding*. Helen placed the warm yellowy brown cake on the table, and its scent sung to me like a fruitful medley of spring and summer.

Helen watched me admiring the cake and smiled, artificial and sweet. A long, awkward stillness followed in which we both gazed at Finn's empty chair. We didn't sing "Happy Birthday," and I certainly didn't rustle-hum (even as I wavered over whether Helen wanted this or not). We only stared at the hollowness of the yellow chair, both imagining Finn seated upon it in our own private ways. Then Helen rose, lifted a knife, and sliced into the cake. She offered me a generous piece.

"Thank you," I said, a polite and blessed phrase.

Helen's eyes reached into mine with affection, and I wondered how many times she wished Finn could speak these words, or any words at all.

"Eat, Willow," she finally said, "for Finn."

True to form, Helen didn't even take a nibble of the cake. I tried not to devour it by measuring my bites with daintiness (for Finn), and savoring the sweetness as I would the forest's most impassioned fruit. Helen took some enjoyment in watching me eat, I could tell, and perhaps this bothered her by the way she stood before I finished and scrubbed the kitchen, her cleansing not nearly as frantic but still present. When completed, she gazed at me with curiosity.

"Will you follow me to my room?" she asked.

"Yes," I said.

I trailed behind her and entered her room with quietness. Helen led me to her vanity, and I stared into the connecting mirror. She pulled the stool from beneath and guided me to sit. Then she picked up a shiny brush from the drawer and wielded it with craftsmanship, taming my hair into silk. Yes, Helen had groomed me before, but never with such softness, artistry even, I'd say. She didn't stop once to lift strands and examine them deeper, as she'd often do. Instead, she spoke rainbow rain. I set these phrasings from Alfred, Lord Tennyson's "The Lady of Shalott" to strong memory:

> . . . Beneath the moon, the reaper weary
> Listening whispers, ''Tis the fairy,
> Lady of Shalott.'

> . . . 'I am half sick of shadows,' said
> The Lady of Shalott.

> . . . The mirror crack'd from side to side;
> 'The curse is come upon me,' cried
> The Lady of Shalott.

> . . . 'Tirra lirra, tirra lirra:'
> Sang Sir Lancelot.

> . . . 'Draw near and fear not,—this is I,
> The Lady of Shalott.'

I adored the *Tirra lirra, tirra lirra* part and imagined all tree sprites rustle-humming, *"Tirra lirra, tirra lirra."* Helen calmed. I could feel it. She stopped brushing and patted my shoulder.

"Your tangles are all gone," she said.

I stood, taking her words as my cue to leave. When I reached the door, she spoke again.

"Let's do this every night. Tame your hair and speak poetry."

Poetry! What a glorious name! More beautiful even than every season's diverse sunset in the forest realm. Oh, more so . . . more so! Nonetheless, I hid my excitement to respect Helen's despair.

"Yes," I said. "Yes."

I closed the door with hopefulness . . . for Helen, for Finn, even for John. That's when I realized he hadn't come home yet. I sat at the top of the staircase and waited for him, as Helen (I dreamed) drifted into a cloud-sleep, and the bluebell house grew stiller, and the wind blew through the book room to tickle my face. I remained until the rumbles of John's old truck sounded.

When he entered—ever so quietly—I didn't make myself known. Instead, I fidgeted in the staircase's shadows and listened as he followed the breeze to the book room. Without a word, he cleaned the glass and then walked outside to return with a piece of wood. John covered the window's aperture, once more as silently as he could.

When he moved to the kitchen, I crept downstairs and peered around the corner. John sliced a piece of cake, bowed his head at the table, and forced one bite. When he rose, I hid again on the staircase and witnessed John trudge to the living room as if lugging Finn's corpse. He kept this heaviness with him as he started and stoked a fire, staring into it with half-moon longing and loneliness. I wanted to run and comfort him.

But Smis appeared to me. *"Stay,"* he whispered. *"Leave him be."* For as much as I hated Smis on this Wednesday, I listened. Again Smis whispered, *"Leave him be."* Perhaps not poetry, but power and sincerity resided in his voice, so I obeyed.

Smis-Speak

I am hated. Still, I exist.

I see Finn in the forest. He climbs Horace for the first time and sits on the branch where his body hung. He doesn't fear. No, he smiles and pats Horace with his glimmer-gold spirit-hand. It is difficult for me to understand.

I come back to the bluebell house and stand behind Scarlet (who now names herself *Willow*). A birthday after a death day in the human realm . . . it never begins or ends well. And all the seconds, minutes, hours in the middle . . . they hang in suspended disbelief of what is, was, and will never be again. Helen throws books. Scarlet throws hate. I respect it. Leave.

I go to the no-place in between this world and that to remember Scarlet Oak's birthday in Horace's hollow. Once upon a time, Horace yielded kindness to me. Allowed me to sit on his branch, offering me (Smis!) company. But on

Scarlet's birthday, he turns from me. Favors his sprite. Fears me. Tells me . . . *"Go away."*

Horace's hollow never belongs to me. I am hollow. I don't belong to anyone. This hurts even more than hatred. When John looks into the fire, I understand.

Chapter 20

Leading into mid-March, I craved the springtime, longing for flowers to bloom and end winter's relentless hold. I tired of snow and whiteness, and even the fires to thwart both. *Cabin fever*, Helen had called it. "You have *cabin fever*, child." I came to know it as that feeling of being cooped up from the world, placed in a box—or in this instance, a bluebell house—with few ties to society or even outdoors. It was true. Grief, winter, Helen, and John (so distant from one another) gave me cabin fever and took my hope. But on March 17, I reclaimed it.

Certainly, up until that point, I'd done my best to divide time between Helen and John. I stayed with their souls (no matter how weighty), kept them company, all the while wishing to place both in a cocoon to meld together and regrow. Of course, this was a musing, but a spectacular one, like poetry. However, on a day when winter and spring bullied each other for favor, the beautiful, dark memory of my birth flashed in me. And so I placed focus on myself and sought to relive it.

All at once, I existed—a soft glow and a tiny cry. But

then, light fractured into a bedazzling shadow that tugged my heart. Fueled my wings with air. Swish-swish, Swish-swish, Swish-swish. I attempted to fly from Horace, only to fall flat against the base of his trunk. That did rattle the sap from him. And I shivered as his branches bled and howled with the wind. But my soul smiled, too, even if my lips feared to follow.

I stopped there. Blocked the memory of what happened a second later. Instead, I decided to wander. I waited for John to enter his workshed and Helen to read in the book room, and then stepped outdoors to light snowflakes caressing buds on trees and flowers. This only stirred my want to roam and hope all the more. I pined to taste Nature, and even the forest realm. While surely I could take the path walked with John to collect the greens, I chose not to do so. Instead, I yearned for a place that had yet to know me.

I didn't want to travel too far away, but far enough. So I dashed along the snow-laced driveway, jumping the metal gate, turning right, and then raced a short distance down the road. In time, my skin boiled to the point that I opened the fox-death-coat. My blue dress flew with the wind as my toes longed to squish the raw ground. Still, I didn't toss my earth boots. It was an unwise thing to do in the human realm. If not Helen, then winter and the calendar would tell you so.

A mile along the road, I stopped, not from fatigue but fear. Guilt, too, told me to turn around. Grief might kill John and Helen if I left only to disappear and never return. That's when a Ford Pinto zoomed straight for me.

I leapt from the road to the edge of the woods and fell, alongside a few tears. With bravery, I stood, moments later, and wiped my face, only to spot Warren Cummings. By the time he reached me and held my shoulders in his hands, I proved well and strong and everything found so commonly in Scarlet Oak, if not in Willow Brook.

"Willow," Warren said, reminding me of the name I chose. "Willow . . . you okay? Man, didn't see you 'round the bend. Should've been drivin' slower, you know. Sorry, Willow."

I didn't utter words but I soul-spoke. Looked into Warren's mysterious eyes and read them like poetry. His want for me surfaced like a beautiful sunrise, a desire to not only see but also warm my soul. That's when I heard a strange sound—not quite a howl—but with equal force.

"Don't be scared. Only my lab . . . Jake. Man . . . dog likes to ride with me on old country roads."

A large, yellowy dog smooshed its dark nose against the window, panting.

"Won't hurt you, Willow. Just wants to make sure you're okay, I'm sure. Dog's an old softy . . . wants to friend everyone."

I walked past Warren and gazed at Jake through the window—our eyes communing with a language of the wilderness. That's when Warren came up behind me and opened the door to let Jake out. The dog pounced me, licked my face, and wagged its tail so fiercely I believed it might fall off. I smiled.

"See . . . loves you . . . even more, I see, than most people. That's a sign. You're something special."

I longed to ask the *whys* of Warren. Like why he chose *this* moment to drive with Jake? And why he was on *this* road? And why he was searching for me in the exact same way I was searching for a place that didn't know me but still did? That's when I surprised myself. Turned. Dashed into the forest, hoping Warren would follow. And he did, with

Jake. He looked only once to his car, worried, I was sure, to leave it roadside. No matter, I ran deeper into the forest as snowflakes dotted me with in-between magic.

I didn't search for tree sprites or smell pine or hear Horace's firm voice coursing my sap-flow, (or Sugar Maple's or Prickly Elder's, for that matter). I only heard my heart-beat and Warren's footsteps and Jake's panting breath. The sounds connected into one moment when all else fell, parted, and opened a pathway to my dissimilitude; I felt like a strange bird that longed to fly without its wings. And so I didn't mentally name things in human-speak (even though I knew them now as *sky, trees, pinecones, birds*). Indeed, I pushed all language past my soul so my spirit could soar. I only stopped once when Warren's footsteps did.

"Whatcha doin'?" he asked, breathless, bewildered. "Mr. Hawes'll have my ass for runnin' after you in the woods. Let me take you home."

I didn't want to return to the bluebell house—not yet—and Jake didn't want to leave, either. The dog rested peace-fully on the ground.

"Mr. and Mrs. Hawes'll worry. Finn died not too far from here, you know. A mile or so down the road. You're gonna scare them to death. They know you left?"

A foreign aching compelled me to step closer to Warren. All thoughts of Finn, Smis, John, Helen, and Horace blurred into an energy I pushed from me, and I pulled Warren in, his eyes the only realm I felt, a knowing and unknowing sky-grass space meant for me. My heart spoke, and a cardinal's chipper *cheer, cheer, cheer, cheer* echoed in the backdrop.

Warren brushed hair from my face. He held my cheeks in his hands. Moved my lips to his. I closed my eyes and tasted him, and he tasted me, lighting me up like sparkly sunlight and its warm, magical want to know everything it touches. The more he lit me, the more I flowed into his breath, until we existed as one heartbeat of extraordinary madness. I understood Nature in this moment more than I ever had.

"Sunshine," Warren whispered when our lips parted, snowflakes falling in between them. "You're sunshine, Willow."

I could have remained in his spell forever. But tree sprites revealed themselves in tiny camouflage to me, all preaching heartache and heartsick and heart-hurt. *"Horrible human-ness,"* they seemed to ax into me. And that's when Jake shot up, growled, and the forest's floor groaned with human weight and madness.

"WILLOW! WILLOW!" John called.

Quickly, I pushed from Warren.

"She's here," Warren said, his voice now broken magic. "Over here."

John's footfall quickened, and he appeared straightaway with breathless fury and wild-wolf eyes. He grabbed my arm with one hand and pulled me to him. Claimed ownership of me. In the other hand, he pointed a silver human-thing (I could not name) at Warren.

"Whatcha doin' takin' Willow here?" John asked. "Thinkin' you have a little fun with her? No business takin' her here. No business."

Fearful, Warren took a step backwards as Jake stood beside him, his fur bristling, fangs bearing, howling.

"Mr. Hawes," Warren stammered. "Put the gun down.

Happened to see her on the road while drivin'. She wandered off in here, and I followed. Knew you and Mrs. Hawes would worry sick about her . . . if something . . ."

Helen's rage-realm found its way to John as he swung the gun, all the while pointing it at Warren.

"I'll book right now, man," Warren said. "I'll book and never come back. Just put that down. You're scarin' her. She's shakin'."

The gun shook with Warren's words.

"Think on Finn," Warren said. "Wouldn't wanna see you go to jail, sir."

Such foolish words! I knew it when John's heartbeat accelerated as he pointed the gun to the sky. BANG! The sound deafened me. I cried. But John wouldn't let me go. In a flash, Jake pounced on John's leg and bit into it. The gun dropped. And that wasn't the only thing that fell. A cardinal landed broken at my feet, its bold red hue mixed with blood. None of us could catch our breath, and the cardinal never would again. John released me, and I stooped low to stroke the bird's wing as John now crouched with his head into his lap, trembling with violence. I looked at Warren.

"Go," I said. "Go!"

I could tell Warren didn't want to leave. But he did just the same—alongside Jake—with his head turned the entire time, watching me. Once they vanished, I tore a piece of my dress and placed it around John's leg to stop the blood. His soul moaned—a haunted forest. Still, I held and rocked him in my arms as if he were a lost child.

"Sorry, Willow," he said. "Sorry."

"Sorry," I spoke, and continued to do so in a whispered loop.

We remained in the snow-tipped forest, close to each

other, until the moon rose to its place, casting its soul-sorry light on our broken pieces. I stood and walked to the fallen cardinal. Covered it with leaves and rustle-hummed Sugar Maple's moonlit hymn. Then I reached for the silver human-thing, and I nestled its cold power in my palms.

Swiftly, John took it from me and placed it in his coat. He gripped my hand, refusing to let go. As we walked this way through the forest, I longed to rest in Horace's warm hollow now more than ever. I was so tired. Hope, undoubtedly, was, too.

Horace-Speak

Scarlet is near. Her spirit glows with the moon. Her soul chills in the snow, and her voice whispers foreign, speaking things I cannot name. Things that belong there in the human realm but live here in the forest.

The boy-spirit knows, too. A voice, such a sacred, sad thing. He knows life truly lives within. Once spoken, a piece chips away like bark. Dies.

Right now, a cardinal's spirit flies to us, perching on the boy-spirit's shoulder. It sings without words. *Cheer, cheer. Cheer, cheer.* Its regal mantra soothes the boy. I imagine his soul smiling with blue roots.

I am growing into the boy, and he is growing into me. Still, I can't help hoping for Scarlet's return. Body. Spirit. Soul. I pine for her. Somehow, I know she pines for me, too.

Chapter 21

When we returned to the bluebell house, John and I didn't reveal to Helen what happened in the forest. Oddly, Helen remained content not to inquire, anyway (not even when she saw John's leg bandaged with a piece of my dress!). Instead, she wrapped me in her arms and thanked God. Yes! I heard her whisper, "Thanks be to God." I fell into her relief and allowed her to comfort me while John wandered off.

First, Helen fed me brown-sugared ham, gravy-potatoes, and bacon-flavored green beans. Then she offered tapioca pudding, watching me with such intensity each time I spooned it in my mouth, I feared I'd morph into the pudding itself. A strange musing, I know. But bizarre things occurred on this day—things I would forever keep from Helen and John.

"I never made you a proper Hawes Easter meal. Let that day pass us with no acknowledgement, and still so much pain. But today it's like Easter Sunday. You came back," she said, teary eyed. "You came back."

Now it was Helen's turn to experience strange musings,

only set to words that I didn't fully grasp. So I focused instead on her food, settling in me like a warm fire as we ventured upstairs. Helen drew for me a bath sprinkled with sea salts and lavender oils and then lit vanilla candles in sconces. Once she closed the door, I dipped my body beneath the languid water and, of course, thought of Warren and how his lips needed to know mine and how kind and fruitful they were.

Once done, I dried off with a plush towel and rubbed honeysuckle lotion into my skin. I smelled like a spring forest, and it carried me deeper into Scarlet Oak (no, Willow Brook) even as human-things crowded around me. I gazed long into the mirror. This morning, my face paled like winter, but now my cheeks flushed with pink, and my once-rough lips softened and reddened in luxuriant rose. My eyes, naturally root brown, sparkled with greens, and my hair shone more sparrow than raven. I looked less sprite and bit my fingernails at the thought. I then studied them but couldn't find one fleck of bark.

I stared again into the mirror and begged it to reveal cold truths. No, not the who-I-was this morning. The who-I-once-was in, on, with Horace—his hollow, his branches, his trunk. Show me the sprite with bark-skin, and gray-black branch hair, and silver-moss eyes, and longing soul, and wandering spirit, all pieces and parts of me fidgeting but still home. The mirror laughed at me (a cruel human-thing). And deep down, I knew that sprite was gone.

Frightened, I bundled my nakedness in a cotton nightgown and found Helen in her room. As I sat at her vanity, she moved to me with grace and gratitude, but didn't speak poetry. Instead, she hummed and tamed my hair with terrible fragility. Her fingers (often frosty) warmed when they stroked my face, yet as she turned me to her, I saw a winter-stalking-springtime sort of stare.

"You are poetry," Helen said, "walked off the page. Living, breathing poetry."

Guilt plagued me, but I managed to smile. Then her eyes dulled, and fear shaded everything poetic about me.

"Don't ever wander . . . leave us again," she said. "You belong with us, now. *This* is your home."

Home—a magical word! *House* existed. But *home* belonged.

"Bluebell home," I uttered, so sleepy.

"See," Helen said. "Poetry."

She brushed my hair a few more strokes and then patted my shoulder. I rose, and she walked me to my room, waiting for me to slip into bed. Then she adjusted my covers and kissed my forehead.

"Goodnight, Willow," she said.

It was the first time I believed her "good" night, because this one was most likely the best she'd experienced since Finn's hanging. After all, unlike her son, I returned to the bluebell home.

Chapter 22

Spring, that whimsical wanderer, carried on into April. Her fertile fingers slid through cracked windows to freshen air and twirl rainbow dust. Forgotten bulbs bloomed in Helen's flowerpots, plants spruced themselves, and the farmland burst into magnificent color. All the while, pollen coated human and earthen-things alike. I welcomed April showers the most, as raindrops bathed me in foreign longings.

Helen and John, however, each experienced spring's rebirth in their own way. Helen spent her time *spring-cleaning* (as she called it). Washing, wiping, sweeping—the tasks were endless (no dirt, scum, or mildew escaped her). In fact, every nook of the bluebell house succumbed to her disinfection, fresh scents deodorized in artificial lemon or bleach. The windows, too, sparkled clear in a way I'd never seen before, and one day, I mistook the view for Nature's authenticity, trying to walk through the glass, only to bang my forehead. I didn't blame Helen. I knew she was trying to shoo all sorrow and erase signs of death. Sure enough, Smis hadn't made an appearance since he told me to *"Leave John be."*

True to Smis's words, I did leave John alone as much as possible since the gun incident. I wasn't missed (for as much as I could tell), as John busied his body through farmwork. Still, he kindly let me know beforehand ... "Spring's the busiest time of the year, Willow. Be outside most days 'til dark. Gotta get the crops in the ground before the weeds take over." He then made a list of all the things he would undertake: plowing, planting, fertilizing, soil testing, pruning, and all sorts of *doing* things. "Best ya stay with Helen. She'll be needin' your help." But the *leaving-John-be* hurt. That silent bond we created slipped from us.

I stayed close to Helen. Sometimes I watched her clean. Sometimes I helped her clean. And sometimes I hid from the clean. But on this day in April, I followed Helen into the clean as she tugged a rectangular lever from the second story's ceiling and pulled a wooden staircase down. She climbed it, and I trailed her into the attic.

Helen set to work straightaway, moving trunks and rearranging boxes. Sweeping the mind of the house, I'd call it, an attempt to purge its dark memories. I didn't assist her. Instead, I stared through the smallest window to spot the pin oak tree's sprite. I knew her proper name must be Pin Oak, and our gazing at one another now happened quite frequently. On this morning, Pin Oak blinked more times than usual, and it was only as I heard Helen scream that I turned from the sprite.

She had tripped on a steel box, and so I reached to help her. But instead, she sat up and patted the floor for me to rest with her. As I did, she brushed stray strands from my face, sighed, and then looked at the steel box.

"Not in its right place," she said, touching it. "Hauntings in here. John's hauntings."

Helen rarely spoke of John to me. Rather, she chatted more and more about Finn. Just the other day, while cleaning the book room, she told me how she took Finn to the library one time, and he arranged three stacks of books and then stood and balanced his body on each, smiling and flapping. Helen loved that, in Finn's mind, he found an imaginative use for the books. She'd said, "Finn created a perch so he could fly with the birds he so loved." But now, Helen spoke of John and his hauntings, and as she said it one more time with a far-off voice, I grew curious as to whether these hauntings had anything to do with Finn.

Then Helen pulled the steel box our way and opened it slowly. She withdrew a small stack of old photographs and rifled through them until she found the one that she wished to show me. It featured a sad, stern man standing next to a woman with a nest of earthy hair and a bleak pout.

"John's parents," Helen said.

She let me hold the photograph, and I stared into their forlorn eyes.

"I never knew John's father, Walter," Helen said. "He died before I met John. But some people hold death by a choker . . . can haunt life just the same. John's father's one of those men. He haunted, and he haunts. I blame him the most."

I looked at John's father—a cruel night of a man—one who'd strip all sparkle from its stars.

"Walter was a drinker . . . addicted to vice. A man who drowned his shortcomings with more drink and more misery. This house, it was his, first, and this farm, too. A tobacco farm, at the time. Lucy's brothers worked it for him, and John, too. John longed to go to school. But he was kept on the farm under Walter's cold thumb . . . made to work . . . only learned how to read when I came along and opened that door for him. John's father stole his youth and dreams, and he stole other things . . . irreplaceable things. I hate him more than death, Willow. I hate him even more than death."

I stored Helen's version of Walter to memory and grappled to understand how drinking was a vice. At that time, I didn't know certain drinks could soul-take. But I listened closely to Helen, and I stared even closer at Walter in the photograph. That's when Helen reached into the box to pull out something unexpected. It was the gun from the forest. I smelled its evil even before I saw it. Tasted its metal. Felt its pain. Helen held it, shaken, and wandered into herself—far from me. When she finally spoke, she did so with the same expression I saw on Finn when he looked right through me in the forest.

"Killed himself," Helen said. "Walter shot himself in the head. Drink and depression did it. John found him when he was just a teenage boy. Found his daddy outside, in the middle of the night . . . near the pine tree I cut down. I know John loved that pine tree because Finn did. But that tree was cursed . . . cursed with Walter's wicked deed. And Smis . . . Smis took Walter, I'm sure. Took him straight to hell."

I struggled not to betray my shock. Helen had said "Smis." Clear as the windows she'd cleaned in the kitchen . . . *Smis!* I took a breath and told my body not to exhale lies. Then I said, in the calmest voice I could . . .

"Smis?"

"Smis . . . yes," Helen said. "Sounds crazy, but this place

was run by crazy. Lucy's brothers, they would tell John all the time while working the land, 'Smis is here. Smis is haunting your house.' They said Smis is the name they'd hear whenever they walked into a shadow on the property, and they were intuitive men, from what John told me. They could see things, hear things. 'Smis . . . ' they'd say . . . 'Southern Maryland in Shadow. *Smis*, for short.' Here, in Southern Maryland, we have our ways . . . our own speak, at times. Makes no sense to anyone but us. You'll learn . . . sometime. Someday."

I could barely breathe. *Smis*—the one word that translated from rustle-hum to human-speak. *Smis!* I wondered if Pin Oak ever whispered Smis's name into the wind, and it blew to Lucy's brothers, informed them of a world beyond their own. Or if he truly did frequent the farm long before me. But before I could muse any deeper, Helen replaced the gun in the box, covered it with the photos, and slammed it shut.

"I've told John a hundred times . . . get rid of that gun. It's evil . . . has no place here . . . anywhere, truly. But John has his own mind . . . feels compelled to keep it, as if it houses the soul of a father that could have been . . . without the drink, the depression . . . the suicide. That's only my guess. Who knows what John thinks, most days. He's always been a puzzle, Willow. One with lots of pieces, some that refuse to bend, comply. But he's a good man beneath it all. He's good, even if things he did weren't. John's *not* his father's son. Never could be. John's hauntings . . . they come from soul, not evil."

Helen's voice softened when she said John's name. I'd never heard her say "John" in that way.

"John's good," she whispered. "Drink and vices,

though . . . both fiends that take . . . neither one fit to open salvation's door. God knows."

There was God again. Even as she claimed she didn't want God, Helen said his name twice in a month's time.

"We all have burdens to bear. This you must know, Willow. Even you."

Helen drew me into her humanness.

"Come, child," she said. "I'm done being haunted."

She shut the box and placed it in a corner of the attic. Then she positioned cardboard boxes near, around, on top of the steel box—a flimsy attempt to bury the past and its hauntings. Still, I helped her.

All the while, I imagined her heartbeat's *tick-tock, tick-tock, tick-tock*—a tender song that wished to love John. Perhaps Helen couldn't feel that *tick-tock* in the tempo by which I could for Warren—all fresh, swift, and hopeful. But if she could love John through past hauntings, she could love him in the springtime. And if she believed in Smis, surely, she could learn to believe in me too . . . someday.

Smis-Speak

I am in the no-place still . . . the place in between here and there. I haunt and shame with this memory.

Horace births Scarlet in his hollow.

I lure her from Horace. Goad her to fly. *Swish-swish, Swish-swish, Swish-swish.* Horace sees me. Fear twists and turns Horace's branches. *Clip.* Severs her wings. Sap oozes from her scar. Horace mourns his sprite. Grieves the loss he wielded.

But I am to blame. Smis gives her a defect. Smis takes her wings.

Scarlet Oak will never fly.

Chapter 23

On a day with more showers than sun, blood came to me. It visited me in the no-part—the body piece a human girl wasn't meant to show. It refused to leave. It soiled my undergarments and bloated my stomach and offered aches and pains. This was terribly human, I knew, not sprite. I rushed to the bathroom, removed my clothes, and entered a warm, sudsy bath. Hours passed in the heart-hurt. Eventually, Helen knocked on the door, and when I didn't open it or acknowledge her, she used a key to unlock it. She looked at my undergarments and then to me with tender eyes.

"Child," she said, "is this your first?"

I refused to speak, only wept as Helen patted my back and took me from the blood for a moment. As she did so, I imagined my soul a cloud, bruised by human hands.

"Come now, don't cry," she said. "A first blood is always the worst. In time, you'll grow used to it. It's magic, truly, even if it feels the opposite. Your body's telling you one day you could be a mother . . . give birth."

What magic had I undone and darkened? It was wrong. All wrong! Tree sprites didn't give birth—ever. Trees birthed us, and we lived and died alongside them. Now I was more human than tree sprite. I longed to run naked back to Horace and the forest realm, to never leave again. No more foolish musings.

But then, Helen handed me a towel and directed me once more to her. She showed me cotton things to use for one's *monthly* (she called it), and then left me to tend to the blood and the humanness and the horror.

When I left the bathroom, she beckoned me to her room. She gently guided me to her bed and placed me beneath the covers. She then brought me warm honeyed tea and sat in a floral chair nearby. She didn't leave me. In fact, she fixated on me.

"You seem a bit old for your first time. I had mine at twelve. You must be fourteen, fifteen, I'd say . . . just like Finn."

Helen's thoughts wandered in my silence. I didn't tell her that I was fifty years old (I had figured it out through both a calendar and memory of my place in Nature's seasons). Sure, it was a guess, but more right than wrong. Even stranger, I also realized that my truest age matched Helen's in human years, even if our bodies weren't in sync.

"It's Nature's way," Helen said, reading my terror. "The passage from girlhood to womanhood, it doesn't come without tears and pain and worry. It's a part of life."

I closed my eyes and sipped the tea, allowing its flavor to coat my taste buds and the honey to sugar all worries, transporting me once more to Warren and our first kiss. Helen's mind drifted too, I could tell, somewhere beyond me. Time then dawdled until Helen finally spoke.

"It took John and me a long time to have a child. Many tries, over and over again, over years and years. John and I had given up when I finally became pregnant with Finn. It was a wonderful surprise. We were happy . . . so happy."

Helen chuckled.

"During that time, John painted up one wall of Finn's baby room in shades of pink. He was certain we'd have a girl. I painted the wall opposite a pale blue. I was certain we'd have a boy. It looked ridiculous, but right in some strange way. Because we did have two babies—one boy, one girl. She died at birth. Finn's twin died. So now you see, Willow, I have loved with the breadth of the ocean, and lost with the grief of rainfall."

It hit me in a flash. John and Helen kept me, loved me, spun me into their Willow because they loved *her* . . . the girl that was but never became.

"When I held my sweet Finn for the first time, it should have eased some of the pain. But it didn't. I knew something was wrong with him, too. A mother simply knows. My girl was gone, and something was wrong with my boy."

Helen's heartache gasped in pink and blue shades. There were too many colors to grieve in one lifetime. Too many.

"But when you came to me on that first night . . . when I was in the heart of suffering, aching for Finn . . . whether it was because my grief was so fresh, or my heart, it beat somewhere else . . . in some other realm that few hearts travel . . . I believed Finn sent you back to me. Finn died and sent you back to me."

She held my hand in hers, and said once more . . .

"Finn died and sent you back to me."

In truths live fantasies, and in fantasies dwell truths. This was a musing I'd only begun to develop. Because in that moment born of Helen's fantasy, a version of truth lived. Yes, Finn died, and in a way sent me to her.

"There were times," Helen said, "that I believed Finn was born the way he was because my baby girl took a piece of him with her so she wouldn't feel so alone, so death couldn't have all of her. That was in the beginning, you see, when I felt Finn was less than, so unlike other children, unable even to speak. But as I grew into Finn, and he grew into me, I realized . . ."

Tears traced a well-worn journey along Helen's cheeks as she paused, allowed them. It didn't take long to compose herself.

"You see, Willow, I realized that my baby girl, she *gave* Finn some of her beauty, to live out for her. And it was the sort of beauty only her mother, her father could truly see . . . because the outside world . . . people . . . they had their own ideas about Finn. But we saw unspeakable beauty, the more Finn grew into this world and into us. Beauty and hope, Willow . . . the same beauty and hope I see in you."

Helen squeezed my hand and pulled the covers to my chin, stroking my hair.

"Rest, child," she said. "I've said too much."

Pain forced my eyes shut. And I rustle-hummed into a fluid dreamworld—part forest, part human—rain calling to me, rinsing my lies, sap, and blood. *"This is where you belong, now."* Whether the raindrops spoke a fantasy or a truth, I didn't care. It was nice to be there, and here. I was Scarlet Oak. I was Willow Brook. I was the girl who never became. Dreams allowed it, and so did I.

Chapter 24

Days passed, but my monthly remained, deepening my sorrow. Even though Smis and I had struck an odd kinship, I wondered if, now that I was less tree sprite, he trespassed in my shadow. After all, I could feel his coldness fluttering near my wing scar. A sliver of Smis, I'm sure, amused in my blood, my humanness, and my newfound voice. Sometimes I closed my eyes and screamed inside of me. He'd echo back. *"No more a strange bird. Human. Human. Human."*

It was on a day when I couldn't hear Smis's voice that my desire to return to Horace overrode all else. Quickly, I put on a T-shirt, jeans, and sandals. Then I crept the stairs, hoping to leave and return without Helen and John's knowledge. Helen, I knew, went to visit her mother while John worked the fields.

As I maneuvered the staircase, however, a police car and Warren's Ford Pinto snaked along the driveway. Once the vehicles stopped, Sandra flung herself from Warren's car, maddened. A police officer dashed from his car to hold her back. I stood at the window discreetly, noticing that the poisoned mushroom woman looked ghostlier, like a cloud caught between the want to storm or dissipate. It was then that John rushed forward. He stood grounded as Horace and wiped his beaded brow.

Instinct urged me to run through the back door and flee to the woods. But if I couldn't see Smis's shadow, I felt him down my neck in an icy shiver, one that redirected me to the attic to hide. I cracked a window and searched for the steel box. Once found, I knelt near it. My proximity to the gun eased me in a strange human-way. I allowed it while listening to the voices below as they ricocheted to me.

"Arrest him. Arrest him now," Sandra said. "This no-good bastard held a gun to my son. I heard Warren tell his friend plain and clear. 'Man, Mr. Hawes pulled a gun on me in the woods. Thought I might die.'"

"Ma'am, we've talked to your son," the officer said. "He's sayin' otherwise. Sayin' it never happened. Just shit-talk with his friends. One tryin' to up the other. Teenagers have their ways. We did, too, once upon a time."

"Warren's protecting a man that doesn't need protection. What he needs and deserves is a cold dark cell."

I peered through the cracked window. John stood rattled with his hands in his pockets, while the officer remained in between John and Sandra.

"He's not denying it," Sandra said. "His silence is his guilt, and that's enough to haul his no-good ass to the station. Question him some more."

"Now what reason would John have to pull a gun on your son? Can't think of one," the policeman said.

"Should've waited long enough to hear it, but I tore into Warren's room and demanded his truth in the name of God. Still, the boy refused me. Never should have sent him

ANGIE WEILAND-CROSBY

along to the Haweses to offer my generosity, warm food, gift giving. Man's never been one to repay hospitality. Instead, twists it into trying to shoot down my son."

The police officer placed both hands on Sandra's shoulders and spoke quietly. But whatever he said didn't assuage her. She roared again, this time with more force.

"He might as well have killed his own son, and now he wants to take mine, too," she said, panting. "He should've been locked up from humanity long ago."

Sandra pushed past the policeman and spit on John's cheek.

"Get her on out of here," John said, his face reddening. "Go, woman. Done lost what's left of your mind."

"Or what? You'll shoot me? You got more of your father in you than you'll ever own up to, John Hawes. Wicked legacy delivers wicked spawn."

"And a horsefly's more God-lovin' than ya'll ever be. You sick . . . always been that way . . . even before the cancer."

"Don't sling God's name around in vain. You know nothing of God. Devil made you, John Hawes. Crafted you with his own wicked hands. Helen didn't deserve to be dragged into your hell."

The police officer patted John's shoulder.

"Sorry, John," he said. "Let's just sort this on out at the station."

"Don't apologize to that man," Sandra said. "Do your damn job, officer. Serve the people . . . not the criminals."

My stomach tightened. I opened the steel box and lifted the gun. It spoke to me in hard shiny metal and evil wishes. Told me to hold it as the police officer placed John into his car and drove off. There, Sandra stood alone near Warren's Pinto, staring with ire at the porch. I lodged the gun on the windowsill with every intention to protect the bluebell house that wanted to be a home.

Gripping tighter, I aimed at that poisoned mushroom woman who wasn't at all good like her son or John. That's when Smis appeared, and strangely enough, I imagined him placing his cold shadow-limbs around me, rocking me in a way Horace had, long ago.

"Scarlet, no," he whispered.

"Willow," I said, refusing to release the gun.

"Willow, no," Smis said. "When darkness branches to your soul, light still finds a way to rise. You're light. You're John's light. Helen's light."

Then Smis vanished. But his cryptic words remained as Sandra's darkness branched to my soul while she rushed the porch and shattered the dangling blue lightbulb. Still, I lowered the weapon. And when she drove away, I crouched beneath the window to cradle John's daddy's gun like a child. I tried to move but couldn't. Still didn't stir when I heard Helen's car.

Helen found me soon enough and nursed the gun from my fingertips. She didn't cry with me or scream. But she did vow, "I'm going to get rid of this haunting, once and for all." She then placed the gun on the floor and held me in the womb of her strong arms. Now it was her turn to rock and cradle me, to whisper, "All will be well." So kind was her rocking (and *All will be well*-ing) that I transported to Sugar Maple. Longed for her wise eyes to meet mine. When I couldn't bear the largeness of the love anymore, I pulled away. Told Helen all wasn't well and what happened. Nevertheless, she drew me to her and rocked me some more before guiding me to bed with heartfelt hands.

"I'll be back with John, child. Sleep. Sleep."

I returned to the dream world—less fluid, more steel. In a place—part human, part forest—I held a gun. Trained it back-and-forth from Sandra Cummings to Nature and her extraordinary madness. I swung the gun in a loop—a cold silver spectrum. Finally, I shot. But then awoke. Didn't see who I killed.

Horace-Speak

In my forest realm, things are happening. Aged, dear Stein leans closer to me. Sugar Maple even morphs from him and visits when she can. She's grown older, slower, sager. The boy-spirit cheers when he sees her wizened face and holds her frail hands. They look inside each other in a way I can't see.

Sugar Maple always ends her visit in the same way. She caresses the boy-spirit's cheeks and smiles with her three moss teeth—each a kind, textured world. She strokes the cardinal's spirit that glows on his shoulder. She rustle-hums, "*All is well.*" Then she points to what rests high on my limbs. A cardinal has built a nest on me and refuses to fly far from it. Instead, it sits in the nest, gazes at the bird-spirit and the boy-spirit below. *Cheer, cheer, cheer, cheer.* It sings most of the time. I imagine the cardinal to own a hollow like me, and in it the bird-spirit flies.

I'd say that I'm lonely. But pieces of me are not. I have

fine company. Sugar Maple and her wise tree, Stein. The boy-spirit and bird-spirit. The cardinal in its nest. Prickly Elder, even.

Still, if I'm honest, my hollow is lonely. Nature is extraordinary. Nature is mad. Nature is magic. But Nature can't fill the womb Scarlet left.

And so, I wait for her return. I wait for Scarlet Oak.

Chapter 25

After my nightmare, I refused to return to the dream-world, and so I heard Helen and John the moment the Impala rumbled down the driveway. I cracked my door, listening, until they moved to the kitchen and assumed their seats. Then I tiptoed the staircase and shadowed my frame. Their words muffled and mangled, so I decoded what I could (at times, I amazed myself with my strong will to know and understand).

". . . A gun, John. Did you hear me in the car? Willow was holding your father's gun."

"I heard ya," John said. "I heard ya jus' fine."

"Get rid of it . . . or I will."

John remained silent.

"And Sandra," Helen said, "she's getting sicker. We don't know what she's going to do from day to day . . . even Warren said that. The boy told the police, emphatically, that you didn't do it . . . that you were never in the woods. We heard him. Sandra heard him. Is she trying to say her precious boy's a liar? Sandra's not herself. The cancer's taking her. Her mind's a tangled dark forest. Heart's always hung out there from time to time . . . but now her mind's catching up."

Still, John didn't speak, and there existed a long, pregnant pause.

"Tell me that's the truth of the matter," Helen said in a forceful whisper. "Tell me you didn't really pull a gun on Warren. You wouldn't, John. I know you wouldn't. You told me you just had a run-in with old man Hayden's German shepherd when you found Willow wandering down the road. That's all."

I peered around the corner just as John lowered his head, shameful.

"You . . . did it?" Helen asked, a question she'd already answered.

"Woman's always got crazy runnin' 'round her blood . . ."

"Crazy is holding a gun on her son. Youth may wear blinders. That's the only excuse I have for Sandra being my best friend. But what could that boy have possibly done to drive you to that? Boy's a good kid in a bad situation. Can you imagine caretaking for his mother . . . all by himself?"

"That good ol' boy . . . he done cross the line with Willow in the forest. Felt it."

Helen quieted for a spell and then moved her chair closer to John.

"You never told me Warren was with her that day. You said Willow wandered . . . like Finn . . . she wandered. Couldn't find her way home."

"Ain't that enough to scare ya shitless?" John asked. "I thought I'd keep the other part to myself. You got enough on ya plate."

Helen rested her hand on John's and then patted it.

"Willow," John said. "Girl's fragile as a bird. Got her

some strange ways . . . young . . . too young. Not to mention the girl and speakin' . . . it ain't always her thing. Boy will take 'vantage of that in a heartbeat."

"Thank God Sandra didn't know Willow was with him. Can you imagine what she'd do? If she knew the girl that . . ."

"Done kicked her . . . and you done chased down the road? Heard ya talkin' to her 'bout it. Knew it was Willow that kicked her. Can't hide her forever, Helen."

"I'm not sure why Willow did it," Helen said, "other than she was protecting you, me. Sandra was here the night you brought Willow home. She was here trying to dress herself up kind and concerned, but Willow could see it from your truck, I'm sure. Sandra's hateful. Always has been."

"Gotta protect Willow," John said, "'cause I sure as hell ain't protected Finn when I shoulda or he'd be here."

The room quieted. Helen longed to weep with John, this I could tell. Instead, she rubbed his hand in much the way Horace patted me with his branches if ever I cried.

"What's done, we can't ever undo it," Helen said. "And I'm still mad as hell at you, John Hawes. But I can't go on like this . . . hating the one man I loved more than my own life. Loved enough to push my mother, my father, all the people behind me who didn't make an effort to know the man I loved. Didn't give him a fair shot. They were blind. But I see your heart, and there isn't a mean heartbeat in it. You're a good man, John Hawes. It was worth it to be your wife, Finn's mother. All of it was worth it . . . up until that dark day . . ."

"Aww . . . Helen, you was much better at grievin' Finn and our baby girl. The showin' of it. The cryin' . . . the cursin' God, even as you beg him to save ya . . . Finn, her. Kept goin' to church with so much hope. Too much hope. And me . . .

locked it all up inside. Ain't wanna look at it . . . feel it. And when I did, what I told myself I'd never do . . . drink like my daddy . . . it all come out . . . all the pain. Ain't the true me that did it . . . was the drinkin', the pain . . . man's beast. But, by God, I'm still to blame."

"Stop . . . here, now. I forgive you. You weren't yourself, like you said. I forgive you, John."

Helen squeezed his hand, brought it to her lips, then held it against her cheek, and in that gesture, I knew love swam somewhere in the muck of grief. I imagined—once upon a time—their love bound by the sweetest sap. A towering, sunny, tree kind of love. As I imagined it, I saw John's tears fall on Helen's hand. They stayed like this for a long while, and I framed it in my heart—a picture to forever keep. Eventually, however, John searched Helen's eyes, breaking the spell with words.

"You know . . . Willow . . . she ain't ours, Helen. You know she ain't."

Helen gazed into John, stretching her fantasy to him, willing it, even.

"Never talk on it . . . how she come to me that night. But the girl ain't ours. We keepin' her from her folks and where she belong."

Helen stood proud and sure, like Horace.

"She is," she said. "I thought, in time, you knew it, too . . . so I never had to say it. She is ours. Don't you see?"

Helen created the most heartbreaking smile I'd ever seen.

"Finn sent her to us, John. She's our girl . . . grown up . . . like Finn, you see. She's so like Finn. Same age. Speaks his language. Hums. Walked out of the same forest that took our son. Finn gave her to us. She's ours."

Now John stood, haunted. He wobbled backwards and placed his hands on the counter to catch his fall.

"Sure, I taught her how to speak. Never could with Finn. But she talks in the way I feel Finn's soul would . . . if given our voice. Each time she does so, my heart tells me she's ours. Her voice . . . it shakes me alive. Willow speaks for the both of them, you see. Speaks beauty."

John didn't speak at all.

"I'm not crazy. I'm not. She knows and feels things. She's beyond us, and a part of us. She's with Finn . . . still. I feel it as I look into her eyes that know not to stay one color. Her eyes change. So, must we . . . enough to accept new thoughts, ways of seeing, hearing, being . . . because Finn's still alive. Finn lives through her."

"You dreamin' up one of your pretty poems, Helen," John said with sadness.

"Willow is poetry . . . just as Finn was . . . is. It's not up to us to kill that sort of beauty that comes from someplace past humans. Someplace of God. A fair God, kind God . . . not the God that humans bend and twist to their will. I have to believe in just this way . . . all of it. Otherwise, I'll die, myself. I'll die. 'Cause I can't live in a world without Finn. I simply can't."

John neared Helen. Placed his tender callused hands on her shoulders.

"Not goin' back there, Helen . . . the seein' and believin' things that ain't there. Thought you was doin' better with it. Thought . . ."

"It's TRUE," Helen said. "ALL of it. As true as it was on that night . . . what I saw . . ."

John lowered his head into his hands. I wanted to remain hidden because I surely couldn't be the girl that Helen needed. I didn't even know how to truly be Scarlet Oak or Willow Brook. Still, my heart walked me into their light.

"My tree," I said. "Finn . . . and my tree."

Helen rushed to me, knelt at my feet, and placed both my cheeks in her palms.

"Your tree?" she asked. "What about your tree and Finn?"

But my words slipped from my soul and into the forest's realm of secrets. *The forest doesn't take kindly to revelation.* Horace preached this dictum often. So, of course, I couldn't tell John and Helen. Not now. Perhaps not ever.

"A dream," I said. "It was a dream."

Helen sighed and hugged me tight.

"No more dreams of Finn and trees," she whispered. "Bad omens to put the two together. Now let's put you back to bed."

I went and wrapped my arms around John, and he returned the embrace gently as the sky tucks in its stars at daybreak. I missed him so, and I missed my forest father, too. In fact, for a heartbeat, I imagined Horace's branches around me, protecting me in a way only he could.

Chapter 26

When I woke the next morning, I rustle-hummed. I did so to remember who I was and where I came from and the tree that birthed me. Oddly, as I spoke my native language, I felt a pull to Finn's room, and so I moved in that direction and entered with hope.

Straightaway, I cracked the window to study the oak tree's curvatures, bark, branches, and budding leaves. While doing so, I rustle-hummed my name and my tree's name, hoping Pin Oak would reply. Nothing happened. Still, I searched for the tree sprite as John began his work in the fields and Helen slept unusually late. When she didn't materialize, I ran outside to the oak tree and stood silently at its base.

I can't say for sure how long I looked up, trying to unravel Nature's secrets (some of which I already knew). But as the morning wandered along, there finally came a time when Pin Oak stirred in her camouflaged bark and vines a short distance up the trunk. Once I spotted her, my eyes drew her into focus. Pin Oak tucked her wings in tidily and wriggled her body, ill at ease. Still, I knew she wanted me to see her, especially since she now more fully revealed herself. She was half the size of a pencil and razor thin. Her silken stick hair gently framed her acorn skin and ivy eyes, and I'd say her soft energy made her perhaps one of the most beautiful sprites my soul ever met. I studied this loveliness for a spell, until she scurried up her tree and, once perched on a branch near Finn's window, smiled.

I raced inside. Flew upstairs to Finn's window to find Pin Oak still on the tip of the closest branch. She pointed her largest finger, motioning for me to come. Of course, a tree sprite was only allowed to rest on one's birth tree; to do otherwise showed the utmost disrespect. But I was in the human realm—and here, things were very different—so I considered it perhaps a measure of courtesy to rest on Pin Oak's tree. At once, I lifted the window, careful not to wake Helen. The sun splashed my face with warm memories as I thought about how Horace's leaves danced with its light in the springtime. Indeed, a tree and the sun knew each other intimately. They were old faithful friends.

With this wise thought in mind, I climbed on a branch as Pin Oak scooted inward to greet me. Oddly, she then rested on her back as the leaves cast intriguing shadows on her face. She didn't gaze at me—not at all. Instead, she meditated with Nature's extraordinary magic, I presumed. Polite, I waited, but still worried that Helen or John would find me. Finally, to break the silence, I rustle-hummed—ever so softly. Pin Oak's eyes mirrored the gauzy clouds above, and it was only when the last of them vanished that she spoke the faintest rustle-hum I'd ever heard. So fragile. So frightened. The strangest sort of hum.

"Hello, she said. *"Hello."*

She sat up and, I believed, intuited my desire to know

things about the Hawes, the bluebell house, the farm, and most of all, Finn. Relieved, I rustle-hummed in response.

"Hello, and good day. Your oak is beautiful and kind, and very strong. I wish I knew his name."

I wanted to also liken her oak to poetry but refrained. I did, however, show Pin Oak through rustle-hum and mind-visuals that I meant her no harm, that I was pleased to share her company, that while living human was my choice, it in no way lessened who I was by Nature. I ended on this note.

"I was a tree sprite. I mean, I AM a tree sprite. My name is Scarlet Oak. But the Haweses know me as Willow Brook."

I didn't elaborate about the two names, as my voice quivered. I simply rustle-hummed more. Spoke of my scarlet oak tree, Horace, my realm, the forest, my wings, clipped, and everything and anything I could reveal of my fellow tree-sprites in tiny detail, such as how Sugar Maple adores her naps and Prickly Elder loves to bark orders. I wasn't sure if she'd encountered dogs, and so understood the context of *bark.* But I rustle-hummed it all the same and placed Warren's dog in my mind as a visual. She nodded and smiled. Then she patted her tree and rustle-hummed his name.

"Sylvan."

There came a time, however—no matter how pleasant our exchange—when I wished she would speak more to me. I didn't want to scare her with requests and hadn't a clue how to proceed. Certainly, I couldn't frighten her with the image of Finn hanging or his spirit rocking. No, that wouldn't do.

So, perfect as a rose, I blossomed a visual of Finn standing on a pile of books, flapping like the happiest bird. At last, Pin Oak gazed in my eyes—long and soulful—and she smiled the width of the sky, and I soon understood that she not only knew Finn but also loved him. I allowed her time to graze in my mind's positivity. And she did so in much the way a hummingbird sips nectar from a flower.

But then my thoughts wandered. Flashed to Finn— alive—leaning against Horace with sorrow. Pin Oak shook. Her eyes glossed and her tiny hand grabbed and squeezed one of my fingers, longing to tell me something.

"Willow," I heard. Curt. "Willow."

As Helen's head popped through the window, Pin Oak camouflaged deep into the branch. I shielded her movement from Helen.

"What are you doing on *that* tree?"

I leapt back into Finn's room while Helen studied the tree. She didn't move, barely breathed, as she examined the oak. It went on this way for an unfriendly amount of time until, sharp as her butcher's knife, she slammed the window and locked it. Then she turned to me.

"What were you doing?"

I froze like winter when it feels strong enough. Couldn't thaw my words even if I wanted to. Not here. Not with Helen's eyes clawing for my voice.

"You said something about *Finn* and *my tree* last night," Helen said. "Said it was a dream. But in your dream . . . was it *this* tree?"

I nodded. *Yes . . . this tree. Not that tree. Not my tree, and Finn hanging from it, and the heartache of it all. This tree . . . a hopeful pin oak . . . home to a benevolent sprite. A sprite that loved Finn. No, loves him, even in absence.*

Helen brushed hair from my face and studied me in the exact manner she did the tree. Then she softened. Spoke more in a whisper.

"I suppose you belong in this room as much as Finn did. If you want, you can move in here. Sleep in his old bed. But that tree, Willow, Finn loved it, but it isn't a good tree. Just haven't had the heart to chop it down."

Helen's eyes traveled faraway, but she came back to me sooner than I expected. She hugged me and then approached the mural, staring at it, allowing the skyline to swoop her to the past.

"I used to have a blue wooden rocking chair right here against this wall," she said. "You see, Finn was a fussy baby, so fussy. Only one thing worked to calm him . . . when I rocked him in this chair, singing the lullaby 'Rock-a-Bye Baby.'"

Helen now sang with the most haunting, beautiful voice.

"Rock-a-bye baby, on the treetop . . . When the wind blows, the cradle will rock . . . When the bough breaks, the cradle will fall . . . And down will come baby, cradle, and all."

Helen hung her head low with a few teardrops. I held her hand, and she turned to me with her wild grieving eyes.

"I wish I hadn't sung that song to him," she said.

I squeezed her hand in the same way Pin Oak squeezed my finger moments before. There was so much I wanted to tell her. But I didn't.

Instead, she spoke.

"In time, Willow, we knew Finn was different. He didn't speak. He rocked a good deal. He went someplace else inside of himself. Someplace we couldn't reach. My heart broke with worry and fear. But John, he'd come in here as I rocked Finn to sleep some nights, and he'd tell me, 'He jus' needs a little help, is all, Helen. Jus' needs a little help.' John's voice was small and tender, but I couldn't listen to it. I couldn't hear his pain threaded in the tenderness. I was too lost in my own. You see, John was strong for me, for Finn. Saved us during that time. Pushed us to the other side . . . the beauty, love, and gratitude for Finn and his wondrous magical spirit . . . always a home to me, to John, to . . . you."

I thought about Finn's broken spirit in the forest realm. No wonder. No magic. No shimmer. At the same time, Helen stared at me, her fantasy fermented to stone. Finn left, and resurrected me—her daughter.

"Beautiful Willow," she said, and nothing more.

We stood that way, holding hands for a long time, mesmerized by the mural and hope's ethereal flight. My wing scar tingled in a lovely way, and when it did, I tilted my head to the window and spotted Pin Oak. She smiled at me, and I did the same.

Chapter 27

O nce Helen decided I should stay in Finn's room, she didn't waver. During rainy April days, we boxed clothes from the dresser, old toys from the closet, and a few books, all while Helen took time to pause, weep, tell a story, or wander in memories. She kept some things: the pale blue romper, the miniature bird figurines on Finn's dresser, the mural ("Erasing the mural," she said, "it'd be like erasing Finn's soul."). Boxes eventually piled in the hallway like sad, overgrown mushrooms. Yes, a strange musing. But still not so much considering mushrooms in the forest realm either nourished or ailed, and Helen's packing of Finn's story, I sensed, did much the same.

When the room grew barer, we stood amidst its deep hollow: the hollow bed, the hollow dresser, the hollow of Finn. But the bird figurines—they spoke a silent soul-language—as they told me Finn still lived here. I could somewhat feel his spirit present, even with the knowledge that it rocked not here but near Horace.

Helen lifted the tiny cardinal figurine, and smelled it. Then she turned and placed the cardinal in my palms so I could see, touch, and sniff it. After I'd done a little of everything, she closed my fingers around it.

"Yours, now," she said. "Yours."

I cradled it as if it were the cardinal John killed in the forest. Grief welled in my soul. But I refused to release teardrops. Not when Helen needed my strength.

"This was Finn's favorite," Helen said. "I think he'd like you to have it."

"Thank you," I said.

Helen smiled through tears.

"John whittled wood to make this for Finn, and I painted it. John doesn't make a show of it, but he's an artist of sorts . . . a woodworker. The one thing his daddy did right, I suppose, teaching him woodcraft. In John's spare time, he makes things in his workshed . . . soul-things, I like to say. Useful things. Beautiful things. Most of the furniture you see in this house, he made it. May not be what's in these days . . . chrome tops, Formica . . . but it gives this old house character."

Now it was my turn to smile at the same time I cringed. John created magic in his workshed. But he carved, cut, whittled from trees to do it. Perhaps Helen read my conflict or confusion, because she stared deeper into me, spoke more.

"You see, Willow, the woodcraft, and even the farm work . . . I think that's what saved John. Laboring, tilling, and caring for this land and the fruits of that labor . . . that's his religion . . . his gateway to God, even if he doesn't go to church. John's a complex man, you see . . . an intelligent man . . . perhaps not by society's measure, with its degrees and doctrines . . . but by God's measure. His farming alongside Nature and her grandeur. His woodwork. His handcrafted art. Clearly, he's an artist."

Now I smiled with Helen. Pushed my concerns into God's hands. From what I'd heard, God seemed capable enough to take it on.

"You know," Helen said, looking around the room's expanse. "We can buy you some new things. Spruce this place up. We'll donate Finn's things to the church. Would you like to come with me, Willow?"

Before I could reply, John entered the room. I didn't know what John thought of me since Helen revealed she believed I was their dead daughter, especially when I found him staring at me, and then gazing off. But I did know one thing for certain about John. He possessed strong views for keeping Finn's room intact.

The past few days, John even avoided the room. But now, as he looked to us, beaten, and then glanced to the mural, tears floated his soul like a lily pad, I imagined. He didn't seem angry (he was, the night before, when Helen packed Finn's baseball mitt). No. Instead, he rooted his body tall and reverent, like Horace.

"Hopin' Finn's flyin'," he said. "Flyin' with the birds."

Helen glided to John and wrapped her arms around him from behind. This was lovelier than a poem, lovelier. I watched as they blended heartbeats set to Finn. Then Helen rested her head against John's back and breathed with him—both remembering the son who said goodbye. Now, I couldn't stop myself. I sobbed into my hands.

"Willow," Helen said. "Come here."

I fell into the fold of their love—their arms around me—the epicenter of their shared heartbeat. I wept and wept and wept until the rain parted ways and a slice of sunshine tapped our backs.

After our sun-soul moment—an ode to Finn—John carried the boxes to the truck. Helen prepared lunch in the kitchen. She sliced fresh tomatoes, turkey, and cheese, and placed all of it on wheat bread with dollops of mustard. Next, she arranged strawberries in crystal bowls and swirled whipped cream on top. Then she poured fresh-squeezed lemonade in sparkly green glasses.

"Let's sit on the porch," Helen said. "Make it a meal."

John appeared shocked with the suggestion, but he smiled into his shock.

"I think Finn would like us to sit there, feel the sunshine, smell spring's fragrance . . . enjoy it."

I helped Helen bring the teapot and teacups inside, wash them, and make chamomile tea. John removed the ax, placed it in a corner of the porch, and dusted the table clean. Together, we brought our plates out, and the crystal bowls of strawberries, and the lemonade in sparkly green glasses, and placed them on the table. Helen returned with the teapot and the teacups and poured us warm tea alongside our lemonade. Nervous at first, we stared at the food and one another. Then Helen bowed her head, and John did, too. Respectful, I followed them as Helen prayed.

"Bless us, oh Lord, and these thy gifts, which we are about to receive, from thy bounty, through Christ, our Lord. Amen."

Helen brightened as she raised her spoon first and ate

a strawberry. But she didn't speak anymore of the Lord, or Christ, or Amen. Neither did John. So, I wondered about God—and if Lord, Christ, and Amen knew God—until Helen interrupted my thoughts.

"Willow, in the springtime, every morning, afternoon, and evening, we'd sit here and have our meals as a family. Even in the rain, Willow. Even then. Finn loved being outdoors. Just seemed more of himself outside."

"Finn would smile . . . eat and smile," John said, shaking his head.

I looked at the ax in the corner, curious.

"That old thing," Helen said. "You want to know why it's here. Well, Finn and I, we'd see John off for the day, after breakfast. He'd kiss our foreheads and then pick up his ax and venture out to his crops. It's an old farming superstition . . . to place your ax upright to the skies to protect the harvest from bad weather. John never worked a day of his life without doing just that."

John grew silent. I'd only seen him take the ax into the fields once, and that was after Finn's funeral.

"Perhaps he'll get back to it," Helen said, eyeing John. "Perhaps."

Now the talk died down a bit, and we ate in Nature's warmth and fragrance, and certainly in Finn's memory. I could feel him with us—a faint laughter in the breeze. When we finished, John told us he'd clean up and he walked us to the truck to tuck us inside. He then moved to the truck bed and patted the boxes with his eyes closed. Helen wound down the window, and John squeezed her hand before the truck rumbled and inched up the driveway.

Chapter 28

I fixated on John's reflection in the truck's side mirror as we moved—John Hawes, a weathered tree of a man. Grief undulated him like branches in a gale, but his body appeared to feel it, accept it, own it, all while reaching for blessed light. For a beat, I didn't want to ever know why Helen blamed John for Finn's hanging. And when we arrived at the towering church, I stared at the colored fragmented windows (that didn't want to know why, either). No, these stained-glass eyes only wished to stretch for light, too. In fact, hope shimmered here, even if Helen didn't. She turned to me with tears.

"It'll be just us and Father Will," she said. "He knows we're coming."

Helen patted my leg, and then we proceeded to carry Finn's belongings up the steps, placing them alongside the grand arched doorway. When we finished, I heard footsteps, and the double door opened to Father Will. His clothes were the color of soil and lilies. I didn't focus on his face or his eyes.

"Good afternoon," he said. "Happy to see you."

He looked at both of us—not the least bit shocked by my presence. Helen didn't speak.

"Finn's things," he said, looking at her, "we'll find them a good home."

She nodded, and now Father Will stared into me.

"I don't believe we've properly met," he said. "I'm Father Will."

"Willow," I whispered.

"One of my girlfriend's daughters," Helen said, "a girlfriend that moved away long ago. But we still keep in touch . . . letters, the occasional phone call. She offered her daughter's help to us. At first, I thought it'd be too much. But Willow, here, she's been more than help to us. She's been a great comfort. A blessing, you could say."

Father Will nodded. If he experienced skepticism, he didn't allow Helen to see it. He respected her story. Left it alone.

"Come inside," he said. "Stay a while."

Helen wanted to leave. But I didn't. I walked through the double door, forcing her to follow. The church bloomed before me like springtime set to human-things: the altar—a fully realized tree, pews—grass to rest on, windows—clouds of color, and statues—beautiful flowers.

"Sit," Father Will said.

He sat in a pew and turned to face us.

"I hope you won't mind if I speak," he said. "You're free to listen or rise up and leave. However, I find that, in times of grief, it helps to give it a voice, a place to go. The body can only hold so much for so long. Let me take a piece of it on, no matter how small."

"Finn loved birds," I said to fracture Helen's silence. "We kept his birds."

Helen appeared shocked, I'm sure, to hear my strange, bird-like voice speak to another. But through mine she found hers. She stared at the pulpit of the church and spoke.

"Finn loved to watch birds fly off . . . wander to places unknown. I used to think he may have been a bird in a past life. And it was a good life. One he'd return to, if he could."

I soared with this visual for a moment—Finn free, flying—until Father Will's words grounded me.

"I think the life you and John made for him . . . it was a good life, too."

Helen didn't look convinced.

"You both gave him all a child needs in this world: Love. And Finn, he reflected it back to us. Maybe not in a way people understood. But God did . . . because God made him, for you. God hand-selected Finn for you, for John . . . good people."

Helen finally looked at Father Will. No more flying with Finn and his birds.

"Those are all pretty words," she said, "pretty thoughts. But none of them take the pain away. None of them bring Finn back to us. And if that's the case, God then hand-selected to take Finn from us, and put us in unspeakable, undying pain . . . the kind that won't ever grow wings and fly off."

"Who says we're supposed to live a life free of pain? Not God. He gave up His greatest gift, his son, for us. That's true pain, there. But I'm not God . . . even if I speak for Him. I'm not His voice. Mine is still human, and so sometimes even I don't understand."

Now Father Will grew silent, and I detected sorrow quiver in his eyes.

"And I can't forgive myself for that day . . . the day John

brought Finn to church and left a broken man. I keep thinking that, if I handled things better, your lives would be set on
a very different path. Finn would still be here. Still be with
the parents that loved him more than life. I know I'm meant
to trust God's path for all of us. But some days even I find
it challenging. Some days, I feel very far from God, if that's
any consolation to you."

Even as I didn't comprehend the word *consolation* at the
time, I understood that Father Will meant to swim with our
family's pain.

"John never talks about that day," Helen said. "But it was
my grief that set him on the pathway to church. When my
daddy died, I was inconsolable. I couldn't get out of bed,
even breathe. Couldn't take care of Finn the way he needed.
It was John's last-ditch effort to revive me . . . taking Finn
to church, going himself, thinking that after all these years
of me pushing him to go and him refusing, that this tiny act
would lift me up. It was a kind act on John's part. But he
didn't think it through."

"No, Helen. We failed you, John, and Finn. This congregation failed you, and no one more than myself."

Helen lowered her head and wept into her hands. It took
time for her to compose herself, but when she did, she stared
with the sun's power at Father Will. It was obvious that she
wanted to hear more.

"John, he had his way with God, there's no doubt in my
mind," Father Will said. "He was close to God everyday,
even if he never came to church. John's spirit rises with God
each morning he works that farm with heart and soul. Just
because someone comes to church doesn't mean that body
is present with Him. I'm quite certain John and God have

had many conversations. Silent ones. Those are oftentimes the best conversations to have."

Father Will reached across, patted Helen's shoulder.

"A good man, John is."

Helen shivered, and then gazed, steadfast.

"John's father forced him to church to pray at the same time he twisted scripture to justify abuse," she said. "I understood why John refused to go to church after his father died. I should have let him be."

"You loved him . . . love him," Father Will said. "Love is oneness . . . but it doesn't always know one way."

Helen stared long and hard at Father Will.

"Please," she finally said, "tell me what truly happened that day. I've heard John's version . . . in piecemeal. But I'd like to know yours."

Father Will lowered his head. Sighed before he spoke.

"John showed up late for Mass that day . . . during the sermon, in fact . . . and that was the first thing that seemed to aggravate the congregation. To this day, I can remember the gospel I was referencing . . . Ephesians 4:30-32 . . . 'And do not grieve the Holy Spirit of God, by whom you were sealed for the day of redemption. Let all bitterness and wrath and anger and clamor and slander be put away from you, along with all malice. Be kind to one another, tenderhearted, forgiving one another, as God in Christ forgave you.'"

Father Will's voice trembled.

"John and Finn held hands as they walked the aisle together. Can see it like it was yesterday . . . John wearing a proper blue tie. I'd never seen him in a tie, before . . . and Finn wearing a blue tie, too . . . humming as he walked . . . like a humming bird, I imagine, now . . . but at the time, it was distracting. Seems maybe he hummed with a want to see, speak, know, feel. Regardless, he seemed happy, curious. There was only room to sit in the front row, and that's where John took him. And as they sat, some offered looks of contempt and others rude *shush*es. John managed the best he could to tune it out, I'm sure, and I managed the best I could to finish the sermon. Ended it short, in fact. The congregation was more than aware, and on any other Sunday would have been more than grateful. But not this Sunday."

Father Will paused, and we waited patiently for his voice to return.

"As the Mass progressed, there were things Finn found pleasing, I do believe. And there were moments when it all seemed too much for him. Some people, they still spoke their *shhh*s if not with their voices, their eyes. And I tried to move the Mass along, to pretend all was usual, a typical Sunday. But when it came time to extend the sign of peace, and the chorus sang "Peace is Flowing Like a River," and the community reached out to shake hands to all except John, well, that's when I moved to John, extended my hand, and Finn, he flew from the pew, past me and onto the pulpit. He hummed and he squealed, and I now believe he was feeling and speaking to God with the voice He gave him . . ."

Helen grabbed the pew to anchor herself, and I cradled her hand.

"Some people were silent, uncomfortable, and some perhaps feeling God through Finn. But then there were the others . . . the people who grew louder in their protests of Finn. Words like . . . 'Get that kid outta here . . . or 'At least sit him on down in the cry room with the babies,' or 'He don't belong. God don't invite the uninvited . . . atheists.' Worst yet, Sandra Cummings . . . 'He's a sin, John Hawes. A

child that never should have been. You have no right bringing him into God's home.'"

Helen shook in her skin, but Father Will continued.

"Finn processed that evil energy, I know, and he shrieked
and grew terribly upset. His face turned red, and he stamped,
and his body seemed outside of his control. John rushed to
him, lifted him from behind, and carried him out alongside
the congregation's ugly words and behavior. When John
slammed the door, I left the pulpit, went to the rectory, and
didn't return. The congregation had to see themselves out
that day . . . the day Mass never ended. And my silence, my
complicity, to this day . . . it haunts me, Helen. I didn't know
how to handle it. A human moment in the house of God. A
terrible human moment. I faced my own shortcomings as
a leader of this church, and I'm so sorry, Helen. So terribly
sorry."

Helen didn't speak. She didn't weep or move. And so I
looked into Father Will's eyes and did all these things for
her.

"Time to go," I said, standing, pulling Helen up with me.

"Time heals," Father Will said. "But it doesn't take away
what was."

Helen looked at Father Will in the strangest way.

"No, it doesn't," she said. "I should've stayed with John
that night. I knew something was awfully wrong with him.
Finn and I never should have left him when my mother
called . . . needed us right then, right there. I should've
stayed."

"Helen . . ." Father Will said, reaching out to hold her
hand.

As Father Will rooted himself with regret on the pew,
Helen withdrew from him, walking off.

I raced to hold her hand and guide her along the narrow, lonely aisle, past the double door, through the entryway, and down the steps. I opened the truck's passenger door, and I placed her on the seat. Then I took the wheel, driving for the first time, through town, along smooth roads and country roads, until I reached our dirt road.

When we returned home, I unpacked Helen from the car—a shell of herself—but one that wished to place John inside, exist in the hollow with him. I cared for them both that evening, tending to their shared anguish deep into the night. In doing so, I cooked a warm meal, cleaned the kitchen, spoke when they couldn't, stayed with them until they fell asleep beside one another.

Then I retreated to the silence of Finn's room. I cracked the window, but didn't search for Pin Oak. Instead, I held the cardinal figurine in my palm and connected deeply with its soul, its energy. I imagined a young sun-smiling Finn playing with it.

"Tirra lirra, tirra lirra," I whispered while flying the bird against the hopeful sky-mural.

Sylvan-Speak

Willow sings "Tirra lirra, tirra lirra" late into the night. She plays with a bird made from pieces of a tree, probably thinking it's alive. She believes other lies, too—like she's a wingless tree sprite. Maybe she isn't fully human, but she'll never be fully sprite again. Perhaps a fairy. Fairies wander near and far without remorse. Their magic blooms allegiance only to oneself. Perhaps she's fairy-human.

No matter, she befriends my sprite—to know Finn through her. I tell my sprite, *"STAY AWAY, Pin Oak. Stay away. Willow is not loyal or true."* But still, my sprite listens . . . not to me . . . but to her.

"Tirra lirra, tirra lirra," the fairy-human sings. In a whisper, I hear Pin Oak sing *"Tirra lirra"* in my hollow. I tremble. It's obvious she feels me, so she whispers softer, but still deeper.

Pin Oak is *my* tree sprite.

Spring will leave. Summer will come. The fairy-human will go.

Fairy-Human-Speak

"*Spring will leave. Summer will come.*" Sylvan tells me only this, never what I want to know.

In the forest realm, I met summertime naked with a wing scar and a body brown as Horace's bark. My eyes gleamed a green that saw past the grass and the leaves and the vines, into the soul of all things. I'd spin my hair into a sparrow's nest and sweat water I imagined squeezed from the sun. I'd eat berries and drink the rain.

But now, I am more human, less sprite. I wear clothes that fit my skin and shoes that walk before me. I brush my hair and speak poetry and wash my wing scar in a tub. I eat human-things, cooked in ovens and chilled in refrigerators. I ride in trucks and on tractors (John sometimes even lets me drive). I sleep in a bed and wake to human voices and sing "Tirra lirra" as I go to sleep.

"*Spring will leave. Summer will come.*" Sylvan tells me only this, never what I want to know.

Chapter 29

Spring left us with beautiful healing threads and memories. On Mother's Day, John gave Helen a quilt that Lucy handcrafted with meaningful scraps of Finn's clothes patched into it. On Father's Day, Helen gave John Finn's old baseball mitt (she returned to church to reclaim it). With both exchanges, I stood present to the waves of their emotion that culminated in a warm embrace.

Helen covered me each night with Finn's *mother-quilt* (she called it), patting the colorful squares. And John placed Finn's old baseball mitt on the bookshelf with the bird figurines. I imagined the figurines flying, and John kindly catching them with Finn's mitt. A comforting musing. Nothing strange or dangerous about it.

But then summertime blew in with secrets. The wind felt like Horace's hollow when angered—a heat that couldn't cool. Helen told me, "Summertime can't lie . . . summer's sun, it's powerful, honest . . . won't rest until truth is told." I worried over what she meant, and for John and Helen, Finn's spirit, and myself. I fretted for Horace, too, and sometimes even Smis (because even Smis needs someone to care for him). No, this was a lie. I didn't fret *for* Smis, but *because* Smis hadn't appeared to me for so long, and what that meant for all of us.

It was on a sweltering night in late June that Warren Cummings haunted me more than Smis. I couldn't shake it. All day, my mind spun stories of wandering off, locating Warren, and then John and Helen finding us. Still, I stared at the hopeless yellow phone—its hushed *ring, ring, ring*—and willed it to speak Warren's voice. When Helen noticed, she said, "Nothing good comes by way of the telephone . . . it only haunts . . . tells you Finn died in the forest. Hung from a tree." Helen's declaration shocked me (she'd been far more agreeable, if not happy). Immediately, the fate of Finn's spirit and my role in it trumped my desire for Warren. I pushed him from my thoughts if not my heart.

That night as Helen brushed my hair, she didn't speak at first. I looked into the mirror at my face and her eyes. And as I did so, I pined to know more than John and Helen's grief, and even about the bluebell house becoming a home. Human greed or grace, I wasn't sure which I felt. But to this day I can still hear Helen's nectar-barbed voice, when a poetic line unraveled from her like dark sunlight.

"He met her on life's darkest road; her soul became his moon."

She didn't say who penned those words, so I figured that they were her own. The mother beast that she was, I'm sure she sensed my secret longing for Warren. Or maybe, she wished to be that moon for John once more. But before I could decode her, swift and exact she walked me to Finn's room (we still named it), and she tucked me beneath his patchwork clothes, kissing my forehead.

"Be your own moon," she said in a whisper.

Helen then found John downstairs and I listened to their footsteps—imagining them drummed heartbeats—as they retreated to their room for the night. I moved to the window, anxious, wishing to give Finn's spirit to them in glimmer-gold. But then, selfishly, I took. For this very thought allowed my conscience to look past their sorrow and into me. Only me. That's when I searched for her—Pin Oak.

She hadn't made an appearance in weeks—not even a tiny wave hello. Instead, Sylvan seemed angry and guarded. In fact, every time the moonlight stroked his branches, I read his disenchantment with me. Still, I didn't cease searching Sylvan. In this moment, I even closed my eyes to rustle-hum, hoping his sprite would respond. That's when I heard a light tap at the window and found not Pin Oak, but Warren Cummings on Sylvan's branch. Excited, fearful, I opened the window.

"Willow," he whispered.

The moon seemed to birth Warren Cummings from her wonder, he glowed so deep and beautiful. Then he smiled, a soul-hungry sort of smile.

"I just couldn't stay away," he said. "I was only gonna stand outside your house, imagine seein' you. But then, there you were . . . the moon lightin' you up like you were meant to be there . . . for me. Man, I had to climb up. I know it's wrong. But I couldn't walk away."

I hesitated. Thought of the one word I *should* speak—the same word I spoke with Finn before he died—*NO*. Then more words of *no* (I should have spoken them . . . but never did!) . . . *No, Warren, I won't come to you. It's wrong. Go. Leave. No. Your mother's evil. GO.* But then Warren extended his hand to me, and my mind raced with my breath, pushing me through the window. Shamefully, I didn't think of Warren's mother and her evil toward John. Only focused on Warren.

We descended the tree with ease together, and as we did I wondered if Warren was more sprite than human or if the tree conspired to help us . . . No, rid us once and for all. But there wasn't time to think much more because Warren grabbed my hand once we hit the ground and we ran the driveway, hopped the gate, and sprinted to his Pinto a short distance down the road.

Before we entered, I kissed him. Not once. Twice. I longed only for the forest of him—the wilderness of what we were—limbs entwined, moving on a dusty road under the moonlight's grace (not greed). I didn't think of John and Helen, the bluebell house-turned-home, sour and sore Sylvan or his sprite that eluded me. I only experienced us—Willow and Warren. Then he opened the door, and I sat down, the car moving breathy along the country road, music spilling into our space, a sensual voice "Shadow Dancing."

"I know I'm askin' for trouble, takin' you off like this," Warren said. "But I don't wanna get *you* in trouble."

I didn't speak, and it took some time before Warren released his voice to me. He spoke of many things that I stored to memory. How he worked at his father's automotive shop for two summers straight to pay for his car. He mentioned his mother, and how the cancer was taking everything . . . she didn't go to church, and she didn't look herself ("a ghost of who she was," he said many times), and how only he and his uncle were left to caretake for her . . . that his dad divorced her, left the state . . . couldn't handle her or what cancer may bring . . . "Went far away as the moon," he repeated several times. He also said "sorry" a lot. "Sorry my mom overheard me talk about Mr. Hawes and the gun in the forest." "Sorry Mr. Hawes went to jail." "Like, so, so sorry. Didn't mean for that to happen."

I wasn't sure Warren Cummings was sorry for taking me away, though, and strangely enough, I didn't care. After all, I imagined battling Smis to steal more time with Warren. A surprising, dangerous musing! Indeed, to ax it, I rustle-hummed deep inside me, wondering all the while why I thought of Smis and Warren in the same breath. I didn't know. I didn't *want* to know.

So I gazed fast to Warren and then Nature's enormity. Her extraordinary madness hoarded the night—stars, trees, fields—even as we ambled along a human road, and still when Warren parked his car on the side of it. He looked at me, and I averted his gaze; it had the ability to loosen pieces of me I hadn't met—fresh, fearful pieces that longed to be loved.

Warren opened the car door and pulled me out. He locked our fingers, walking us through a moon-soaked wildflower meadow. Like a love poem, I tried not to feel too much . . . too soon. But I did. I felt my legs move, my hand hold his, my hair blow, my body speak a strange language in a strange world where only we existed. Perhaps this was oneness, I mused, traveling someplace beyond myself, even as we reached the edge of a forest.

"Do you trust me?" Warren said. "The place I want to take you . . . it isn't far."

I followed, and we walked a short while in the misted honeysuckle heat until the forest grew sparser and I heard a brook flow and soon spotted it moving over large rocks. And when I looked beyond and saw a few weeping willow trees in the distance, I couldn't breathe or speak. The moonlight rippled across the brook, dipping, inviting stars. Not the cruel stars that mocked Finn's death. No. Sensual stars. We sat and stared at Nature's finest, mesmerized.

"This property," Warren finally said, "belongs to my uncle. It's always been my favorite place . . . my place to go when the world stops making sense. Tonight . . . the world makes more sense than it ever has."

Warren stroked my hair, smoothed it, and then fingered my scalp. My body spoke in the place where blood flowed. I struggled not to listen. But that place was charged with Nature's breath, and so I turned to Warren, and he tasted my lips again and again. I wanted more.

Warren pressed his hand beneath my clothes to the spot that ached for him, and his finger entered me—a cold and warm pain. I shuddered and withdrew, shocked with its intensity, newness. Warren respected my body's cues, and turned me, placing my back against his chest. He held me gently, and we stared into the moonlight as it tampered with the forest's secrets and our lonely turned to knowing souls.

"I'm sorry," Warren said. "The just being near you . . . it's enough."

I relaxed again, against Warren. Stargazed. I thought of Finn. Yes, Finn. Because without Finn, I wouldn't know Warren or this moment. And I wouldn't know that Warren's place, it was me. Willow Brook.

In time, we drove in silence back to the bluebell house. Warren wanted to escort me up to the door, but I refused. Instead, we kissed goodbye and he told me that we'd see each other again soon. Warren remained fixed behind the metal gate as I walked the spiraling driveway, and he watched as I climbed to the window. He didn't wave goodbye and leave until I entered Finn's room. Now I fixated on Warren Cummings moving away with the moonlight. Oddly, again, I thought of Smis.

"No," I said, forcefully. "He's too full of life for you to take him."

Smis—the master of secrets and longings— didn't appear to me. Smis would stay away, wouldn't he? Make my ending with Warren a mystery.

Horace-Speak

As summer scorches my forest realm, Smis comes to me in the form of Scarlet's shadow. I can tell he truly longs to rest on my limbs like the days before I birthed a sprite—to listen to my soul-speak that wafts all worries away with the wind. But instead, he stands a painful distance from me and speaks.

"Scarlet Oak names herself Willow Brook, now. She's more human than sprite. She keeps secrets ... with a human boy." Over and over again Smis-speaks. *"Scarlet's more human than sprite. She keeps secrets ... with a human boy."*

I mourn my sprite and weep for my human.

"She still belongs to me," I tell him.

Smis frustrates with my loyalty—an unwavering tie to Scarlet Oak-now-Willow Brook. He hasn't the capacity to understand what is bound by sap. Smis only knows emptiness, and an unspoken wish to fill it with love's good company.

And so, I apologize for shunning him long ago. *"Sorry,"* I say. *"Fear made me turn you away. But come closer and be with me. Fear is gone. I love you. Still, I love you."*

The boy-spirit climbs down my trunk to approach Smis, reaching his glowing spirit-hand to give. Smis doesn't take. But I know he feels a little less lonely . . . just like me. Smis is simply misunderstood.

I no longer fear Smis. But Scarlet-Willow and I—whether connected by sap or soul or memory—we are child and parent. I can't help but love her more.

Chapter 30

The next morning, I watched John from the window as he met the searing sun and humidity with his ax in hand. As he walked, I could sense Helen with him in some way I hadn't seen before—a beautiful silent oneness—and still I felt her when he placed the ax upright, stared to the heavens above with goodwill. He then moved purposefully to his plow and did what farmers do—the tending to Nature's earthen-things, things meant to either grow or die.

I checked on Helen in her bedroom to find her asleep. As her eyelids shaded and fluttered, I imagined her in the most radiant dreamworld, a place where Finn stood incandescent beneath Horace's sun-split shade and soul-spoke to her. The more I focused on it, the more her mouth's corners uplifted. In fact, she unleashed a smile I'd never seen. I moved to kiss her cheek but stopped midway, fearing she'd smell Warren on me.

Now guilt wriggled raw. I wondered what Horace would think or say or do if he knew about Warren. I missed him something awful, so I opened the window and stretched to sit on Sylvan. The old tree allowed my presence but didn't speak or comfort me in any way. Pin Oak did not show up for me either, and so I leaned my head to the left to look past Sylvan's branches and commune with summertime's sticky sun-drenched secrets. In time, John drove off in his truck, and Helen popped her head through the window.

"Be careful on that tree, Willow," she said.

Then her voice softened as she studied me.

"But I do understand. Sometimes life tells you to tilt your head, sideways squint, peer through a new perspective. Just don't stay out there too long."

I stayed out long enough to relive each moment with Warren. I closed my eyes. Inhaled the woodsy, wild scent of Warren Cummings from memory. Then I opened my palms, imagining that I held his beautiful blue soul.

Stop! Don't think . . . don't think . . . don't think of Warren's soul. Smis will come . . . take it . . . just like Finn. Smis. Smis. Smis. You won't leave me alone . . . even when you leave me alone. Where are you? Why won't you show me your shadow?

My thoughts ran away with me (there were many more), and that's when I spotted Warren's Pinto amble along the driveway. So I crept inside—quickly—and peered through the window with discretion.

The car parked, and when Sandra Cummings slipped out, panting, I worried she'd discovered my Warren Cummings secret and intended to tell Helen. As she moved to the porch, I noticed that she appeared frailer, slower, whiter. Still, that wounded ghost could most likely limp up those steps and shatter once more the hanging blue light that John had replaced. But I didn't move to warn Helen. Instead, I hid in the hallway's shadow. In time, I heard Sandra's feeble *knock, knock, knock.*

Helen looked through the door's peephole and then turned her back and ventured straightaway to the kitchen. So Sandra knocked harder—the noise not at all a match for her frailty. When that didn't work, she coughed. Kindhearted enough, Helen opened the door.

"Go home. Get in bed, Sandra," she said. "You've no business driving around in this condition . . . going to kill someone, if not yourself. And you've sure as hell no business coming here. I told you at the station. Don't you ever step foot on our property again. You're lucky I'm the only one here."

"That's exactly why I drove down the driveway," Sandra said. "I saw John wasn't home. I need to talk to you Helen. Set things right by God."

"By God?" Helen said, her anger rising.

"Yes."

"Wait here a moment," Helen said.

She closed the door and gazed up the staircase. I peeked around the corner, and in a rolling-rainstorm-of-a-woman stare she told me to *dare not* show myself. I knew by this time, however, that look originated from a fierce mother's intent to protect. So I obeyed, insomuch as I didn't go downstairs. But I also didn't move to Finn's room. At this time, Helen opened the door and allowed Sandra to hobble into the kitchen and sit, the chair moaning and creaking over her presence.

"So, tell me," Helen said, "what God told *you* to tell me. Then promptly leave this house. Never return."

Sandra's words were labored.

"You've suffered, Helen . . . more than any human I know. And I wasn't . . . no, haven't been the truest friend to you. I want to apologize, acknowledge my wrongdoing.

God's words . . . they're as good as gold. And He told me to speak my truth, and apologize."

"For what specifically would you like to apologize?"

Sandra coughed again, and I heard something slam onto the tabletop.

"Drink the water," Helen said. "Speak, then go."

There was a pause, and that's when I defied Helen. Crept downstairs. Hid around the corner.

"You know the doctors aren't giving me much time. Cancer's taking Warren from me . . . taking everything . . . my dignity . . . my . . ."

"Specifically," Helen said, "are you here to apologize for accusing my husband of pulling a weapon on your son? For being plain hateful? Or is there something more? Something regarding John's visit to church with Finn?"

Sandra didn't speak.

"So, let me refresh your memory if the cancer's taken that too," Helen said. "Did you tell my husband, in the house of God, of all places, that my boy was a sin? A child that never should have been? That John had no right bringing him into God's home? Did you say these things?"

Still there was silence.

"Did you say these things, Sandra?" Helen said, as she pounded her fist on the table.

"There was a time," Sandra said, "when we needed each other . . . were the best of friends for one another . . . before John . . . before . . ."

I peeked around the corner to find Helen's back to me and Sandra's ugliness on full display. My wing scar ached and my soul tormented. I wanted to slice through my skin, grab my blood-sap rage, hurl and splatter it all over Sandra.

But Helen shook me from my imagining as she stood and slammed her fist once more on the kitchen table.

"Tell me, Sandra! Did you say those things?"

Sandra's eyes glazed over and her skin whitened even more. She looked down to the table.

"DID YOU?"

"YES," I yelled, stepping from the shadow. "YES, SHE SAID THOSE THINGS. SHE HURT FINN! SHE HURT JOHN! SHE HURT YOU!"

Sandra Cummings startled, her face glazing in a strange way, with eyes distant and close.

"LEAVE," I said. "LEAVE OUR HOME!"

I rushed to Sandra, but slick on her feet, Helen darted and dragged me into the book room. I breathed too fast—the kind of seeing-Finn-hanging-and-dying-fast.

"Take a breath," Helen said. "It's okay, Willow. Stay. Stay here. I know how to handle this. Don't move. Stay."

Helen stared into my torment, quivered, her anger for Sandra clipped by her love for me. And I swam in her quiet-rain forest realm of mother-love, her tears meant for me. She stroked my hair, whispered, "Stay," once more, and then rushed from the room. I didn't move or eavesdrop. But I did hear Helen when she guided the poisoned mushroom woman to the door and opened it with these words . . .

"Here, here . . . it's okay. You're seeing things, Sandra. Hearing things that aren't there. Taking you home. Taking you home myself. There's no girl here . . . no girl. Let's get you on home to bed. Rest you on up."

215

I rested on that red oak chair beneath sunlight and the spider plant until John came home and found me. He held out his hand.

"Willow," he said, "what's wrong? Where's Helen?"

Traumatized, I didn't speak or stand, and so John knelt before me. He placed his solid hand on my cheek.

"Come on out to my workshed. Be with me for a while. Helen'll be home soon. Tell me what's what."

I nodded, and John walked me hand in hand to his artistic space.

"Makin' somethin' for ya, Willow," he said. "A gift. Be givin' it to ya soon. But for now, sit on down, rest up, ya hear . . . and I'll clean on up . . . with your company, that is."

I sat on a stool in a corner and watched as John wiped and swept, and listened as he whistled almost like a bird. Our souls spoke without words, and I nearly eased in John's presence. That is . . . until I spotted something. It gleamed in silver. I looked away and then back to the box that was tucked behind some cans and boxes on a shelf. No matter how much my soul longed for peace, evil visited the bluebell home in Sandra Cummings, and evil lived in that steel box.

True to John, I came to the workshed. I sat on down, but didn't rest up. Not when the gun that killed John's daddy spoke to me, too.

Smis-Speak

It isn't that I've vanished, left her. It's that Scarlet Oak's left me, vanished. Willow Brook doesn't truly want to see me. Humans never do. Fairy-humans, either, it appears. They keep me locked in steel boxes, hidden in dark places, and look at me only when forced. Never with a smile, a whistle, laughter. None tell me to "sit on down, rest up, ya hear." Still, I visit, watch, listen.

I tremble in Sandra's shadow along a country road. I hear her cry when Helen refuses to heed her sorrow. Sandra's soul is buried deep in darkness, and hatred won't illuminate her heart, help her dig out.

I linger in Helen's shadow. She clasps her hands on the steering wheel and stares straight ahead. She longs for where her hands are meant to be—around her baby boy who grew into a child but never a man.

I sit in Willow Brook's shadow. I wish my shadow solid form, with arms and hands to hold her, to give. For a death-beat I lie to myself. Say that I can. But now, Willow sees the gun, not me. Willow believes that the gun, Smis— we are interchangeable—soulless. Death. That's all.

Chapter 31

Summertime slipped into a routine that I depended on, and Smis's absence became a part of it. Mornings belonged to Helen—housework, reading, even writing (she told me the other morning, "Willow, you form your letters with true artistry."). I loved the letter *W* best. The afternoons belonged to John—farm work, listening, sometimes laughing. The evenings belonged to our family—shared over a hearty meal—and then to Helen and poetry as my hair tamed beneath her brush before it grew wild in Warren's fingertips. The nights, they always belonged to Warren and our secret.

Most nights, as John and Helen slept, I climbed down Sylvan, sprinted along the driveway, and met Warren by roadside. We drove to our spot, our souls aglow with the fireflies. Our lips tasted and our fingers learned as we became ourselves and one in the same breath.

As Warren dropped me off each night, I walked, mindful, along the driveway, communing with Nature and her extraordinary madness. Sure enough, Nature was my ally, a fragrant place of quiet to dive deeper and read my soul like poetry. Indeed, she was also my soul's reflector: the buzz of stars, the whisper of dark, the hum of trees, and the thrill of beautiful, dangerous secrets.

In this mindset, I always kicked off my shoes, once reaching Sylvan—climbed with bare feet, kissed his bark, and caressed his grooves with my fingertips, rustle-humming all the while, *"I am still a part of a tree . . . a part of my great scarlet oak, Horace."* Although Sylvan never spoke to me, I hoped he and Pin Oak listened.

But whenever I returned to Finn's room, rapture left me. My body chilled, even in the heat, and a longing for some sort of return to who-I-once-was took hold. At the same time, it washed, as tears that would never return. I gazed through the window's looking glass, apart from (not at all a part of) Sylvan. Each time, I searched for Pin Oak with silent desperation. She never found me.

This was my routine for weeks, until I awoke on a *holiday* (as John called it). Indeed, on July Fourth, my everyday life ruptured into the birth of something far more beautiful . . . and dangerous. Something that threatened all my secrets and could render irreversible change.

In the morning, Helen and I spent more time in the book room than normal as she spoke of July Fourth and fireworks. "Finn would cover his ears in distress as they lit up the sky," she said. "But once the color exploded . . . and the sound faded away . . . his smile . . . such a magical thing." I wondered if Horace had seen Finn's smile and if he would agree it wandered in magic's realm.

In the afternoon, I helped John weed his strawberry crops, and I listened as he told me Helen's same story of Finn and fireworks, but with a different language—earth poetry. "A crack . . . a pop . . . Finn'd cover them ears . . . and

then . . . by God, Finn smile with the stars . . . that bright."
I smiled as he spoke and laughed as he laughed, and grew quiet, reflective, when he did.

Later, John and Helen taught me how to shuck corn and snap peas from their pods. Then we savored these same vegetables alongside brown-sugared ham and pineapple for dinner, and enjoyed fresh strawberry shortcake for dessert. As the sun grinned around us on the porch, we smiled for Finn—the simplest, most beautiful language. When we finished the meal, we cleaned the kitchen together until it sparkled, and then John studied Helen. Finally, he spoke.

"Do you mind much if I take Willow with me for a bit?"

"I'll go read," Helen said. "Wouldn't mind a little time to myself."

I could tell Helen wasn't going to read but instead take that alone time and place Finn's memory inside of it. I squeezed her hand before following John outside. We ventured deep into his farmland and sat just as Nature opened her agony—the sun floating on the sky's blood and fire, and then falling. We held hands in the silence. Watched the sun lose her horizon. Give her soul to the night.

"Willow," John said. "Ain't showed ya much but this small slice of world . . . here on the farm. But I wanna show ya this. God's poetry."

John never mentioned God or poetry, other than Helen's love for it.

"I feel somethin' . . . dunno if I can say it's what others say it to be . . . but I feel somethin' with me, reaches through me, and finds its way to Finn. Think that somethin', God if ya wanna call it that, gave ya to us. And my worst fear's that jus' the same . . . God'll take ya away. My heart . . ."

John covered his heart but didn't speak. I knew he meant

that if I left him, his heart couldn't take it. I wondered if John already knew about my wanderings—far from home—alongside Warren Cummings. I also considered that he was trying to communicate that he knew without articulating it in naked language.

"Used to take Finn to the fireworks . . . but not too close to people. The closer you get to some people . . . the further ya are. Finn and me . . . we sit at the edge . . . gave him room to be. People . . . most ain't got the gumption to see God, even though they say they know Him. People ain't seen Finn because they ain't seen God. But to work the soil, live under the sky . . . all its colors . . . ya see. I saw Finn . . . see Finn. Boy was amazin'. Still amazin'. God's child."

John lowered his head—a tear rolling down his cheek.

"Willow, sometimes the little things in life are more than enough. Even a smile. Little enough, won't ya say?"

I nodded.

"And while you sure given me some things to smile on . . . Finn took my truest smile with him. By God, he did."

John locked his fingers into mine, and squeezed them, a language protective as Horace's hollow.

"But I still got these hands to hold on to ya, Willow . . . keep ya safe."

I placed John's single tear on my fingertip—a sacred gift.

"Love," I said. "Love."

John smiled, even if it wasn't his truest smile, and when night rolled in with bugs and stars alike, we walked hand in hand back to the bluebell home. I heard booms and ricochets behind us, fireworks from afar. Or perhaps just musings in my mind. We walked on, silent, and John turned in early with Helen to their room.

In Finn's room, I studied the night's largeness and darkness from the window, Sylvan only a piece of it. My heart ached for secrets that live and have no will to die. Within this heart-hurt, I still climbed down Sylvan, winded myself along the driveway, and jumped the metal gate. The barbed fencing caught my yellow sundress, ripping it. Quickly, I pulled the fabric against my stomach and sprinted to Warren's Pinto. He opened the door like always, with the moon's smile, and once he closed me in, sped away, excitement tapping his fingertips on the steering wheel, his music echoing louder, more forcefully. For the first time near Warren, my head throbbed and my body squirmed, ill at ease.

"Too loud?" he said, noticing.

"No music," I said. "Nature."

I rolled the window down and let summertime's fiery wind blow my hair and moisten my face. Warren turned off the music, somewhat used to my strange ways.

"Like . . . I have a surprise for you," he said. "Thought I'd take you somewhere . . . not near Leonardtown . . . not our place. But I'll have you back before midnight, I promise."

I didn't say no. But I didn't say yes, either. I sat still, as John's words refused to leave me, replaying in my mind: "But I still got these hands to hold on to ya, Willow . . . keep ya safe."

"Can't be a true Fourth of July without fireworks," Warren said. "And even if you talk so little . . . or maybe 'cause you do . . . there's one thing I can't get outta my mind. In another life, you told me you'd like to be a bird . . . fly. Gonna give you both, Willow . . . fireworks, and wings to fly."

I didn't protest, even when my stomach ached and my heart told me we were traveling too far from the bluebell home. When we arrived, I was surprised to find so many cars, so many people, so many large, moving human-things with so many lights, so much sound. Disoriented, I closed my eyes.

"You okay?" Warren asked. "We can go if you want."

I opened my eyes and nodded.

"We're in Valley Lee," Warren said. "Like . . . this carnival is awesome, and the fireworks will be, too. You'll see. You won't ever wanna book from here . . . go back to that lonely quiet room of yours."

"I . . ."

"I know," Warren said, speaking for me. "You don't want to be seen . . . don't want Helen and John findin' out. No one's gonna know who you are. They haven't shown you to anyone. And even if we see some of my friends . . . we won't talk to them. They know I get in my moods . . . gotta lot goin' on with my mom . . . just wanna be left alone . . . do my own thing."

For the first time, Warren's words didn't calm me. Still, I opened the car door, allowed him to hold my hand and pull me into the loud disharmony of cars and crowds and then into human's extraordinary madness—the carnival. As I walked dizzily, head pounding, the rides, games, food stands, and carnival goers mimicked a skyline crammed with Nature's entirety—stars, sun, moon, trees, grass, flowers, rain, snow—*too much, too much, too much*—the incessant chirp of cicadas, the rolling roar of thunder, every scent of every season . . . none of it where it belonged. Candy colors and windswept movement—all of it—EVERYTHING spun my nervousness to greater heights, high, high, higher than my body's panic when Prickly Elder hovered above me with his sour egg breath and stiff crusty wing.

"Cool, right?" Warren said, unaware of who I truly was and where I truly belonged.

I didn't speak. Words couldn't possibly find me when everything spoke too loudly and smelled too much, moving too fast around me.

"Come on," Warren said, walking quicker.

Once we stopped, we stood still behind many people.

"The line's a little long," Warren said. "But it moves."

I didn't mind standing still. I closed my eyes. That's when Warren kissed me, and even his lips didn't feel the same. I returned to John's words, "But I still got these hands to hold on to ya, Willow . . . keep ya safe." John would know. Of course, he would know the carnival was too much for me. He never would have brought me here—would have taken me instead to sit in a field and watch God's poetry. John and Helen, they were family . . . and Horace, too. Warren wasn't. He was a boy who took me to a place that said my name, and then a place that couldn't possibly know my name. Warren didn't truly know me or my secrets. No one did . . . except Smis.

It was as I thought this very thing that Smis—strange as all strangers—appeared, even if I didn't see him. Only sensed his energy. Yes, he lingered behind me in line, whispering, *"I'm here, Willow. I'm here for John, and for Horace. I'll keep you safe."*

My mind wandered. Smis wouldn't keep me safe. He wanted to take Finn to the Dark—no light, no safety, no love. Still, I grew a little less alone and a little more with Horace in the forest realm, and so when Warren pulled me to a hard red seat and placed a steel bar over us with a smile, I was a little less afraid.

"Haven't you ever been on a Ferris wheel?" Warren asked, reading my awkwardness.

"No," I said.

"You'll fly, Willow. Fly! And the fireworks, I timed it just right . . . so we'll see them while we ride."

The Ferris wheel started to spin—high, higher, highest— looping round and round and round. It soothed me. Calmed me, even. I smiled for the first time. Warren placed one of his hands over mine as I gripped the steel bar, and he turned my face with his other hand to kiss me. My heart remembered who-I-was with Warren, and so I softly kissed him back. *BOOM!* A blue and white firework exploded. Startled me. I opened my eyes. Jumped. The seat rocked a little.

"Don't move too much," Warren said, "unless you wanna rock this thing . . . make the ride way awesome."

I stilled and oriented myself as best as I could.

"Look," Warren said, pointing to the skyline.

I stared into the moon and the stars and the night's secrets. I longed to exist with Nature as I knew it, but that wish burst, and in its wake a firework seared and broiled the sky with artificial rouge color and a gunshot sound that spun me to the forest realm. No, not to Horace, but to John, Warren, and the dead cardinal in the woods. I couldn't release the thought, which then pushed me to Finn hanging from Horace, and my eyes looking into his, and Finn's only word, *NO.* Then, *DEATH, DEATH, DEATH* took, and gave me *SMIS, SMIS, SMIS,* and then I took Finn's soul, and now, here I sat beside another human boy whose soul I pined to know, to take. I cried. Rocked. Moved the seat violently. I couldn't stop. No, I rocked and rocked and rocked, like

Finn's broken spirit. Then I shook. Hummed. Not a human-hum at all. A rustle-hum, which scared Warren. He froze in his fear . . . until . . .

Warren hummed with me, a beautiful human-hum that mirrored my pain and spoke to who-I-was, who-I-am . . . and told me (in the rocking) that he did know me (he knew my soul), and I wasn't alone with all of my secrets. He was with me. Loved me. And it was this gesture that broke the rocking and allowed my spirit to soar on the last loop of the Ferris wheel. I flew alongside the boy I loved, Warren Cummings.

When the Ferris wheel stopped, Warren took my hand, and that's when I noticed Smis. He rose with Warren's shadow. I hadn't the time to acknowledge him, however, because Warren lifted me in his arms, placed me over his shoulder, and as I closed my eyes to all human madness, he sprinted as best he could, brushing me past people and noise and smells to the Pinto's safety. He then placed me down and drove a short distance away, into Nature's quietness. At once, I patted his hand.

"Stop the car," I said.

Warren put on the brakes, and I moved outside to sit on the hood, my yellowy dress blending with its color.

"I want to see the end," I said.

Warren held me close as the show's grand finale shimmered, soul-spoke with the sky, and it was in this moment—in the *pop* and *crack* of the fireworks—that I knew Finn would unveil his amazing magic smile. So I blew my anxiety far away and grounded myself to the moment. You see, I didn't forget to smile for Finn.

Smis-Speak

Warren does not hum to Willow. *I* hum to Willow, for Willow, by Willow, in Warren's shadow on the Ferris wheel. Warren fears, silences, freezes, until kissed, but I hum so Willow won't fear. I hum to tell her someone understands her . . . even if it's only old horrible shadow-contortionist Smis.

But here is where Smis ends . . . in the artificial shadow of the fireworks. I don't hum, and I don't even think of following Willow where she'll go next. I think only of this memory from our early days in the bluebell house . . .

"Can't outrun me, there in the forest realm, or here in the human realm," I told her. *"Can't win."*

"Can't lose," she said, and then Helen put the strange fox-death-coat on her. I wish I could wrap Willow tight in that coat right now . . . because she *will* lose. She just doesn't recognize it, yet.

She knows I'm here. Knows it. She soul-speaks, "*Go,
Smis. Go. I'll be okay.*"

I give to her what she demands—her fairy-human free
will. I disappear. Leave. Submit to her (can you imagine?).

My shadow's never felt so heavy.

Fairy-Human-Speak

Warren and I are here at our place, in our forest realm. I stand at the crossfire of fairy and human.

I stand with buried sun, and moon aglow. Hair wind-blown, lips shining with stars, fireworks memory.

Warren slips my clothes from me.

Naked, my skin drinks summertime's heat.

My wing scar aches, longs, and so I imagine fanning wings the color of the Fourth of July's sunset.

I rest my back on forest grass, give my fairy body to the human boy whose soul I love.

The night takes us.

"Willow," I hear him whisper, "Willow."

In my name, I taste his love.

I smile for me . . . magic.

Chapter 32

When I walked from Warren to the bluebell home, Nature couldn't soothe my ecstasy or pain. I begged Nature—begged. *"Please quiet my aching parts. Love me still."* But my oneness with Nature fell to separateness. I couldn't hear her, even if she soul-spoke. And so I ran and climbed Sylvan, sat on his branch closest to the window while bunching my dress and dangling my bare feet. Then I cried.

Through my teardrops, I closed my eyes to relive Warren Cummings—the moments that divided me from sprite to fairy-human. I wept and wept and wept, but still, I didn't regret them. I couldn't pluck Warren from my heart, no more than I could the wolf lichen on Horace's trunk. We were one, too. Beautiful in our strange Warren-and-Willow way.

While I grieved in gorgeous pain, Pin Oak walked on dainty twig feet to me with secrets of her own. I opened my palm, and she hopped on. As I lifted her to my eye level, we studied each other's souls until there came a time in which I understood she wished to drink my heartache and take it for herself. I refused her. Intuitively, I knew her fragile body housed too much suffering.

This empathy drew me from my pain, and magically, for the first time, this happened—I could read her mind, not just her soul! And so I gazed deeper into her, longer, and in a fuzzy flash . . . I saw five-year-old Finn smiling, holding Pin Oak in his palm. I waited patiently for her to reveal more. The images sharpened: Finn pulling his hand inside, taking Pin Oak to his dresser, placing her there, allowing her to play with his bird figurines. Finn watching Pin Oak with his sky-wide smile—the same one that carried John's smile.

I could have remained there all night, mind-gazing, knowing Finn, seeing Finn as he was when he lived in the bluebell home. But the creak of Finn's door severed the spell. Helen walked to my bed and patted the pillow I placed beneath the covers while Pin Oak scampered from my hand and raced to camouflage. I protected her from Helen's viewpoint. Then I slipped through the window and stood in the dark's striped moonlight until Helen turned on a lamp.

She approached me and placed her finger beneath my chin. Raised my eyes to meet hers and then searched me for lies, for truth. Satisfied, she stepped back, staring at the rip in my yellow dress and then at every piece of me that couldn't lie because summertime didn't allow it.

"You weren't just out on that tree tonight," Helen said. "You were with Warren."

I didn't speak.

"Answer me . . . the truth," Helen said.

"Yes," I said. "I love him."

I feared that the rolling rainstorm of a woman would appear—roar, rage, thunder—but Helen only moved backwards and sat on the bed.

"Boys lie," she said. "Tell you they love you to get what they want. So, tell me, Willow, did Warren give to you, or did he take from you?"

"He gave," I said.

Helen motioned for me to sit and then held my face against her heart. As I cried, she rocked me and rocked me and rocked me.

"Cry, my love, cry," she whispered, "like you never have before. The sky paints beauty for those broken enough to feel."

Even if she viewed me as broken, her hold grew gentler, like Horace's limbs in full greenery, and her *shhhh . . . . shhh . . . shhh*s mimicked the wind's voice while tucked in Horace's hollow. My soul ached, longing for my birth home.

But Fear told me, *"Never. Never. Never will you morph your way back into Horace's hollow. Never."*

Horace-Speak

As was expected, I named her Scarlet Oak when she was born. And then my heartbeat fluttered with hers, only for Smis to tempt her to fly from me. I severed her wings. My impulse to protect only disabled. And then I wished to label—rename her Twig Oak. She was a tiny twig of a sprite to begin with . . . and then . . . no wings. Twig Oak—a much more suitable name, because without me she would snap. Break in two. And so, I kept her close . . . sometimes too much in my hollow. I kept her very close. That only took her musings far from me. And now, in body, she's even farther from me.

But there are moments when the boy-spirit looks into his soul in my hollow and smiles. That's when I feel Scarlet very close in a different way. Not with proximity or soul-speak or dominion, but simple love. And then I read love from our distance, and I know my sprite left me to save another. The boy-spirit connects me to her, and in these fluid, sparkling moments, I realize Scarlet was never an ordinary sprite but an extraordinary sprite.

She wasn't made to be me, but for me . . . to cherish, to grow, to give, to let go, to wait until she returns with her name, her secrets, her story.

Chapter 33

Helen and I kept my Warren Cummings secret from John, and in doing so, I promised not to see Warren. Helen ensured my compliance by finding Warren roadside one night, ordering him to stay away while also spewing wicked lies (I presumed) to keep him far. She didn't offer room for me to tell untruths, either. In fact, each night she rested in bed with me, remaining there until well past midnight. When she left, I always woke and stared through the window, reliving every moment with Warren. Pin Oak kept me company in my yearning, offering silent soul-speak.

Then August galloped to us with a powerful, honest sun and scorching heat, while truth swam in my hollow. For three mornings straight, I rose, barely ate, vomited. I stayed in bed, unable to perform the things I was accustomed to doing, and, of course, I could hardly keep this from Helen. Not when she fastened her body at my side most moments, eyes diving into mine, rummaging through my private romantic memories. Satisfied that she'd found her answer, she traveled to the drugstore, returning with a bag and ordering me to the bathroom, where she placed a white stick beneath my urine. We waited together for it to turn pink.

"As I thought," Helen whispered. "You gave too much to Warren . . . too much. You're pregnant."

I cried, but Helen didn't. She understood many things, and I did, too, noticing the half-hearted smile she tried to conceal at the same time she clucked her tongue and disparaged Warren Cummings. Swiftly, she placed me in bed. Fussed over me, dampening my forehead with a warm washcloth. She then brought me a hard-boiled egg and saltines on dainty china, as well as ginger ale in one of her fancy teacups.

"We mustn't tell John . . . not yet," she said. "Don't know what he'll do when he finds out. It won't be a pretty picture."

Again, I sobbed, and so Helen rubbed my head and read poetry. I fell asleep to the start of Walt Whitman's poem "There Was a Child Went Forth."

> There was a child went forth every day,
> And the first object he look'd upon, that
>   object he became,
> And that object became part of him for the
>   day, or a certain part of the day,
> Or for many years or stretching cycles of
>   years.
>
> The early lilacs became part of this child,
> And grass, and white and red morning-glo-
>   ries, and white and red clover, and the
>   song of the phoebe-bird,
> And the Third-month lambs and the sow's
>   pink-faint litter, and the mare's foal and

the cow's calf,
And the noisy brood of the barn-yard, or by
the mire of the pond-side,
And the fish suspending themselves so
curiously below there, and the beautiful
curious liquid,
And the water-plants with their graceful flat
heads, all became part of him.

The field-sprouts of Fourth-month and
Fifth-month became part of him,
Winter-grain sprouts and those of the
light-yellow corn, and the esculent roots of
the garden,
And the apple-trees cover'd with blossoms
and the fruit afterward, and wood-berries,
and the commonest weeds by the road . . .

When I awoke, John stood near my bed. I could barely face his smile (which I knew wasn't his truth). He brushed a strand of sparrow hair from my face.

"Helen'll take good care of ya," he said. "You'll be jus' fine, ya hear? Jus' gotta bug . . . is all. A bug."

I only wished my pinky held a ladybug right now—and *that* was truth—not this, not the "child that went forth," one that would become a part of me only to grow apart from me. Mostly, I worried over if he or she would have wings and how in the human realm that handicap wouldn't do. Of course, I also remembered my isolation in the forest as a wingless tree sprite. I wept.

"No need for them tears, Willow," John said. "Be better before ya know it."

Little did he know there was more need than ever. A need to cry, hide, even be with Smis. Yes, in the dark of that night I spoke, begging Smis to take me and my child to his realm of nothingness. *"My baby can't survive here. Not here. Impossible."* I said these words many times.

Smis, the great shadow-contortionist, kindly answered my call. He appeared through John's shadow and held my trembling hand as John said, "It's okay. It's okay." Smis then rustle-hummed and soothed me, communicating that Horace loved me (a strange musing for Smis!). Then he inspired with these words. Yes, *inspired!*

"When you reach for what feels impossible, you grow into a beautiful version of what is possible."

That's when John rose and walked past the dresser. Curiously, he patted Finn's baseball mitt before he left. Smis then lingered in that area, pointing to the mitt before he disappeared. I had never touched the mitt out of respect for John and Finn. But now I moved to the dresser and placed it on my hand. I felt something foreign, and upon wriggling it out, found a tiny folded note. Immediately, I noticed John's writing (a treasure itself). But then the words, oh the beautiful words!

Sunflower Dreams

You and me, son,
We're that someplace in between
Running through them sunflowers
Knowin' every step's a dream.

Daddy

I read John's words many times. Poetry! Then, it dawned on me. My vision of Finn running through the sunflowers that I handed Helen in my palms on the day of his funeral—it was real. John and Finn loved large in that sunflower field. I cried for this truth, so much so that when daylight found me, I thanked Smis by opening my eyes.

Then I experienced life—all of it—the seed in my hollow, Finn's bird figurines, Sylvan, Pin Oak, the farmland beyond. In this euphoric state, I realized that Smis, the great shadow-contortionist, and I, we also inhabited that "someplace in between." I loved him for it. Thanked him, too. After all, in my greatest time of need, Smis showed me—no, *us*—that we mattered.

Chapter 34

Summertime stretched well into September. To conceal our growing secret, Helen bought me dresses that sailed with the wind and offered many creative excuses to John. "Willow has her monthly, John. Loose, flowing clothes help a girl feel better." Or, "Willow couldn't sleep last night . . . let her sleep this morning she'll eat breakfast later." Or, "Summertime's ending, that's why her tan's blown clear from her and her face looks paler." When John asked my reasons for not working the farm with him, Helen told him, "Willow wants to learn to write poetry." This wasn't a complete lie, but still, it wasn't complete truth, either.

At times, John listened to Helen with a cocked head and curious eye. But he didn't push or argue. He simply went on his way, communicating solo with the soil and God. I missed my alone time with him in *God's country* (he sometimes called it). I missed so many things, most of all Warren. But I knew Warren couldn't live around the secret we created. It was too fragile—and so was John. I especially feared John's reaction to the pregnancy when I thought about the gun in his workshed.

Then came the night when Helen grew ill (no doubt wore down from her hawk-like vigil over me). The flu slapped her to sleep early, and she didn't wake to check in on me later that night. I slipped onto the front porch in my nightgown and bare feet to sit beneath the dangling lightbulb and rustle-hum my heartache to Nature, all the while, breathing in her smallest version of freedom. I closed my eyes. Inhaled the last vestiges of summer's perfumed allure. Even recaptured the first time I studied Warren Cummings descending the spiraling driveway to me. Here I stood—in this very blue-lit spot—near an ax, a teapot, and teacups, longing in wild foreign parts of me. Tantalized, I moved deeper into memories of Warren. But my womb cramped, disrupting the magic of firsts and seconds and all moments that followed.

So I opened my eyes. Stood to return inside. That's when I spied Warren Cummings in the distance. He owned the moonlight's vulnerability even as he stood rugged behind the cool metal gate. I wanted to fly and fall into his arms. But Helen's sensibility took over as I approached him. I didn't unlatch the gate. Only stood behind it to meet his broken gaze.

"Couldn't stay away," he said. "I come here each night . . . real late. Look up to your window . . . hopin' to see you."

"You mustn't," I said.

"I know," Warren said. "Ms. Hawes, she did her best to keep me away. Said she'd tell my mom, and then my mom would tell the police about you . . . how you assaulted her. I couldn't let that happen, Willow. But, still, I can't stay away from you, either."

As Warren spoke, I wished more suffering on Helen (just a little bit more), even as I knew she aimed to protect her family.

"I miss you," Warren said. "Can't eat. Can't sleep."

There was so much to say—but our seed tugged my words with a rope—hanging every hopeful thought.

"Can't speak to say anything to me?" Warren said.

Tears brimmed his long dark eyelashes. He lowered his head and wiped them dry with his fingertips.

"If John knows about . . ."

"Knows what? That I love you? What's so wrong with that?"

"John, the gun . . ."

"You gotta chill. He's not gonna kill me. He'll be mad as hell for a while, but he won't kill me."

"I'm leaving," I said. "Going home."

"So, where's home, exactly? Man, for once, talk to me, more than a few words at a time. You never speak of your real folks, where you came from, none of it."

"Go. Go now. Forget."

"Forget? I couldn't forget you if I tried. You're everything that keeps me from giving up in this godforsaken place called life."

"I can't be," I said, my heart writing its obituary as I spoke. "Sorry, Warren. I can't."

Warren lowered his shoulders and stared at the ground for a long while. He then took a breath, and he stared at me with so much will, unutterable belief.

"Always thought my grandma was a bit off her rocker when she'd say these words. But they were her favorite. She liked to sling them around to young people when they weren't mindin' her. But grandpa told me once that they were his words. He spoke them to her when she had the want to run off and not marry him when they were so young."

I met Warren's gaze with curiosity.

"He told her . . . 'Meet me in the middle of your story when the soul is worn but wise.'"

Hope and beauty laced into these words.

"Willow, you know, I'd wait until the end of your story if need be just to have the chance to love you."

Warren reached to hold my hand. I allowed him to do so at the same time I willed our love story to end, shatter right then, right there. Perhaps in another lifetime we could meet up in the night's skyline as beautiful stars. Shine together as worn, wise souls.

I held this hopeful visual for one too many heartbeats. Then I turned from Warren. Ran as fast as the wind could breathe me back to the bluebell house. I then shut and leaned against the door. Cried in silence—a slow-moving teardrop for every piece of our story that braided us into a tragic love poem. I stayed in this spot for hours, even when my seed ached. Indeed, I didn't leave until Helen's coughing upstairs demanded I return to Finn's room.

There, I peered through the window—Warren's silhouette no more—all of me emptied except for my seed and the forest's strict principle Horace delivered to me at birth: *"Keep secrets close in the sunlight and the shadow."* But now I knew differently. Secrets kept close only torture the heart in both sunlight and shadow.

I would speak this to Horace one day. Set his trunk straight.

Chapter 35

On September 20, 1978, summertime bellowed that it had lied too long. Truth charged across the farmland as a wayward storm, its lightning a wicked smile as thunder roared and rain pummeled the windowpane. In the forest realm, I always delighted in Nature's sore temperament, and I often sat on Horace's branch to face it head-on. Now, I longed to return, and it was in this moment that I realized my truth. *In the backwoods of Nature's soul I left my wild true heart.*

Saddened, I opened the window, allowing the rain to drench me. That's when Pin Oak appeared wet—tinier than ever. She wobbled on the branch closest to the window. Tapped her feet and tilted her head back-and-forth. I placed my palm outside, hoping she'd come to me. In time, she did. Even allowed me to pull her through the window's aperture and into Finn's room.

Never had we both inhabited Finn's room together. I worried she'd morph into largeness, even as I knew from memory-gazing that she forever remained small with Finn. Of course, this was unusual; sprites assumed human form when detached from their birth trees—a failsafe adaptation meant to increase our safety. But still, here Pin Oak was, petite. Curious, I placed her on the dresser and watched as she quieted her body enough to sit beside the cardinal figurine and stroke it while pulling her twig legs into her chest. She cried tears so little, so large.

Her love for Finn—it was greater than mine. Not imagined in a musing, nor impulsive with a craving to own his soul. Her love simply existed without a want for more. And when beneath soft lamplight she rustle-hummed in the bird figurine's shadow, I grasped the reality of things. Pin Oak loved Finn in truth, never lies.

I bent to her level and stroked her twig hair. I rustle-hummed my apologies for her loss. She held my pinky finger in her small hand. A moment. A sacred, honest moment to keep.

BOOM! The storm raged. Lightning blinded. Pin Oak jumped. She thunder-danced, tapping her feet. Her steps pounded wilder, and her eyes widened, inviting me into her dark pain. I didn't blink or turn away. I stayed with it. And suddenly, her eyes took me where I needed to go . . . deep into her secret, Finn's secret, John's secret, Helen's secret, *the* secret.

While traveling into her haunted bluebell story, my senses collided. And this is how I felt . . . where it took me . . .

First, summer's honeysuckle tears, and wounded thunder, and lightning with electric sound fizzing on my tongue. A crack nearly hit Sylvan as Pin Oak perched on a branch close to the window. I could see John, in Finn's room, wearing a loose blue tie. He paced the room, back-and-forth, back-and-forth, back-and-forth. He held a whiskey bottle in one hand and his father's gun in the other.

John drank the evil brown liquid, and the more he did so, the wobblier he became. Cries of rage and heart-hurt hurled from his storm-turned-inside-out. He rocked and screamed, rocked and screamed, rocked and screamed.

Then he stopped. Knelt on Finn's floor. Placed the gun to his head. Dropped it. Took more swigs. Collapsed. Cried. Yelled . . . at his father, God, the church folk. Enormous unstoppable pain, larger than the sky and its fury.

When it passed, he stood upright—Horace's posture at its best. That's when the peaceable beast took him—the most dangerous beast—the one waiting to feed.

Perspective then shifted to Nature's distance. Lights. John's truck, rumbling, racing, then a shrieking STOP. Helen darted from it and looked to the window. She then glanced to the passenger seat at Finn.

"Stay," she said. "Finn, STAY."

She rushed to the house. But now, John had already climbed onto the tree—his bottle . . . gone, his gun . . . gone. His body moved closer, closer, closer to Pin Oak. He looked into the eyes of a creature he couldn't possibly believe. He stared—a bemused inquiry. The moment passed.

He held a rope, and he fastened it tight around the branch. He prayed.

"God forgive me for doin' as my daddy done. Watch over Finn. Watch over Helen. Forgive."

He placed the rope around his neck. He fell, dangled, a stormy-shell-of-a-man. Lightning struck, and Helen screamed through Finn's window.

"NO! NO! NO!"

The scream echoed—a nightmare's melody. Desperate tiny twig fingers struggled with the rope, working to undo its hold.

"NO! NO! NO!"

The NO came from Finn. I knew this NO well. The voice I'd heard before he died. Perspective shifted to Finn beneath the tree, looking up, yelling . . .

"NO! NO! NO!"

Pin Oak's fingers fiddled quicker, harder . . . until the rope loosened and John fell to the ground. Finn blanketed his father's body—crying, holding, loving. Helen raced to them both and pulled Finn from John. Stroked her husband's head.

"I've called for help," she said. "Hold on, John. We're here. Hold on. Hold on. Hold on."

Helen and Finn stayed with John as rain softened, thunder lost its voice, lightning shied away, and artificial red lights flashed. Men rushed and examined John's body before carrying him off. Helen and Finn hurried along with them into the red flashing vehicle. It sped away.

On Finn's dresser, exhausted, Pin Oak buried her head. Her eyes left mine to travel once more (I imagined) into the largeness of her secret. I lifted my pinky and I stroked her wings, which fluttered and sobbed with her. My wing scar burned. But I didn't weep. I gave to her—didn't take anything more.

Outside, the storm clouds lost their gray and the sky radiated in dark blues. The rain whispered on the windowpane. I took Pin Oak in my hand once more, walked with reverence, and then pushed my palm through the window. Before I delivered her to Sylvan, she held my pointer finger and squeezed it—a tiny *thank you.* I let go, and she was gone.

In my aloneness, I shivered in heart-hurt, and it was then that Helen moved silently behind me. She placed her arms around me. Held me tight. She then turned my body around to draw me into her truth.

"Finn's fairy," Helen said. "You see now . . . she's real. One terrible night . . ."

Helen stopped herself, and I nodded as a quiet moment passed, the two of us peering through the window.

"Summertime can't lie," Helen whispered. "But this is truth. Finn's fairy rescued this family at a time when we could be saved."

Smis-Speak

One stormy night, I ran beside the Finn (who once lived in body-spirit-soul) to the pin oak tree. I held his hand in quickened sorrow. When he screamed "NO," I did the same.

When his daddy dropped, and Finn dropped with him, I watched their Love. Law said, . . . *"John should come with me."* The heart said, . . . *"Let him stay."* Some believe I don't own a heart. But Smis and heart (I know) are one and the same.

I should have taken John on that night. I should have walked him far away. Finn told me "NO," and I listened.

Death told me *not* to offer a second chance. But I did.

Because the truth is that Love's voice spoke louder, telling me to give a second, and a third, and fourth chance. Infinite.

Of course, I said *that* wasn't possible. Because a Grim Reaper, he only gets one free pass to save someone in his sorry lifetime of shadows. A little known fact.

But even now, as I sit from a distance in the forest and watch Finn's spirit with his bird and tree, I know. Love has the power to give infinite chances.

Smis only holds the pitiable power to say *"No."*

Chapter 36

Helen didn't speak anymore of Finn's fairy, that night, and I didn't tell Helen what Pin Oak revealed to me. Instead, she helped me change my wet nightgown, placing the mother-quilt over me and rubbing my stomach before kissing my forehead. When she left, I struggled to tuck away the secret. But my body, fidgeting, couldn't. In time, I heard a tiny knock at the window. I sat up, the sky now cloudless, the moonlight bright. Pin Oak smiled in its clarity.

I left my bed and opened the window once more. Pin Oak rested on her branch, and I could tell she didn't wish to come back inside. Instead, she pointed her finger and motioned for my eyes to come back into hers. There was more to show, she promised. I wasn't sure I wanted to know anything more, but I submitted. I entered her memories.

Pin Oak sat on Finn's dresser amidst the bird figurines. Finn was there with her, sullen, in the thicket of heart-hurt. Pin Oak stilled when Finn stilled. She rocked when Finn rocked. And when Finn horror-hummed, she peace-hummed. Time then moved in hyper-speed, and the sun rose and set, rose and set, rose and set. Still, Pin Oak stayed with Finn in the heart-hurt and the stillness, in the rocking and the horror-humming, and the sun-rising-and-setting-of-it-all after his father's attempted suicide.

Of course, Helen entered the room here and there, holding Finn, rocking Finn, crying with Finn. And on the third day, as first daylight pursed its sunrays through the curtains, she beckoned Finn to come. They left the bluebell house together as two and returned in the Impala with John as three—a family. When John stepped from the car, his neck and right arm were bandaged, and his right cheek shimmered in purplish-black. Finn, however, beamed (didn't bruise). He held his daddy's hand. Smiled larger than magic.

Pin Oak offered due respect as she sat quietly on Sylvan, offering private time to the family before she scuttled from her branch to the windowsill, crawling into Finn's room. She jumped to the floor, scampered and climbed the quilt to Finn's bed. It was empty. Then, she leapt to the floor—took in the entirety of Finn's room from the tiniest of perspectives—before moving to the bottom of the dresser, to the mural, to the doorway. She fit beneath its crack and tiptoed to John and Helen's bedroom. The door stood ajar.

Pin Oak now peered into the room's beautiful fractured light. John rested on the bed with Helen close to him while Finn slept at peace in between. He filled the spaces of his parents' breath and cuddled into their warm, safe Love. All the while, John and Helen gazed at their child with a sunrise smile. Relief.

Pin Oak attempted to withdraw, but I begged her with my eyes to let me stay here, longer, warmer, safer . . . Love. She allowed me to fixate on the image until her eyelids began to droop from weariness. Pin Oak then cleared her mind, and all rustle-hums ceased. She nodded to me. But I imagined her saying in human-speak, *"One pure moment holds the power to create infinite Love. And, Willow, no matter John's hurt, and hanging, and heartache . . . this was one of those moments."*

Horace-Speak

The boy-spirit wanders tonight.
He moves from me to Sugar Maple and her old
    tree, Stein.
Back-and-forth.
Back-and-forth.
Back-and-forth.
Be with me. The night is lonely, I say.
He stops pacing, cramming and squishing
    himself into my hollow, miniaturizing as
    compact as Scarlet used to do.
With tiny spirit-hands, he touches his soul
    nestled cozy in me and weeps in peace.
I finally realize this truth. The boy is no longer a
    stranger to me, or even a spirit.
No, Finn is warm safe Love.

Chapter 37

Autumn blustered into being, promising to bleed color into leaves that would eventually fall. Each morning, I avoided John, not only to hide my pregnancy but to also conceal acknowledgement of his secret. My love for John didn't lessen. Still, I feared the stormy sliver of him. And I didn't want to be the fairy-human that urged him to find his daddy's gun or a rope or another human-hurt thing.

I thought about John and this God I'd come to know through the Haweses. I couldn't imagine that God intended John's pain to crack in this way. He sounded too grand and complex—too beyond this realm and every other to do it. No, humans were to blame. In fact, human sin shattered his sorrow like the trapped entrails of an egg. And once his shell was gone, that pain had nowhere to go but ooze, drip, even hang. And Finn watched. Recorded it. Waited for the *doin' as my daddy done.*

Now Finn's death haunted me more than ever while waking or sleeping, existing in my musings, daydreams, and nightmares. I wondered over Finn's *why*. *Why* did Finn do as his daddy done, and his daddy before? What happened before he entered my forest realm? In a loop, I replayed the night he hung. Finn did it *like his daddy done* . . . every step and movement, in a sense. But Pin Oak showed me more. She revealed the memory of warm, safe Love, that of Finn sleeping peacefully between his parents.

Since I couldn't ask Helen or John, I posed questions to myself. Was Finn's hanging and *No* a hopeful return to his daddy and what happened after? The one pure moment that created infinite Love in his parents' bed? And was his spirit rocking a hopeful return to the warm, safe Love of his mom's rocking chair? Was Finn's every action in my forest realm a misread desire for this warm, safe, pure Love?

My mind didn't conceive of this, my heart did. It believed, and I hoped—no, prayed—to this God (I'd heard of) that this was the proof Smis needed to send Finn to the Light. I also prayed that Horace, in his hollow, had grown into giving Finn's spirit warm, safe Love, and his soul the same.

Sometimes I cried. Pin Oak showed up when I did and rapped at the window. She'd kept me good company, lately— never hiding from me. In fact, she shared Sylvan, allowing me to sit on his branch alongside her whenever I wanted. But now she refused my invitations to Finn's room.

However, when her first leaf colored, she plucked and offered it to me through the window—a token of friend- ship between her realm and mine. I understood. The blue- bell house wasn't her home. She belonged with her oak and would live and die beside it as good sprites were meant to do.

I fit into the bluebell home for now (perhaps forever), and as this healed and haunted me even more so, I attempted to shake my worries through my *studies* (Helen called it). Together, each afternoon, we worked on reading and writing. Helen told me things like, "You are very smart. Your comprehension is improving. Your writing is legible and interesting. Your phrasings are intriguing. Like poetry . . . gorgeous." I wondered if my child had a hand in it, a human seed learning how to form and teaching me the same.

I showed Helen just enough to make her smile, but certainly not all of me. Like how effortlessly I now understood language, how swiftly I could read, and how easily I could write my letters. I didn't reveal how imaginatively my mind could wander. You see, I didn't want to give away all of my magic. Some of it still belonged to me, Horace's sprite.

One night, I wrote this poem in secret:

Sunflower Man

John Hawes, Sunflower Man.
He rises.
Offers me shade.
Sometimes, even room to grow.
Smis shadows my sun-lips,
Cracking them.
Truth will be told.

The words—maybe mine—maybe not. After all, at first, they seemed to flow from the great beyond, some other realm I hadn't yet met. But then I felt Smis's shadow midway through, and considered that he may have used my own fingertips to seal the poem's dark end. Fear took hold—so much so that I ripped, balled, and dropped the paper into the trash can. Still, a beat later, I picked it all back up. Placed the poem's pieces together underneath my mattress.

It was then that Smis appeared in the corner of the room. He stayed only long enough to prove me wrong—to show me that he didn't wish a cruel ending. In fact, he spoke his own poetry before vanishing.

"There are days when even Hope bows her weary sunlit head. It's okay, a return is inevitable."

Quickly, I gathered and wrote his message on paper, resting it neatly beside my fractured poem. Something about being close to Smis through poetry soothed me, and I managed to fall asleep to only a few nightmares.

The next afternoon, I sat on the porch and watched John in his fields. First, he used the plow. Next, he fetched a scythe and lashed the crops. His strength bulged through wet clothes, and his fury (imagined or otherwise) sliced me back to his hanging, and Finn's hanging, and even Helen's axing of Finn's pine tree. I could hear blood-red screams. Taste soil-drink. Smell fire. Feel a rope cinch my stomach. See the mean-spirited Smis.

To counterattack all of it, I rushed to my room and lifted the cardinal figurine, flying the bird along the sky-mural while imagining my child's small hands around its wooden feathers. Soon, Helen opened the door. She smiled at my play.

"You okay?" she asked. "Ready to come to the book room?"

"I'm tired," I said.

"You don't look well," Helen said. "You must take care of yourself . . . for the baby. Rest."

I waited for Helen to walk downstairs and enter the book room before tiptoeing down the stairway. I needed space to breathe. Craved closeness to John (even in the far), and so I left the bluebell home and walked to the sunflower field. Of course, Finn rested here, and I couldn't bear to ever look, to imagine his cold body buried deep beneath the earth. Hauntings. Human hauntings.

Still, I sat nearby, hoping the warm, safe breeze would calm me. I didn't look down once, but rather up to the sunflowers, admiring the humility in their hugeness. They swayed, soul-spoke in the wind's lullaby while reaching for checkered sunlight, and I communed with them—experiencing no-time. In this space, my thoughts emptied. Body stilled. Tiny seed slept. All at one with Nature's extraordinary calmness. I stayed here with it until John's voice rippled into the quietness.

"Never seen ya near the sunflowers, Willow," he said.

I turned to meet his eyes. Sunflower Man. Here in this moment, as I smiled back, I lived my poem, and worried that Smis might shadow my sun-lips and crack my truth. But instead, John handed me a shiny red apple.

"View's awful pretty right 'bout here," John said.

I fiddled with my dress, especially when John looked down and I did the same.

"I'm sorry," I said.

I was able to read the ovular ivory tombstones lodged into the ground:

Finn Hawes, Beloved Son, 1964–1978.

Hope Hawes, Beloved Daughter, 1964–1964. A heart-beat of a life, Love eternal.

At the bottom of both stones, beautiful swirled etching read:

Life's Double Blessings.

John looked up—a silent prayer—and we moved a respectful distance from the tombstones to sit.

"Autumn . . . used to be my favorite time of the year. Colors . . . so pretty. Made my hard work on the farm somethin' like magic . . . to look up and see them."

John was contemplating how the season lost its magic the moment Finn hung.

"You been awful quiet, lately. Been thinkin' on it . . . on tiny things, too . . . and how ya like that mouse I seen last spring, hangin' in between bluebell flowers. Silent . . . small . . . holdin' on to life's prettiness."

John missed me, thought of me, wished I was who-I-once-was. My heart hurt.

"Willow, still ain't sure who ya are, and how ya come to be . . . come to us. All's I know is Helen and me . . . we couldn't have made it, this past year. Couldn't have survived without ya. Best I can do is think Finn did send ya . . . in some way."

John took a bite of his apple and looked at me to taste it as well. I bit into the fruit's tang and juice.

"Haven't told a single soul this," John said. "But Helen . . . woman thinks Finn had hisself a tiny imaginary friend . . . Finn's fairy, she'd'a called it . . . and it supposed to live on a tree outside Finn's window . . . supposed to save me one night . . . from myself. But if that's the truth of things . . .

fairy shoulda save Finn that night . . . shoulda save Finn on that tree. Undid his rope."

John ruffled his hair with his fingertips.

"If magic ever was . . . or coulda been . . . then that magic shoulda save my boy. Helen like to tell me . . . fairy's still on Finn's tree. But I tell her . . . magic couldn't be."

I couldn't breathe. Somewhere in John's rolling farmland of quiet fury—and all the wounded pieces in between—he struggled to believe that a fairy should have saved his boy. *Me.* That *I* should have saved his boy.

I thought about the tree sprites and how they considered humans lesser-than—no magic. But John—this human—held magic. For he could walk through all of Nature's seasons with a secret and then speak it in a sunflower field, eating an apple, alongside the fairy-human-thing he wanted to believe and disbelieve, love and hate all the same.

Truth rattled and roared, threatening to crack me. My mind tormented. *If John knew I watched his son die, he would hate me. If he knew our voices screamed "NO" in unison. That I failed to undo the rope as Pin Oak had done before. That it was my fault. Me. Me. Me. How couldn't I have known to do the thing Pin Oak knew to do on impulse? And if my theories about Finn's hanging were accurate, then Finn had counted on ME to do that thing Pin Oak had done before!*

Shame flooded my wing scar. Grace, I hoped, sheltered my seed from it.

"Gonna lose sun if I keep to sittin' here talkin' 'bout fairies."

His voice garbled as my mind turned to Smis, who was set to take Finn's spirit to the Dark. *What to do? What to do? What to do to change all of this?*

Death's enormity rippled through me, and I swam in it, nearly drowned, even as my expression grew rock-still as the tombstones. John now stood and threw his half-eaten apple into the sunflower field.

"You sit here a while. Sunflower's good company. You need more sun, I keep tellin' Helen, 'Give the girl more sun, and she'll be back to her ol' self again.'"

He then patted my shoulder and proceeded to walk off. A moment later, he turned to me.

"My late momma . . . she used to tell me . . . 'Soul kneels ya down to pray. Spirit lifts ya up to love. Mind wanders. Heart speaks.'"

He placed his hand over his heart, tapped it, and then smiled. Even if I knew it wasn't his truest smile, I mirrored it back to him, placing my hand to my heart and tapping it. He then walked slowly from me, and I mourned John Hawes, Sunflower Man.

I imagined us meeting in a different way. I would still be Scarlet Oak, and he could be a strong, kind tree next to Horace. I mused on this imagining, divorcing myself from no-time and wrapping myself up in it all the same. I didn't move until John began to slash his crops once more with the scythe. *Thwack. Thwack. Thwack. Thwack.* My body couldn't bear to hear the pain.

Chapter 38

Autumn bloomed in the human realm alongside my pregnancy, and with it came a need to learn how to mother. Helen told me the proper term was *nesting*—a fierce urgency to clean and organize before the birth of a child. She likened it to a bird preparing a home for its babies. Being both a strange bird and fairy-human, nesting flew to me in the form of baking sweet confections.

On this morning, I wanted to make an apple pie after spotting the basket of homegrown McIntosh apples in the kitchen's corner. Helen helped me peel the apples, as well as slice and spice them. I kneaded my fingers in the dough, slapped and rolled it, and then arranged it into a pretty full-moon shape in a glass pie pan. Then I gently folded in the apples, covered them with dough and pressed the edges fancy as stars. Afterwards, I cut slits to sniff the cinnamon and nutmeg and sprinkled sugar on top. Finally, I placed it in the oven. Only felt a little sick. It seemed my will to see, smell, and know the pie before its completion proved stronger than my nausea.

As the pie cooked, Helen and I sat at the table, mostly in

quietness. That was, until she decided to *baby-speak* (these talks often left me in a state of panic). In these moments, Helen delivered a plethora of information. Today, it went something along these lines: "Willow, this is what you do when a baby cries . . . This is what you do when a baby sleeps . . . This is what you do when a baby drives you mad . . . This is what you do when a baby takes you."

"A baby takes you?" I asked, stopping her lecture.

"Yes," Helen said.

"Where?" I asked.

"Not where," Helen said, "but who."

I was confused, so Helen patted my hand.

"A baby takes you, Willow. Who-you-once-were—the baby takes it—and in its place, another-you forms. And you may fight it. You may moan. You may cry. You may think it's hardly fair. But only time will help you see that the another-you formed is, in truth, the you-that-was-meant-to-be, and then you won't even be able to stand alone in your skin, the love is so fierce . . . this new mother-skin, with all the same parts inside but none of the same parts. All soaked and blessed in the love that only comes from giving to a child that took from you."

I couldn't process all of her words, even as I stored every single one inside for future replay.

"You see, dear, it's like autumn outside. Autumn knows a mother's heart. It gives and then lets go. Motherhood is all about giving and letting go. And mostly, the child takes."

Still, I struggled to comprehend.

"Willow, the most important thing you need to know," Helen said, staring in my eyes, "is that the baby takes your heart. It's yours no more."

I tried to imagine owning Horace's heart, but Horace

would never submit to this notion. He'd name it one of my foolish musings.

"You took my heart," Helen said. "And so did Finn."

Now it was my turn to pat Helen's hand, as shame returned.

"I'm only Willow," I said.

"Yes," Helen said. "My Willow. My Hope."

John struggled to make sense of a fairy that spared him but failed to rescue his son. And Helen baked a sweet fantasy that Finn sent Hope back to her. It killed me, how much they gave to me, and how much I took. Thankfully, the timer dinged its desperate ding, and I rushed to the oven.

Heat pressed against my mother-skin as my seed rustle-hummed in my womb with a want to take my heart. I imagined my child with half-baked limbs reaching well past my womb, holding my heart in unformed fingers, reshaping and replacing it to the proper spot. Then I lifted the pie with red quilted potholders and placed it on the stovetop.

"Let it cool," Helen said. "I'm off to put the laundry on the line."

Helen left me in the kitchen to delight in the pie's scent, as well as taste the pleasure of a somewhat-aloneness that would soon be taken from me, too. In doing so, I wandered to the window and watched her pin my dresses on the line— the fabric moving like ghosts in the wind. That's when I grew into no-time. My heart stilled and beat, stilled and beat, stilled and beat. Then I snapped out of it, moved to the oven to slice a hearty piece of pie, and raced upstairs to Finn's room. I sat in the blue rocking chair and savored it.

Soon I heard a tiny knock on the window. There was Pin Oak, smiling. I returned the gesture, but in the way I believed John did so—not my truest smile. Then I brought my dainty plate to the window, eventually climbing through and sitting on Sylvan's branch with her. I could hear Helen's voice in my head, "Willow, you can't ever climb on that tree, now. You could fall . . . lose the baby! It isn't a safe place to be anymore."

Pin Oak, however, seemed safer to me than anything else in this moment. In fact, she existed in her realm as my warm, safe Love. I thought of how she offered me her first colored leaf, and so I placed the tiniest bite of pie on my fingertip and gave to her. She took it in her small palm and ate it with a shiny twig-lit smile. We stayed here for a long stretch—no rustle-hums, no human-speak. True silence. Truer friends.

Sylvan, however, loathed the silence and friendship. Angered, his branch shook and spoke. Worried, Pin Oak looked to me. She motioned to scurry along back to the human realm. As I tried to do so, the plate dropped. Broke. I moved with more caution to the window, only to find Helen's reproach.

"Willow," she said. Curt.

She took my hand and maneuvered me through the open window to the safety of Finn's room. I turned to look for Pin Oak, but she was gone. Instead, Helen held my face, positioning it to her and away from the tree.

"Finn's fairy may be good, true . . . but that tree is evil. It doesn't want you on it. Leave the fairy be. Your *baby* should be your only concern now . . . not Finn's fairy."

I closed my eyes to Helen's anger and disappointment. Everything was too much, too soon, too . . . sad.

"Please go," I said. "I want to be alone."

"You *aren't* alone anymore," Helen said.

"The baby *won't* take me," I said, my eyes fiery (I could actually feel the fire in them).

"Already has," Helen said. "Already has."

Helen slammed down the window. Locked it.

"No more fairy. No more tree."

She then banged the door as she left, as if that sound would cement things—rattle me to march to motherhood's rules.

I was relieved when John came to me later that evening. He stood and stared at Sylvan for a good while. Surely he didn't tell me *"No more fairy. No more tree."*

"Pie was good," he finally said. "Been cookin' lot for us . . . wanna give ya somethin' . . . my secret somethin' been workin' on when I can. Made it with my own two hands."

John withdrew a tiny wooden figurine that looked like me except for one thing—there were wings, colored with the Fourth of July's sunset.

"Know Helen . . . she ain't want no speak of angels that flew off on us . . . but figure she ain't mind too much if I give ya a fairy . . . one that looks like ya. Fairy supposed to save me, one night. You save me each day, Willow . . . from myself. So I gotta believe in that . . . if not the fairy itself."

John placed his delicate artwork in my palms, and I studied it in silence while bottling all tears. But my soul still spoke, and John listened. He placed his large hand on my cheek, and he smiled the sort of smile that didn't lie.

"Go on . . . you can put it with Finn's birds . . . see ya playin' with them sometimes. Always make me smile."

I placed the fairy figurine next to the cardinal figurine. The moment I did so, Helen popped into the room. John motioned with proud eyes to his wife to look and see. She walked to the dresser and picked up the figurine. I reached to grab it, not wanting Helen to take my fairy from me. That's when it fell and the right wing broke. Swiftly, I scooped her body while Helen lifted the wing.

"No problem here . . ." John said, taking both pieces and studying them. "I'm awful good at fixin' things right up. Fairy'll be right as rain . . . good as first born."

Helen and I gazed into our larger secret from John.

"Thank you," I said to John. "I love the fairy."

"Knew ya would," John said. "Knew ya would."

"Get some rest now, Willow," Helen said. "Your fairy's in very good hands. She'll be okay."

Helen smiled, warm and sweet as our apple pie, and in her smile I spotted relief. If I played with *this* wooden fairy, I wouldn't play with *that* fairy on the evil tree that could harm my baby. She hugged me and then held John's hand as together they took the fairy's pieces. I had no choice but to let go. Still, I wasn't fully alone. Not when my seed willed itself a voice. Soul-spoke to my conscience, *Tirra-lirra*ing my secrets.

Sylvan-Speak

Now, the fairy-human sings "Tirra lirra" to my sprite. She knows and shares human-things with Pin Oak. She even grows a human seed inside her. I've tried to like her. But can't. Won't. Not like I did Finn.

Yes, once upon a tree, I liked Finn Hawes. I listened to his rustle-hums—more sprite than human. I gazed into his Nature eyes (some magic in them). I smiled when he smiled. Permitted him on my branches. Even allowed Pin Oak to leave me to play in his room.

But on that night, when Finn's daddy hung, I told Pin Oak, *"NO. NO, Pin Oak. Not our place to intervene."*

Pin Oak didn't listen. She chose Finn. And there stood Smis . . . always ready to take.

The fairy-human may lead Pin Oak straight to shadowy, soul-sucking Smis, and if Pin Oak defies him once more—it could be our last breath. Sylvan . . . Pin Oak. Gone.

Chapter 39

Morning chilled the sky in deep blues, and Sylvan faced me barer than days before, with only sparse patches of blood-red leaves. It was the anniversary of Finn's death. True, the calendar's numbers didn't fully match up. But on Thanksgiving last year, sure enough, Finn hung. I asked Helen and John one week ago about the holiday. Helen simply said . . . "Death." John then told Helen, "Ain't no good, teachin' her that. Thanksgiving Day's supposed to be good . . . a givin' day, Willow . . . a day of thanks and givin'." But Helen lowered her head, and said, "Finn died on Thanksgiving. Nothing good, giving or thankful about that."

I stared deeper into Sylvan, and my body quivered. I didn't want to leave my room. Didn't wish to see John, or Helen, or think of the boy-spirit I once knew (only briefly). But Smis arrived, stood in my shadow, and whispered . . .

"It's time."

"I have my proof, and even if I didn't . . . you're good, Smis," I said. *"You've been good to me. You've given to me. You would never take Finn to the Dark. You won't do it."*

"Return to the forest," Smis said. *"We've business to tend to."*

His shadow dissipated. Left me to worry. I then reflected on my pact with Smis. One cycle of seasons to bring proof Finn's death was not an intentional ending. But was this my only mission? Wasn't there so much more? Didn't I long to heal traumatized parents and a boy's broken spirit? But had Finn's spirit healed? Had John? Had Helen? Had I? Was it possible (even with magic) to cure grief—to morph it as one must into healing? I doubted so. I heard Father Will say that time heals. But does it? Or does time only turn the heartache into something else? Someone else? Does grief ever go away?

No. I failed. Scarlet Oak—the-sprite I once knew—she was foolish in her musings and spunk and desire to reach for the impossible. Scarlet Oak, a wingless tree sprite, believed she held the power to challenge Smis, to abolish despair, to overturn Nature's law. But now, I was Willow Brook, the fairy-pregnant-human who knew, understood, this was foolish. I befriended Smis (didn't challenge). I added to grief (didn't abolish). I fell in love with Nature's law (didn't overturn).

For fifty years (human time), I walked autumn, winter, spring, and summer in an unbreakable loop. But never had I traveled the seasons in this way or changed so much. I was a fairy-human who read books, wrote poetry, used human-speak. Scarlet Oak, Horace's sprite, she died—ended. Willow Brook lived on.

I knew, however, that Willow Brook must return to Horace, to Finn's spirit, to my former community, and to Smis (most of all). There, first I would greet Finn's spirit with apologies, goodwill, regret, and sorrow, telling him in soul-speak, *"I tried my best in so many ways."* Afterwards, I would then beg Horace to understand and love me no matter.

Burdened, I searched for Pin Oak to soothe my heart. But I couldn't find her, just as I couldn't find Scarlet Oak. I gravitated to the dresser and held my fairy figurine, gliding my finger along the glued ridge of her wing's brokenness. I thought of every sprite I knew, especially Prickly Elder, Sugar Maple, and Sycamore. Such loyal sprites, good sprites. What would Prickly Elder rustle-hum to me? What kind of cruel visuals would he ax in my head? I couldn't feel much empathy for him. Still.

It was while fixating on Prickly Elder that I realized I hadn't heard John and Helen's bedroom door creak open. Even if I hadn't calmed the rolling rainstorm of their anguish, I could still give on Thanksgiving. Cook them a meal and nourish the tiniest teardrops of their pain.

I tiptoed downstairs and set to work. I prepared the pancake recipe Helen told me Finn loved, sprinkling flax and chia seeds into the batter, along with cinnamon sliced apples. Yes, of course. If Helen ate what used to "light Finn up like a rainbow . . ." perhaps one bite, maybe two, would refresh her. As I arranged pancakes into neat stacks on china with a dollop of butter and swirls of maple syrup, I told myself that surely this breakfast would make them smile. Confident, I placed the meal with fresh orange juice on a tray.

Once upstairs, I nudged open the door to find Helen and John seated on the bed's edge with their heads bowed in silence. They didn't notice me. But I studied them—two oak trees that wanted nothing more than to offer each other shade, company, solace . . . but couldn't, wouldn't. Instead, they towered and drooped apart. I so longed for them to bend to each other.

"Come," I said. "Eat."

Both looked at me with heavy eyes. I didn't move to them—so close, so far. I knew not to do so by their joint expression. And so I traveled back downstairs, resting alone on Finn's chair until the pancakes hardened beneath clumped butter and runaway syrup. Hours passed before Helen and John appeared to sit at the kitchen table. Neither one lifted a fork. They looked once at each other, but not to me.

I stayed with the awkwardness, recalling sunlit meals on the porch—the kindness, togetherness, resilience, (even laughter, at times). But, like Finn's invisibility in their sphere, these memories, too, felt impossible. Dead. I didn't speak. Only sat and mirrored grief back to Helen and John.

Eventually, John wandered to the fields and Helen went upstairs. I soaped the plates and glasses with warm water, dried them, and replaced them in perfect order on the shelves. I swept the floor. Mopped it. Cleaned the windows to a pristine sparkle. All the while, I rustle-hummed and my seed slept.

I retreated to the book room to search the shelves for comfort. The book "Trees and Other Poems," by Joyce Kilmer, spoke to me, and I leafed through pages, searching for Horace's wise words. I found the poem. Flew upstairs to Helen's room. She sat on her stool, gazing faceless in the vanity's mirror. I inhaled her sadness and listened to imagined whispers of her dead son.

My neck then tingled. I knew what to do. A tree took her son's life, but I *must* show her that a tree could still be good—that a kind tree was caring for her son's spirit. Then I'd let her know I came to take some of her grief. Place it like wings on my back. Fly off with it.

"Can I read a poem for you?" I asked, my voice a whisper.

I longed to dream in our poetic realm—a bridge between human-speak and rustle-hum. And so I swam my tears into a deep sleep so my voice could be heard. I spoke, not in a whisper but not too loud. Indeed, I spoke truth. Not a lie.

Trees

I think that I shall never see
A poem lovely as a tree.

A tree whose hungry mouth is prest
Against the earth's sweet flowing breast;

A tree that looks at God all day,
And lifts her leafy arms to pray;

A tree that may in Summer wear
A nest of robins in her hair;

Upon whose bosom snow has lain;
Who intimately lives with rain.

Poems are made by fools like me,
But only God can make a tree.

When I finished, I looked at Helen, hoping she'd see the truest me, and then find my warm, safe Love for my tree, Horace. But before I could say anything more, Helen stood. Slapped my right cheek. Her hand hurt more than Prickly Elder's wing-slap. More so! Shocked, I caressed my cheek as sleeping tears woke. Was she slapping me, God, or my tree? I didn't know. I don't believe she did, either.

"How could you read *this* poem to me . . . on *this* day?" Helen asked. "Finn died on a tree!"

"I'm sorry," I said.

Helen's eyes grew dark before she sat on the stool and then closed them.

"Leave me alone, Willow. No food. No poetry. No worry. I just want to be left alone."

I left, wanting no more than to return to the forest. Instead, I went to Finn's room. There, I listened to the aching soul of the bluebell house and the stir of its human-things. I could hear Helen's pain—apart and a part of it.

In the human-hurt, I gave the poem "Trees" room to speak. As the words danced within me, Horace towered in grace. We were closer now . . . even in the far. I rested my head on my pillow and touched my stomach. "Tirra lirra," I whispered. "Tirra lirra." The little seed hiccupped. *Be well. Be brave.* I closed my eyes and let sleep take us both.

Horace-Speak

I am here. I am close, and far. I am apart, and a part of you. Finn is with me—close, and far. I am apart from and a part of him, too.

I've come to love him.

Sometimes he scoops his soul from my hollow, climbs my trunk, sits on my happiest branch, and offers his soul with glow-hands to the sun and the moon. Sun-speak. Moon-speak. Finn-speaks.

The tree sprites rustle-hum more and less of you (I know, because they visit us often). They've come to love Finn, too. Sometimes Finn makes even crusty Prickly Elder smile.

When the night is too full of stars, and Finn frightens, rocking his spirit-body, the tree sprites circle me, hold hands, and rustle-hum until he calms. All but Sugar Maple. She isn't well.

Finn stays with Sugar Maple when the sun rises and falls. He rustle-hums to her, soothing her to rise and fall.

The forest is still here, and Smis comes often. He never approaches Finn. Only watches him. At times, I believe Smis loves him, too.

I still miss you, even as I love Finn.

You are still close, and far, apart from and a part of me.

Scarlet Oak.

Willow Brook.

Extraordinary you.

Chapter 40

I dreamed that Horace communicated to me, and it traveled so peacefully that it influenced my surroundings, once I awoke. Slowly, I moved to the window. Sunlight shimmered like Finn's soul in the quiet spaces of Sylvan. And so I stared at the twinkles, glimmers, movement on his leaves and branches, wanting nothing more than to lose myself in it all day. I'd allow it a pathway to an imagining, one in which I miniaturized on Horace, even with a human child in my womb. But I knew none of this was possible. In fact, it was time to return to the forest realm as Willow Brook.

To soothe myself, I found Helen's record player and brought it to Finn's room. I put on a record, watching it spin and spin and spin. "Ave Maria" soul-spoke, its glorious sound softening Grief, turning her from stone into fluidity and moving her from my soul to my eyes. Tears fell down my cheeks. A presence—Grief. A tangible presence. I walked to the window and gazed past Sylvan's sparkle to find Helen and John in the distance. The music reached past me, floated through the gleam, soared to Finn's parents, and circled them hypnotic in much the way I experienced the Christmas angel chime.

Again, Helen and John sat together. But this time they did so on soil, fingers interlocked, sun grazing their faces as eyes combed the horizon. I wondered if they were silently speaking to Finn together—perhaps by way of the sun's rays. Of course, I knew differently. Finn's spirit rocked distressed in my forest realm, and his soul sat lonesome in Horace's hollow.

Still, I watched Helen and John through music and handholding and shared sunbeams and longing for Finn. All of this together showed me that perhaps I did offer solace. Because now their heart-hurt was shared, not separated. Oneness in a moment of sunshine. A moment when I was not a part of them but apart from them.

I stood there for so long, watching, aching, giving . . . so much so that I believed I was Grief herself.

Smis-Speak

Grief speaks to me when no one else will.

Chapter 41

Helen and John only returned inside when the sun dipped to the earth apologetically and began to say its goodbyes. A piece of me believed it may never return. "The sun will never return in the same way," I whispered to my seed. I wanted to cry. But my body couldn't. Grief dressed itself up as human and hid within me, a master illusionist. Grief and Smis—what a pair. Human shadows.

I listened for Helen in the kitchen. Would she bake a cake as she did on Finn's birthday? *No!* On a death-day, Helen slapped, stilled in the sun, silenced. I longed to bring a cake to Finn—the brown-sugared pineapple confection—the taste of warm, safe Love. I'd give some to Pin Oak, to my seed, too. But then reminded myself this wasn't the time to think of sweet things. It was time to leave.

Bang. Bang. Bang. Noise clamored from the book room. I crept downstairs and found the door slightly open. John and Helen worked in harmony to complete a job I'd never known they wished to do. John ripped wood strips from the bookshelf and banged fresh wood in its place as Helen handed him nail after nail, studying him closely as he worked. Here and there, she'd glance at the book piles on the floor, as if worried they'd grow limbs and wander away.

I was a silent observer, even when I thought Helen spotted me. I didn't move but stayed with them—apart—curious, all the same. I left only when my seed whined for me to go to the kitchen. There, I sliced plain white bread and placed grapes in a bowl, eating and washing up alone. No roast turkey. No corn pudding. No peas or turnips or cranberry bread. No pumpkin pie with whipped cream. No family. Nothing that I saw or read the other day in the picture book *Cranberry Thanksgiving*.

In time, John and Helen finished their shared task, whisked to the bedroom, and shut the door louder than usual. I crept upstairs and into the hallway. Listened even when I shouldn't have.

"I wanted to tell you. I'm telling you now," Helen said.

"But ya kept it to yourself . . . how many months?"

Helen's words dropped like boulders.

"How long did *you* keep me from *your* pain? How long did *you* pretend you were okay? Everything was okay? Being Finn's father was a blessing? But one church visit, that's all it took, to crack you wide open and make you lift the bottle."

"I dunno what to say to ya, Helen. Did my best," John said, his voice childlike.

Horrific, grave silence took over—worse than the peaceable beast—and in it I imagined their pain as giant, inaudible dragonflies slicing and flying through skin, feeding on their hearts. Blood everywhere. The dragonflies only ingested it. Fueled up to spew horror-speak through human lips.

"You lied," Helen said. "For *years* upon *years* to me . . . to Finn . . . to yourself, most of all. 'All he needs is jus' a little help. Jus' a little help.' And *I* believed *we* were that little help that made him absolutely beautiful. But it took ugly voices from ugly people to make that untrue. 'Cause if that's what it took to break you, then you must've thought the same things, and those awful things just lifted that bottle upright and poured the venom down your throat. Told you to hang yourself from a tree. To end your life, and in doing so . . . ours."

"NO,' John said, forcefully. "No. Y'ain't understand."

"If I did understand . . . Finn would still be here. If I understood just a fraction of who you were, are, John Hawes . . . Finn would still be here. 'Cause he never would have seen what he saw. I wouldn't have allowed it."

"You think you can control everythin'. You think 'cause you gotta room full of books, you know more, or 'cause you gotta God or a church . . . always somethin'. But y'ain't know everythin', Helen. Y'ain't God."

"I know that if you hadn't have tried to hang yourself, Finn never would have seen it to do what he did. You know he mimicked us. Liked to copy the things we did."

"And who's supposed to be watchin' him Thanksgivin' . . . the night he wander off on his own?"

"*We* were," Helen said. "*We were*. We were his parents, and instead of being his parents . . . doing what good parents do . . . inviting over family, friends, saying grace, carving the turkey, serving, eating, laughing, slicing the pumpkin pie . . . you and I were up here . . . left Finn downstairs with the Thanksgiving dinner, but no family, no friends . . . alone, unattended . . . while we did what we're doing right now . . . in this room, arguing over the night you tried to kill yourself."

"*NO*," John said, emphatically. "Was fightin' over ya crazy. Over the fairy you said ya saw. Did you ever stop to think how hard it was, takin' care of ya both? Y'aint ever go to get help after Hope died . . . jus' left it to me to take care of ya both."

"I'm *not* crazy," Helen said, as something slammed against the wall. "I've never been crazy a day in my life. There *was* a tiny fairy that lived on that oak tree . . . still does . . . and she was Finn's fairy. The fairy loved Finn, played with Finn. I used to watch them from the hallway. Watch them in their own creative world . . . loving each other. And that fairy—Finn's fairy—she saved you from your demons, that night. Untied that rope. And now, Willow's come to us . . . a double blessing, still. She *is* our daughter. She's ours. And now she's giving us another gift . . . a baby. Can't you see that?"

"All's I see . . . a boy took 'vantage of her, and that I shoulda used my daddy's gun that day in the woods to scare him more. You think people's gonna jus' let this go? You think Sandra's gonna, when she finds out? Or do you think they may check up on who Willow is, where she come from . . . and know she ain't ours. And if she ain't ours, who is she? Took her from someone."

"She's ours, John. Ours. Just like that fairy was Finn's."

Again, silence arrived, but this time more like the peaceable beast.

"We ain't done much of anythin' right," John said. "We ain't let Finn go to school. We shoulda let him. May have been a special school, but they'd a know how to do right by him. We shouldn't have kept him on a farm . . . away from the world."

"What did you propose we do? Give him to people . . . cruel people the likes of Sandra Cummings? We kept Finn protected, and nurtured, and most of all, loved. We gave him a gift."

"We kept him from pain . . . so the boy ain't even know what it was . . . ain't even know it was hangin' from a tree . . . pain. And now we gotta girl that ain't ours, and she's got more pain inside . . . growin' . . . gonna take her."

"She has *us*, John. She has us to take care of her."

"Like we take care of Finn that night? Shoulda been watchin' him. Knew Finn like to wander . . . 'specially when we fight. But we say . . . 'Here's the door . . . go on wanderin . . .' we too busy fightin' over things we ain't ever gonna change."

"Oh, John," Helen said in a sad whisper.

Again, quietness blunted all sound, and I imagined them holding hands as they did in the field earlier. Eventually, however, John chopped the silence.

"Think we gotta do somethin' together . . . get on rid of all this pain. I gotta idea to do it, too. Been thinkin' on it all day. Let's say we ax down that tree. Axin' the tree in the forest that took Finn . . . like you axed that pine. You and me together, this time . . . ax that tree."

I gasped. Helen and John's dragonfly-pain wanted to feed on *my* tree. Kill it so a piece of their horror could sprout wings and fly off, and in doing so, slay me and my unborn child. There wasn't time to think. Only act.

I raced to Finn's room. Threw on the fox-death-coat. Opened the window. Pushed myself onto Sylvan's branch. The tree quaked, angry, and twice I almost fell. Still, I moved (didn't search for Pin Oak). I reached the trunk, scaled down. Bare feet pounded autumn's cool ground to John's workshed. I pulled open the door, found the steel box, whipped out the gun, and placed it in my coat's pocket.

I sprinted up the snaked driveway—wind smacking my face, moon lacing my sweat in silver. I ran faster, faster, faster . . . longing for wings. And then they arrived, but not of my making. No, I heard the *Swish-swish, Swish-swish* of Pin Oak's tiny wings near my ear. She landed on my right shoulder and refused to fly off. I rustle-hummed to her. *"Go. Go. Go. Be with your tree. Be with Sylvan, as you should."* But she refused. No time to argue—I took her.

We raced past sparse spruces, oaks, and apple trees, dead sunflowers, corn fields, tomato plants, potatoes buried deep, old toolsheds, silos, barns, tractors, plows, mailbox, barbed gate. Nature urged us on, and humanness whispered hor-ror-speak. I didn't stop to listen or muse, see or smell, taste or hear . . . feel. I ran and breathed with Pin Oak. One Grief.

My seed spoke. *"Slow down. Slow down. Slow down."* But the axing of Horace drowned my seed's voice. *Thwack. Thwack. Thwack.* I pushed through the metal gate. *Sap is stronger than blood. Sap is stronger than blood.* My bare feet echoed the words as they struck the road.

Pin Oak feared. I could sense it. Still, she longed for Finn. She climbed under my coat, my dress, down my back, and grooved into my wing scar, melding with me. She became my wings. Yes! Like a faithful truck's engine, Pin Oak moved me forward. And so I feared less. Loved more. Ran quicker. Heartbeat one with Nature's extraordinary madness.

Sylvan-Speak

I kept Pin Oak close . . . so close. You see, she was born with a disability. She lacked the power to morph-as-she-must into largeness, once she detached from me. A tiny twig-sprite was all she would be . . . could ever be. She was so small, I had to keep her close. I only allowed Finn to know her. They were kindred spirits. It was enough.

Four seasons ago, Pin Oak flew after Finn in the dark. Rustle-hummed to him, *"GO HOME!"* Finn ran. Flapped. Horror-hummed. Pin Oak wanted to follow.

"Come back to me," I called. *"Like Finn, you are too small. Come back. Stay."*

Fear and loyalty pushed her back to me, and Finn hung. Died.

Tonight, we fought as Willow moved on us. I surprised . . . no, shocked myself.

"Go, Pin Oak," I said. *"Go."*

Pin Oak froze in grief, fear, and loyalty—her wings paralyzed.

I wobbled my branch. Shook her free. *"Go, Pin Oak,"* I said. *"Go as you must! You haven't a disability . . . but a different ability . . .* a diff-ability (I nicknamed it, and in human-speak!). *Your unique magic flies—soars—inspires!"*

Pin Oak hesitated and then smiled. Flew off.

"Pin Oak, you are large," I whispered with the wind, *"LARGER than me. FLY!"*

Part Three

*A Return to the
Forest Realm*

Smis-Speak

If I fall, leave me to rest.
I'll awaken
deeper
yet.
Smis rests in the no-place.
It's nearly time.

Chapter 42

I leapt into the forest realm—Pin Oak fluttering on my back. Moonlight milked the trees and a white fog slid in wisps, cool, damp breath directing me. I followed the moon and the mist. Welcomed the leaves that flew, tangling my hair. My stomach twittered, and my bare feet battered wet ground, pine needles, sticks, acorns, and soil. Still, my mind created an inspirational line to keep us going.

Autumn whispered to the wind, "I fall; but always rise again."

As this mantra echoed within, I sprinted past the loveli-ness of trees. Elms and maples, beeches and spruces, pines and oaks. Each a world, and a part of the world—the same, and different. The tree sprites hid, and I didn't seek them out. I kept running, loving, all the while rustle-humming to them. *"You are beautiful. You are extraordinary. I once was you—magic, too. Accept my return with grace."*

But just as swiftly as hope fueled me like a prayer, lights chopped into the forest. I heard the rumble and screech of John's truck in the distance. Doors slammed. Human voices bashed into the wind. I quickened my pace as Pin Oak ascended my back, her fingers searching, anxious. I slowed only to allow her movement, and once she clasped the top of my dress, sprinted once more.

We raced on, deeper into the forest, searching. While I knew my tree's location by heart, my seed obscured this view, taking some of it, forcing me to think harder. The more I thought, the further I diverted from course. In fact, I took a mistaken turn, and then another, pivoting and almost slamming into a spruce, nearly dropping Pin Oak. I stopped briefly to readjust her and then ran again. But this way, it felt wrong, too, and that way, even more wrong.

My heart lost its path as I ached for Horace. My seed didn't care, and my mind coiled and became further confused. I begged the moon to guide me, and when it refused, I implored the entirety of Nature. She, too, failed me. So I searched for human lights to illuminate my way. But now I couldn't see or hear Finn's parents. To stifle my tears, I sniffed pine.

Then I sprinted harder, leaner, longer, with stiff legs and bleeding feet. Pin Oak began to cry.

"Do not cry, Pin Oak," I said. *"It's okay."*

It wasn't okay, and she knew it as she clung to my hair, riding my right shoulder. In this fear, a dark figure flew above and shadowed us before it swooped. Cold, bristly hands grabbed my arms, pulling them back at an angle, as if reconstructing them into wings.

At once, I smelled Prickly Elder's sour-egg breath. But there wasn't a moment to speak because we lifted from the ground and, for the first time, I flew above the forest. Instantly, I flashed to my birth in Horace's hollow:

As I came into being, my body shivered electric and my heart hummed a lullaby from Horace's womb. *Swish-swish, Swish-swish, Swish-swish.* I listened to the sound of my flapping wings as I flew in Horace's hollow. *Swish-swish, Swish-swish, Swish-swish.* I was too small, but larger than the forest. *Swish-swish, Swish-swish, Swish-swish.* I was too young, but more knowing than my body. *Swish-swish, Swish-swish, Swish-swish.* I was in love, and in life, and in magic. *Yes!* This was my first memory of warm, safe Love.

My birth memory arose, more beautiful than spirit or of spirit, I wasn't sure. And as I remembered, I could tell that Pin Oak read my thoughts, especially when she wept with buzzing wings, nearly falling from my shoulder. Poor Pin Oak—so far from her tree. It was too much. So, I put her first. Returned to her and into presence among the wind-flying, the heaven-bound, jeweled leaves, moonbeams, and fog. From this height, I saw the entirety of the forest—an expansive, soulful view as trees stretched like earthen fingers to the sky.

But then I spotted Helen and John's flashlight slicing through darkened gaps—an ax shadowed in John's hand. And there, towering in the distance, I saw Horace with Finn's spirit occupying his topmost branch. Despite the danger, Finn glowed golden, bridging the moon to the sun.

We landed on a white oak's branch. That's when I turned and stared into Prickly Elder as he kept us close, refusing movement. Quickly, I reverted to rustle-hums, pleading my case. With fairy-human eyes I showed him so much, constructing elaborate visuals to help him understand my predicament and Horace's plight. Even as my seed urged me to do so, I resisted using human-speak.

Prickly Elder painted a horrid mind-picture in response. Humans wandering into the forest realm, discovering sprites and destroying Nature's secrets. Trees axed. Decimated. Tree sprites walking with Smis, for Smis, by Smis, outside of Nature's time and magic . . . to Death, Death, Death.

I rustle-hummed to Prickly Elder.

"Never, ever could this be . . . because my humans—John and Helen—they are good humans."

I showed Prickly Elder the visual of John and Helen sitting in the field, looking to the sun, holding hands. And then John and Helen in bed with Finn—the sacred spaces of their family. I revealed Helen's love for me, John's love for me, even Warren's love for me. It only saddened Prickly Elder all the more. No rage. Just sadness.

I came short of showing Prickly Elder when John lifted Helen from the ground after she axed a pine tree. But I wanted to because it was love even in the grief. However, I did point to Finn's parents with the ax in the distance, and rustle-hummed as best I could . . .

"They want to kill the tree that took their son."

Prickly Elder bludgeoned a visual of my death alongside Horace into me. His eyes blinked and then he rustle-hummed.

"You must sacrifice yourself to safeguard the forest's secrets. You defected us. That was a poor choice. Now choose right by us . . . to save us. Die beside Horace, as a dutiful sprite would."

I gazed deep into Prickly's eyes and struggled to read him, but couldn't. I listened for his rustle-hums. Only they, too, cocooned into silence. I tried to show him my body, at one with Warren's, and the tiny seed growing in my hollow.

"You see, I can't die," I replied. *"My child will die, too."*

Prickly Elder only turned from me and looked for Helen and John as they moved closer to Horace. I angered. Flashed to the Prickly Elder I knew. The slap-me-in-the-face, pompous codger of a sprite, inflexible as his tree trunk. I reached for the gun in my coat pocket, slid my hands over its cool metal, and wrapped my fingers around it. Pin Oak patted me.

"Leave it to me to speak," she rustle-hummed in my ear.

Pin Oak flew to Prickly Elder's frosty cliff of a shoulder, and she planted her twig feet on him, like vines to bark. When he looked at her, she tapped his lips with delicate fingers and spoke a language he knew. Slowly, I sensed Prickly Elder melding into Pin Oak's memories. I, too, experienced every beautiful heartbeat in her love story with Finn.

Finn flying Pin Oak on a cardinal figurine.

Finn feeding Pin Oak warm pancakes, syrup dripping down her chin.

Finn flapping and leaping, Pin Oak on his shoulder.

Finn crying and Pin Oak cupping his tears, drinking them.

Finn laughing into Pin Oak's smile.

Finn squinting into her mind, humming into her soul, staring off into faraway and close worlds created only for them. A human and a tree sprite—One—Magic.

For the first time ever, I witnessed Prickly Elder release a teardrop. He loved Finn. *Yes!* Pin Oak, extraordinary as she was, read his affection all along. Quickly, she showed Prickly

Elder the end. Horace axed with Finn's spirit in Smis's shadowed hand, en route to the Dark. And Finn's parents more human . . . less human in unspeakable pain.

Prickly Elder took Pin Oak from his shoulder and held her gently as an acorn in his palm. His teardrop reflected the colored prism of Pin Oak's kind face, and then quite suddenly his warmth fluttered as he embraced my hand, fingers more tender.

Only a second later, horror axed into me. Echoed.

Thwack. Thwack. Thwack.

I screamed the unholiest scream—a call to action. At once, tree sprites flew with deathly shadows: *Arroosh. Aroosh. Aroosh.*

The ax felled into Horace again.

Thwack. Thwack. Thwack.

My stomach curdled—at one with my forest father—and I fell from Prickly Elder's soft clutch.

Chapter 43

Prickly Elder dove deep, clasped my arm, and caught me before I hit the ground. He then pulled me up as Pin Oak climbed him and clung to his hair. We flew alongside every tree sprite who loved Finn through wandering mist. Magic, we were, soaring beneath moonlight and around half-dressed trees. We dipped and whooshed, flapped and rustle-hummed, whipped and chilled. All the while, autumn's wind chimed with its enchanted twirling leaves. In unison, we were one heartbeat of Nature's extraordinary madness.

As we approached Horace, John dropped the ax and turned to face us. Fearful, Helen grabbed her husband as he stumbled in disbelief. We landed together—the tree sprites then moving behind Prickly Elder, their love for Finn eclipsing Nature's secrets, and my love for them expanding past the star-laced sky.

At first, I walked slowly, passing John and Helen with tender fairy-human eyes. Then I ran to Horace. Placed my trembling fingers on his wounds. Fingered his sap, cradled his trunk, kissed his bark, and rustle-hummed into his pain. I looked up to find one scarlet leaf left on his branch. Now, more than ever, I longed to miniaturize into his hollow and snuggle next to Finn's soul. Instead, I rustle-hummed.

"I'm here. I'm sorry I left."

Horace didn't speak. Shocked, I'm sure. Saddened. Hurt. But in his agony, I felt his love for me, and for the boy-spirit he protected. That's when I searched for Finn's spirit, to no avail. And so I turned to John and Helen.

For a heartbeat, John studied the ax, now lodged in soil. A companion—a foe. He then looked up and maneuvered Helen behind him.

"Who . . . are . . . ya . . . Willow?" he asked. "What are ya?"

"I'm Horace's tree sprite," I said. "This oak . . . he's my father. He birthed me, and raised me, and let me go. He loves me, fierce as the moon and quiet as the snow, aching as thunder, and proud as the sun. Horace is my oak, and I am his sprite."

John shook while staring around, yet Helen left him for me. She caressed my face in warm hands—her fantasy emptied and filled, all the same.

"Horace didn't kill Finn," I said. "Horace loves Finn."

Just as quickly, John pulled Helen back.

"Ain't real," John said. "Grief's killin' our senses. Makin' us see things that ain't there."

Helen released herself from John's grip, replacing her hand gently on his with tearful eyes. At the same time, Pin Oak flew to me and perched on my shoulder.

"Look," Helen said. "See. It's all true. Everything I've been telling you. Right there on Willow's shoulder . . . it's Finn's fairy."

"No," John said, blinking, shaking.

"Yes," Helen said. "Our boy, obviously he could see

things we couldn't. Feel things we couldn't. Communicate with things too small and large for us to know or acknowledge. But here, where he died . . . his spirit still lives. I can feel it. He's free to show us his world."

John keeled over with weighted breath. Gently, Helen dipped to him.

"John, Finn's here," she said. "He's here . . . ready to show us the wingspan of his world. Like a poem—that kind of magic. Words falling off the page in loose limbs and sturdy heartbeat . . . walking straight to us. Finn's here, John. Believe."

John shook his head, as if to do so would return reality to its rightful place.

"Ain't nothin' but our minds fuelin' in grief. Hauntin' us with Finn. We come here thinkin' cuttin' the tree that took him . . . somehow, it'd bring him back. Ain't never happen. And all this 'round us . . . ain't real, Helen. Simply ain't real."

"It's real," Helen said with vehemence. "Maybe the angels that flew off . . . left us, and our Finn to die . . . they've come back . . . as fairies. Brought Willow to us."

I moved closer to Helen and John.

"Finn's here," I whispered. "His spirit's here. My tree's taken good care of him . . . the tree sprites, too. Smis nearly took him to the Dark, not the Light. I begged Smis for mercy. I came to you . . . to try to heal your grief and to change Finn's course. I knew he didn't mean to die, and he surely belongs in the Light."

John quaked with anger and heartbreak. He took a cavernous breath and a step forward. Then he closed his eyes, as if doing so willed everything away. When he finally opened them, he gazed at me with an oak's conviction.

"Willow," he said, "*my* Willow . . . you truly fixin' me to believe you're a tree fairy? You knew and know my boy? Come to heal us . . . knowin' 'bout life, and death? Where we go and meant to be? You know Smis? A damn sight make-believe shadow? Smis's wanderin' in crazy human mind . . . is all! Gotta baby inside of ya . . . that's what's human, girl. Human. Not a grief lie. Human. Now, come on with us, ya hear? Back to the farm, and we'll be takin' good care of ya'll. Takin' good care of Willow Brook Hawes, and her baby . . . gonna be our grandbaby, too."

John bent down. Lifted his ax.

"We don't need to be cuttin' down that tree. Reckon I'll leave this ax here all together."

John tossed the ax toward Sugar Maple's tree.

"See . . . the ax . . . gone. We done wrong by ya, on this day. Left ya alone . . . ignored ya . . . trapped in our own heartache. And all's happened is you went away in ya head, lost yourself, like Finn. But we're here to take ya back, child. Cold, out here. Dark. Sad. Come back home, Willow."

John clutched his left hand over his heart as if trying to keep the explosive organ intact. Push it back beneath his skin. Be human as best he could, and a father (if not to Finn) to me.

"Please, Willow," he said, tears on his cheeks. "Please."

I imagined John's ax chopping my heart to pieces—a sliver to Horace, to John, to Helen, to Finn, to Warren, to Pin Oak, and even to Prickly Elder. Because, like the leaves falling, my heart was dying. And that's when I saw the great shadow-contortionist, Smis, command the Dark as he glowed in autumn's patchwork color. Seeing Smis in color for the first time, it welded my heart back together. In that moment, Smis loved me. He would love Finn's spirit, too.

"My home's here," I said to John.

John looked confused, and I soon sensed the presence of the peaceable beast he sought to tame.

"Why you doin' this to me? Haven't I been through enough? Haven't you seen me cry, and ache, and do my best? Haven't you seen my pain . . . known it in our silence? You come to me, Willow. You make me feel, not think . . . to feel ya, and Finn, and everythin' 'round me. But to feel this . . . know this . . . that'd be too much. By God, my heart . . ."

"John," I said, moving to him, "I was with Finn that night. He came to *my* oak tree . . . to Horace. He flapped and hummed, and cried a bit, and sat against Horace's trunk, so quiet, so beautiful. I imagined him not a strange bird, but the most exquisite bird set to fly off to the moon, to the Light. But he didn't make it. He just needs a little help to get there, that's all."

John shook his head.

"Finn climbed my tree's branch, hung, screamed "NO." I was with him as his beautiful eyes looked into mine before he died, and then pieces of him morphed . . . went where they must. I'm so sorry for not telling you. But I think you always knew. I was with Finn, and that's why you've been with me, felt me, knew me without words."

"No," John said, falling to his knees, sobbing.

That's when the tree sprites rustle-hummed an empathetic hymn. I turned, communicated to please offer privacy. Respectful, their wings raised in unison, they nodded and flew to their trees, morphing into miniature. Then I knelt down beside John and near Helen, who stooped with me.

"It's not your fault," I said.

"John," Helen said, "you didn't mean what you did. It was the first time you ever drank a drop of alcohol in your life. Your body didn't know what to do. Mind was gone. And your wild beast of grief took over. Grief left unattended . . . that's what did it . . . not you. You need to let it go. We can do that . . . right here, right now."

"Let it go?" John asked, wiping tears from his face. "Let it go? How's I suppose to let it go? I ain't never let that go. My boy's dead 'cause of me. Dead! 'Cause of me!"

"You can't go back," I said. "Time and the calendar says it's done. We can only go forward."

"No place for me to go . . . but here," John said, pounding his heart. "In here, where it's dark as night . . . in here, where my boy's supposed to be . . . where I'm supposed to be his light . . . take his hand . . . be his light . . . his daddy that knew not to do what *his* daddy done before."

"Finn wants you to see him . . . to look past your despair," I said.

"Can you believe?" Helen asked, gently. "Willow . . . she's the way . . . to finding Finn, seeing him, hearing him, knowing him. Believe with me. Let's see our son."

"He ain't here, Helen. He jus' ain't here."

And that's when I saw Finn appear with divine grace on my tree.

Finn-Speaks

Here I sit on a tree.
Heartbeat gone.
Soul hums free.
See me.
Hear me.
Feel me.
Know me.
Mom, I'm here.
Dad, I'm here.
Do not hurt.
BE with me.
I'm here . . . with Horace.
I'm there . . . with you.
Sent through you, to you, always.
Love.
Grow.
Like a tree.
Believe in me.

Chapter 44

John Hawes, Sunflower Man, could not believe. He crawled with grief's claws, swiped his ax, stood and lifted it with rage. He thrust it backwards with the forest's force, and he cut into Sugar Maple's soulful tree, Stein, with fury. As I screamed, as Helen screamed, as Pin Oak screamed, Sugar Maple remained calm. She peered from her hollow—so frail, so small—her body wrapped loosely in shriveled bark, and she glanced to my tree with full-moon eyes that beamed upwards to Horace's tiptop branch. There, Finn sat with the cardinal's spirit on his shoulder, showing her that the end was near but still beautiful.

I gazed at how Finn shimmered with the forest's soul, as his legs dangled like faithful leaves and his face glowed in reciprocity of the moon's goodwill. Oblivious, John Hawes chopped once more. But Helen Hawes, she wept as she spotted her son climb down Horace, detach, and run her way. Tenderly, she embraced her son's spirit, rocking him against her chest. In the gaping wound between his father's axing and his mother's rocking, Finn looked at me. The peaceable beast was all but gone, and in its place lived unspeakable grace. In that one glance, Finn forgave me and showed that he knew and loved me, Horace's sprite.

As Finn broke our stare, Smis entered, mournful. Helen cradled Finn more so. John axed Stein, and Smis gave naked emotion. Yes, I nearly spotted shadow-tears, and so I pleaded with brown-root eyes. But Smis's glowing shadow now shaded in woe. I spoke human-speak, plain, clear.

"Please . . ."

"John can't see," Smis said.

"He wants to see."

"He can't feel," Smis said.

"He feels too much."

"He can't know," Smis said.

"John's heart shadows his knowing."

"It's law. I must take Finn."

"Finn's death was an act of Love," I said. "An act to return to the Love of his parents. Pin Oak showed me, clear as rain. Only *I* made the gravest mistake. *I* didn't undo the rope as Pin Oak did before with his daddy. I'm to blame. Not Finn. Never Finn."

Smis lowered his head, and I sensed great shame.

"The universe isn't always fair," Smis said. *"Neither is Death."*

"Love is," I said.

Smis couldn't argue that point. But fear still dimmed Smis's shadow. He looked past me, and as he did so, I realized Smis didn't know all the answers—all of Nature's magic, all of God, or Love, or Law. Smis wasn't all knowing. He only knew the end must come in some way to begin again.

I wasn't all knowing, either. But my body still told me what to do. I looked from Smis to John as he axed into Stein, and then I took John's daddy's gun from my pocket. Trembling, I pointed it at John—my human father.

Chapter 45

"Put the ax down," I said to John. "Now!"

Still, John axed his pain.

"Willow!" Helen said, clinging to Finn. "Put the gun down. It's evil, I told you. Does evil things, even to good people. You're good. Very good."

I shivered. Wobbled. Smis was set to take Finn, and I had no power over it. But John couldn't kill the oldest soul of a tree, Stein, and his honeysuckle of a sprite before her time. I closed my eyes and fingered the cold metal. Quickly, Smis flew to me. Stood in my shadow to whisper . . .

"No."

Plain. Simple. That word, No. It rerouted me to Finn and the hanging and the helplessness of it all. No. I couldn't do it. Not now. Not ever. I couldn't kill . . . even for Sugar Maple. My soul wilted, and I grew lost in no-time—hypnotized by John's axing motion—so much so that I startled when a dog barked. Accidentally, I pulled the trigger. Shot.

The bullet whizzed to the swinging ax, ricocheted, and slammed into Horace's trunk. Shaken, I dropped the gun. That's when the poisoned mushroom of a woman rushed up behind me and grabbed it, as Jake broke free and sprinted far from all of us.

I turned to face Sandra Cummings. Hairless, gauzy, she floated and stammered, yet still strengthened in hate. Her wicked energy, in fact, commanded the forest, twisting its tentacles, hissing at its leaves, kicking up roots, and seizing the brutality of stars. She held John's daddy's gun and challenged me with its smoking mouth. Laughing, then she trained the gun to the moon.

"John Hawes," she said.

John dropped his ax—stunned.

"Come to find your girl on the farm," Sandra said. "Found your truck instead, parked near this spot. Knew you'd be grieving here, and thought it'd be a good enough spot as any to bring you my grievance."

"Sandra," Helen said. "Put that gun down."

Sandra sized up Helen, smiling, clearly unable to see Finn's spirit.

"You know, Helen, I got all of it out of Warren . . . everything. My boy thought I was on my deathbed, so told me about Willow and how you've been harboring her, and he's been loving her behind my back. Shameful, Helen . . . trying to make a sick, dying woman believe things aren't there that were. Knew I saw that awful girl who assaulted me that day at your house. Wasn't hallucinating."

Helen stepped in front of Finn. But Sandra made no mention of his spirit or Pin Oak on my shoulder. Instead, she waved the gun to me, and then to John. Back-and-forth. Back-and-forth. Back-and-forth.

"Don't know who to use this gun on first," Sandra said. "But I'll use it on one of you . . . if not both."

John held his arms out with still, callused fingertips. "Sandra . . . ain't no sense in this. You sick woman. Need to go home and rest. We all do."

"Go home and rest when a girl's come straight from the devil to take my son? She's meant to die. God told me so."

"God didn't tell you any such thing," Helen said. "Come on now, Sandra. I'll take you home. This isn't you . . . it's the cancer . . . the tumor in your brain."

"More me than it's ever been. Can see things clearer, now. The march to death does that to a person. And I'll be damned if I'm going to leave this world with my boy loving the devil. Warren's meant for great things. Great God-loving things."

Sandra Cummings then stared at Horace. Moved a few steps closer.

"That the tree? The one your boy hung from?"

Before anyone could answer, she shot a bullet to the right of Horace's hollow.

"There, Helen. Hurt it for you. God's will, too."

I dashed to Horace. Placed my palm over the wound and rubbed his trunk. I stood beside him as Sandra withdrew a haunting laugh from her soul's hollow.

"Strange, wicked girl," she said. "Has to come from John's side of the family. You know . . . my good, God-fearing daddy used to say only the wicked and the holy can truly see the black and white of things. Everyone else is stuck in between . . . seeing all shades of color . . . and the color . . . that's what gets you mixed up, thinking crazy things. But you and me, John Hawes—the holy, the wicked—we see the black and white of things, clear as day."

Sandra targeted John with the gun, her eyes powdery as its residue, her lips silvery as its concave mouth.

"Your daddy . . . wicked as they come . . . killed himself, he couldn't take the wickedness anymore. And you . . . took after him all right. So, of course, you had a sin of a son. Finn couldn't even speak to hear God. And me, I was blessed with a son meant to soar. That's God's will. You were jealous . . . tried to take him from me in the woods that day, and then let the devil's girl take a piece of his blessedness. Can't let that go. Have to set it right before I go, myself."

"Finn's beautiful," I said. "Love."

Sandra Cummings's eyes flickered, amused.

"Is? Finn *is* beautiful? He's dead. Gone. Weak, like his father and his father before. Not fit to thrive in this world . . . fit enough to burn in the fires of hell. God is Love. Finn, he was sin. John's original sin."

Helen struggled to compose herself. I sensed her wanting to rip Sandra apart—branch by ugly branch—but she refused to leave Finn unprotected. She placed her hands behind her, holding his glowing ears, shielding them.

"Finn's here. Finn is Love," I said. "God and Finn . . . I'm sure they're the best of friends."

"God, Love . . . neither resurrects a boy from the grave . . . a boy never meant to be."

I looked at John, his skin pale gray, eyes shivering. I imagined his heart caving—blood dripping into his wounded soul—creating an intricate maze to the peaceable beast.

I looked at Helen, her body soft, present—an open heart flowing like a pure brook to her son. She hummed. Rocked his spirit gracefully as weeping willow trees.

I felt Pin Oak's fear on my shoulder but more so her Love that never wavered. Only extended into Finn and kept him great company.

I looked at Sugar Maple as she peered from her hollow. She gazed into me.

"Be well, Willow Brook. Be well."

I didn't look at Smis. I couldn't. Wouldn't. I could read him too well.

I looked at Sandra, a walking ghost of a human. Words like the chop of an ax. *Thwack. Thwack. Thwack.* Heart sunk in quicksand and soul darkened beneath soil before its time. Spirit suffocated in the hell of human-speak.

Then I looked to Horace, my great oak. His final scarlet leaf, detached, blew upward with the wind, signaling for me to return home to his hollow. But my feet froze as Finn's voice looped in my mind: *NO! NO! NO!*

I placed Pin Oak on the ground and flew, not to Horace but to Sandra.

John, however, he charged more quickly. Leapt into the peaceable beast. Sliced it open. Roared. John grabbed my arm. Pushed me tender as he could to the ground. Shielded me. And then John faced Sandra head-on, ready to throw away his daddy's gun once and for all.

It all happened so quickly. Sandra shot John. Once. Twice. Three times. In the chest. John dropped before me as the gun tumbled, and Sandra collapsed near it on the ground, spent. Then came the sound I'll never forget.

Haunting.

Beautiful.

THWUMP.

Stein fell with his faithful sprite, Sugar Maple. Landed on top of Sandra Cummings, pinning her to the earth. Sandra didn't blink, twitch, or escape. Instead, Smis moved to her. Stood above her and looked to me.

"She'll go to the Dark, not Finn," he rustle-hummed.

I couldn't revel in Sandra's passing or mourn Stein and Sugar Maple's ending, because John Hawes convulsed before me—eyes open, stretching to the stars. Blood oozed from his chest and dripped on my fingertips, and I held no amount of sap to thicken and prevent its flow. So I placed my hand over his heart. Held it there until his breathing ceased. I rustle-hummed.

"Peace. Peace. Peace.

John Hawes, Sunflower Man.

My human father."

Finn-Speaks

Finn. Finn. That you?
Yes, dad.
I in heaven?
Close. Hold my hand.
I meant to go with ya?
Yes, dad.
Can't move, Finn. Dead.
Try.
Scared, Finn.
Spirit ain't like to fear. Only Love. Be.
By God, it is you, Finn. My boy . . . amazin' boy.
  My smile.
Take my hand, dad.
Fly with me.
Believe.

Chapter 46

Helen Hawes didn't scream, even as she wept. Instead, she knelt holier than a prayer—elegant as a poem. She placed John's callused hand in her right hand, and she held Finn's hand in her left. The in-between spaces lit with moonlight, soul-light, killing the brutality of stars, offering them shimmer-kindness. Love. Large and small and lovely, selfless Love. The kind that released her husband to move on with their son. I cried as I watched with tears meant to drown, resurface, and reawaken—fresher, clearer.

The tree sprites morphed from miniature and stepped largely from their trees. They held hands, circled the family, rustle-hummed a soothing hymn as colored leaves whistled, spun, fell. Nature's symphony. No madness (extraordinary or otherwise). I nodded to them, grateful, and most of all to Prickly Elder, more than grateful.

I glided to Horace, my trusty scarlet oak, and leaned against his steady trunk. John Hawes's deep blue soul departed from his body, flew to my hands, to my owner-ship—Willow Brook—the last living thing to touch him. I held John's soul in my palms, feeling him.

Then I watched John's spirit lift from his body in the richness of yellow-gold and balance on the ground, taking Finn's hand, smiling at his wife in a language only they knew. I watched as Finn smiled into Pin Oak and as the cardinal's spirit flew above Finn's spirit. And I watched as John walked alongside Finn with Smis behind them, a shadow illuminating in a spectrum of beautiful autumnal color.

Smis motioned for them to move to a prism of rippling sparkle-light. As father and son walked hand in hand, John Hawes turned. He waved to his wife, and Finn blew his mother a kiss. John and Finn then flew into God's Light together. I knew, because Helen whispered it to me . . . "God's Light."

John Hawes didn't look at me. He didn't have to, because his soul spoke to mine in the faintest whisper and the divinest sunflower voice. *"Willow, take care of Helen. Take care of the baby. Take care of you. I'll be takin' care of Finn, now. Give me so much, Willow. You give me so much. Bye for now . . . 'til the sun sets and shows ya all its pretty colors. Takes ya back to me.*

Horace-Speak

The fullest soul is a shimmery reflector of Love.
Finn is Love.
And my hollow sings—a mirror of him.
He lights up all of me.
I am happy.
I am!
Good-bye.
Good-bye.
Good-bye.
Finn.

Chapter 47

The forest realm possessed the bodies of John Hawes and Sandra Cummings for the time being, until humans ultimately came wandering to take them and place them in human-things and return them to the deep soil below. I didn't say my goodbyes to John's body before the rescue workers arrived. I knew he wasn't there. But I glanced to Sandra Cummings and shrouded her body with hope for the son she left behind, her son whom I loved. Finally, I bowed my head to Sugar Maple and Stein, and then rustle-hummed her moonlit hymn.

Smis came to me in my shadow and then, respectful, separated, walked away. He didn't turn back. Only soul-spoke, informing me that it wasn't my time to know him, be with him, so intimately. But I shivered in his love all the same— for me, for my tree.

"I miss Finn," Pin Oak whispered in my ear.

"Grieve. I'll take care of you," I rustle-hummed back.

Helen sat on pine needles and damp leaves. She bowed her head and wept a rolling rainstorm of tears, so much that I worried she'd dry up and crack into ash. I touched her hair.

ANGIE WEILAND-CROSBY

Hugged her from behind. But then I left her to grieve—to do what she must—and approached my tree, Horace.

"May I place John's soul next to Finn's in your hollow . . . for the kindest of keeping?"

"Yes," Horace said.

I nestled John's deep blue soul next to his son's in pale blue.

"I'm sorry," I said, unable to stop my human tears. *"We'll never be the same again. I'll miss sleeping in your hollow the most."*

"Things are as they should be. Now go. Stay with Helen. Return Pin Oak to her tree. You're free . . . to live your life as Willow Brook."

"You'll always be my tree," I said.

Horace didn't speak, but I read in his silence that I would always be his sprite. His hollow then warmed in a poetic glow with Finn's and John's souls. I lifted Helen from the ground and guided her to my scarlet oak tree, pointing to his hollow. She stared at Finn's soul first, mesmerized.

"Finn," I said. "Finn's soul lives here . . . always. John's, too."

Helen didn't reach to hold, or own, or tuck away. But she gazed with eyes only a mother could know—eyes that traveled through a forest of emotions and still held fast and true to the only one that mattered—Love. The more she looked into her son's soul, the more she looked into herself. Indeed, I could feel Helen's soul through her clothes, her skin, her blood. It whooshed like a womb—an invisible thread binding her to Finn, as lovingly interconnected as Lucy's nimble fingers to the mother-quilt or Sugar Maple's spiritual hymns to the moon.

In time, Helen eyed her soul mate—a long, gorgeous

gaze—and she smiled, of all things. Smiled! I imagined her heart-speaking. *John isn't good. No. John is tremendous as all the forest's trees. And so is our love . . . never-dying, never-ending, ever-Loving, Lasting, Longing.*

We stayed in the forest until first daylight streamed through the trees—the magic-time when the sun scooped pieces of itself and willingly let them go to morph into what they must. So many sparkle-pieces. So much Love. If only more could see.

Helen and I sat against Horace, Pin Oak on my shoulder, watching it all—Helen's head leaning on me. That's when my soul spoke. *There is mystery and then there isn't.* I stayed with this unknowing and knowing. We didn't leave until the sun rose to a reverent height and the path was clear.

"Time to go," I said, taking Helen's hand in my own.

Smis-Speak

This is my greatest secret.
Death is not the end.
I am living proof.
Beyond Death, We—the Leftovers—still Love,
   Live, Remember.
Love is like the sun and moon.
No beginning, no ending.
Golden reflectors of each other.
This is Smis-Speak left unspoken:
There is no voice for Love.
There is only Love.
Grief shows us the way there.
So, be kind to Grief that rains pure Love.

Chapter 48

Grief didn't leave any of us. Not Helen. Not Horace. Not Warren. Not Pin Oak or her tree. Not Prickly Elder. Not Lucy down the street, or even Father Will. Grief certainly didn't leave me. She stayed. The only difference was I befriended her rather than scold her, name-call her, morph her, shoo her, erase her, no-time her, drown her in drink, ax her, or gun her down. I gave Grief time—her due respect—and I spoke to her in all kinds of speak. I didn't take from her.

"Grief," I said, "I see you, hear you, smell you, taste you . . . I feel you. Thank you. Thank you. Thank you for reminding me that I Love."

Each time I spoke, Grief stepped outside of me, bowed her head in respect in much the way I witnessed Smis do at Finn's funeral. And I walked past her, bowed my head all the same, and then I kept on Living, Loving. And perhaps this was my greatest lesson. I couldn't heal Grief. Didn't want to, even. And I couldn't take her away from another. Grief was a private friend each person (or fairy-human, or sprite, or tree, or living thing, or soul-thing) must tend to in their own way, their own time. But I was still there for Helen, for Horace, for Warren, and Pin Oak, for Prickly Elder, and Lucy down the street, and even Father Will. I was there, Living and Loving in the way only I could.

I stayed with Helen in the bluebell house no matter that people suggested we do otherwise, including Father Will.

"So much sadness here," Father Will said, after John's funeral. "Start fresh, Helen. Start fresh."

Helen simply nodded and kept her musings to herself. But that night she spoke to me.

"Willow, no life comes into being, is truly lived, without some hauntings, and if you can't face them down, tell them you refuse to become a haunting yourself. Then, of course, you have no business staying in a house with haunts. But this house . . . it's our home, and there's more Love here than haunt. Far more Love. I'm staying."

"Bluebell home," I said, squeezing her hand.

"Yes," she said. "Heartaching, and heart-enriching as poetry. Our bluebell home."

After that was settled, we went downstairs and tended to Warren, who slouched on our couch in his private heart-hurt with Jake resting at his feet.

"You'll stay with us . . . the two of you," Helen said, patting Jake's head. "If you want, that is. I know you have your uncle, and he's offered to take you in . . . he's a good man, your uncle. But you have a child that's soon to become with Willow, and we could use a man around the house. I know you're not yet a man . . . wouldn't expect you to do all

John did, step into the shoes of manhood so soon. But you'll have to walk that way anyway, at least by Willow, to fatherhood. We'd like you here if you'll have us."

"I'm sorry," Warren said, "so sorry for what my mom took from you both."

I sat beside Warren and held his hand.

"Warren," Helen said, "I want you here, but you have to promise me you can't take on that burden. It's not yours to own. Your mom was sick, is all. The cancer, it took her mind someplace no one needs to go. You grieve for the mom you loved, but you don't take on her load."

Helen patted Warren's shoulder, and then she went upstairs. I squeezed Warren's hand, and we didn't speak. Instead, we remained on that couch, holding one another all night long as Grief loosened her soul, embodied us in it, rocking, rocking, rocking us to sleep.

Chapter 49

In time, more people knew who I was—Willow Brook Hawes. Helen revised me into distant kin. I arrived to console her and John after Finn's death. Only she and I knew the rest, and Smis, of course. That I was a tree sprite who turned fairy-human, and then offered Warren Cummings a soon-to-be child to replace the mother who passed—a haunting.

Many people were kinder than I'd imagined. Helen even returned to church, and sometimes I went along with her. I'd sit in the pew and listen a little to Father Will. But mostly, I harmonized my growing seed with no-time. In doing so, I gazed at the stained-glass windows, the colored light filtering in and flying like birds to the realm that was now a home to John and Finn.

On a spring Sunday, after Mass, my seed finally morphed into fullness and left me. Her tiny, thin fingers stretched to my face, and she only cried a bit before looking into me with soul-eyes—eyes that already knew too much. Warren sat on the bed beside me, adoring her, stroking her head. But

I discreetly turned her around. Could see them (even if he couldn't)—the tiniest of wings.

Promptly, Smis arrived bedside, cloaked in Helen's shadow, and looked to me with Love for direction. I read his thoughts. He needn't speak them. *Should I take her wings? Would it help you? Would it help her?*

I peered through the window and caught sight of Pin Oak on Sylvan's branch. Her eyes, large and peaceful, smiled into mine.

"No," I rustle-hummed to Smis. *"They belong to her . . . a part of her."*

Warren barely flinched when I rustle-hummed. He'd acclimated to my curious ways (most likely thought I was humming a lullaby), and still, I hadn't divulged who I truly was or where I came from to him. One day, perhaps I would. But not this day, or the next. In honor of Horace, I'd keep the forest realm's secret, for now, in the sunlight and shadow.

Smis, however, he knew most of me—and in that knowing he tipped his shadow-head and smiled—a smile as light and dark as the sunflower field in all seasons. His kind gesture delivered me to one of my greatest fairy-human musings.

A birth . . . a beginning. A death . . . an ending. Both require light and Love to exist. What happens during the in-between, how much light and dark you give and take . . . that's the free will that Horace often spoke of.

"Goodbye," I said to Smis, smiling, thinking of Horace as well. *"Thank you for coming . . . for-giving."*

As Helen reached to hold my baby girl, Smis struggled not to shed emotion. Vanished. He left Helen to sprinkle tears on newborn skin—a baptism of sorts.

"What will you name her, Willow?" she asked, returning her to my arms.

I looked to Warren, and he smiled.

"Hope," I said. "If it's okay with you, we want to name her Hope Oak Cummings."

"Yes," Helen said, her hands blanketing her heart. "Yes."

Then, Helen sat on the bed with us, and we all held onto each other, leaving enough room for John and Finn and Grief to celebrate, too.

Acknowledgements

No one grows into existence alone. We are pieces of a rich tapestry—like the mother-quilt—handcrafted by our loved ones through time. I'd like to thank these maternal weavers. Mom, your fierce pixie dust moves me, always. Nana, your strength lifts my pen. Grandma, your gentleness lends soft touches. Mom Crosby, your confidence pushes me. And Bonnie, your support has encouraged me.

And a nod to my paternal oaks. Dad, your silent depth speaks to me. Pop, your steady devotion empowers me. Pop Pop, your strength of will inspires. Grandpa, your voice sings "Ave Maria" in my sleep. And George, your hum warms my heart.

Summer, there are no words to name the force of this human-thing called mother-love. You taught me this truth, and so did autism. Amber, I hold you close. In your own words, "Even though it's different, now, you're still here, somehow." To my nieces and nephews who house precious souls and "diffa-bilities," I will never cease sharing the wingspan of your gifts. To my sisters and brothers, you have given me the courage to dream big. To my backwoods cousins, my imagination still dwells in our "paradise." Much gratitude to my soul siblings, Eddie and Jennifer, too.

Many thanks to these irreplaceable loved ones for nurturing *Scarlet Oak* into being: Marilyn Jannarone, Jack Jannarone, Tommy Crosby, Hunter Lee Hughes, Denise Sirchie, Patti DiMiceli, Rebel (Dawn) McLeod, Amber Orozco, Brittney de Vicq, Debbie Mattingly Landreth, Jenifer Garcia, Jay Rallion, Allyson McGill, Jocelyn Conway Malone, Sneha Sheeja, Julie Soper, Meghana K S, and Reema Varghese.

To Leah Weiss, I knew in an instant you were my fantasy editor! You worked your magic, and I am ever grateful.

To Melissa Williams, thank you for designing *Scarlet Oak's* interior in a lovely way.

Beautiful Souls on Instagram, you bless me with your kindness.

To my former students, dream, soar . . . never give up!

Cali, my dear Lab, thanks for roaming the forest and human realm with me.

Debbie and Dawn, from girlhood on, you have given to me laughter, love, and support so freely. Thank you!

Allyson, you deepened my passion for story in college, and set me on the path to *Scarlet Oak*.

Denise, your notes and enthusiasm for all things "Scarlet" kept me moving forward.

Patti, you inspired me to embrace this journey as a grand, authentic adventure. You are the bravest spirit, and your angel is my muse.

Eberhard Grossgasteiger, there is mystery and then there isn't. Need I say more?

Hunter, my world only makes sense with you in it. No matter near or far, our souls are creatively entwined.

Tommy, you fanned my dreams with ongoing belief, and pushed me to fly. Your vision and talent serve as my inspiration, and your love is the purest gift.

Finally, to the Leftovers (and we are all Leftovers) . . . Treasure the little things. Love and Grieve Large. Awaken deeper yet. Be well.

About the Author

Angie Weiland-Crosby was born and raised in Southern Maryland, where the forest realm felt like her second home. After graduating from St. Mary's College of Maryland with a degree in English, she traveled the United States for two years before settling in Los Angeles, California, working first as a Hollywood story analyst and then as a teacher. She currently lives in Annapolis, Maryland, with her husband, daughter, Labrador retriever, and border collie pup. She writes inspirational quotes to soothe the soul, and so is never far from nature and always close to the little things in life.

Made in the USA
Middletown, DE
18 June 2022